LORDS OF PROPHECY

M.A. ROTHMAN

Primordial Press

ALSO BY M.A. ROTHMAN

Technothrillers: (Thrillers with science / Hard-Science Fiction)

• Primordial Threat

• Freedom's Last Gasp

• Darwin's Cipher

Levi Yoder Thrillers:

• Perimeter

• The Inside Man

• Never Again

Epic Fantasy / Dystopian:

• Dispocalypse

• Agent of Prophecy

• Heirs of Prophecy

• Tools of Prophecy

• Lords of Prophecy

CONTENTS

This page purposefully left blank.

The Aboveworld

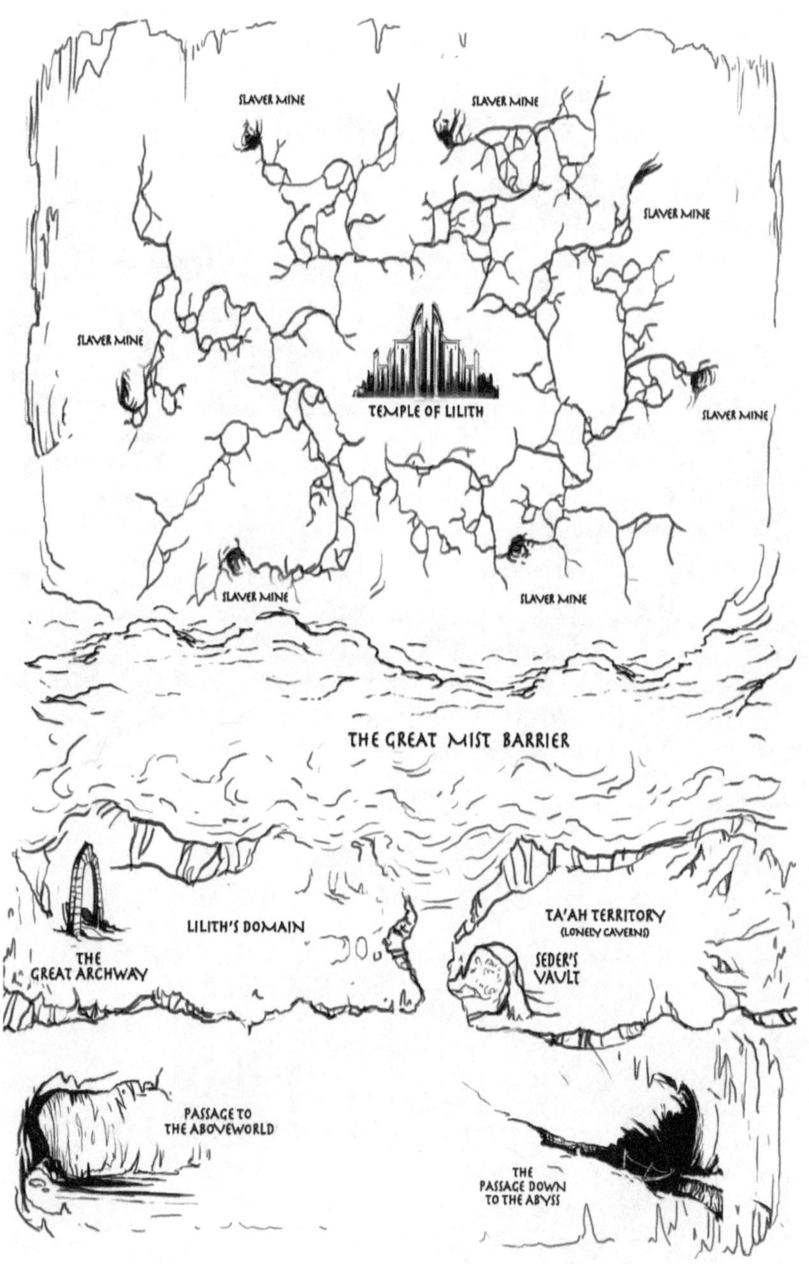

The Underworld

OVERWHELMING GUILT

"I'm a murderer," Arabelle lamented, crouching with a dagger in each hand as her handmaiden held her at bay with an iron-tipped staff.

Miriam crept toward her left, trying to keep her mistress from lunging at her. "Princess, you have to stop torturing yourself over this."

Arabelle leaped across the gap between them, and sparks erupted from the dagger as she scored a hit on Miriam's breastplate.

Miriam's staff whistled through the air as she swung a vicious blow at Arabelle's outstretched arm. Arabelle dropped into a crouch, just barely dodging.

"It's been four years, and the act still haunts me. It was my choice, and my choice alone to take their lives." Arabelle crept after her handmaiden, looking for another opening as she worried over the past. "They hadn't even attacked me! I've kept this secret from everyone but you. How can I allow Ryan to accept me as his bride, having kept such news from him?"

Miriam blinked the sweat from her eyes and snarled as she attacked, sweeping her staff at Arabelle's knees. The princess leaped backward, and Miriam continued her attack with a nonstop flurry of jabs, kicks, and sweeps.

"I won't have this from you again, Arabelle. Your father may be sheikh and you may be my best friend and princess of our people, but I have to say it: you're acting like a little girl!"

Miriam advanced with determination, increasing the speed and power behind her attacks. Arabelle dodged and deflected the blows.

"You've told me many times what happened," the maid continued. "You slew those men in self-defense, or in defense of others. You're being too harsh on yourself, and I won't hear self-loathing coming from the princess of the Imazighen!"

Arabelle ducked underneath one of Miriam's attacks and knocked her off her feet with a tremendous kick to the chest. Then she signaled the end of the sparring session.

"I suppose you're right," she said with a sigh. "Our people deserve better than this from their princess."

Miriam sat up with a groan. "No, they don't deserve *better*. They deserve you. Your acts were always for the greater good, and that's all any Imazighen could hope for." When Arabelle frowned, the maid added, "But Princess, if you feel guilt over the act, then yes, you should share it with Ryan—er, the Archmage. Do it before your wedding, if you feel you must. I'm sure he'll be understanding."

As Miriam began to strip out of her armor, Arabelle noticed a bruise forming on her handmaiden's collarbone. She applied a gentle touch to the spot, and the swelling and discoloration faded.

"I think I'll tell him," she said. "I only wish I could tell him *now*. He's not scheduled to arrive from Eluanethra until the day before the ceremony, and that's almost two weeks from now."

She pictured Ryan as she'd last seen him. She'd been drawn to his kind blue eyes even when he was but a dream of what would be, and over the years, that blue-eyed boy had grown into handsome adulthood. She closed her eyes and felt for his presence. He was many miles away, yet she knew that if she followed her senses to the northeast, her vision would lead her directly to him.

"Why don't you use your ring?" Miriam asked.

Arabelle's eyes popped open, and she saw Miriam pointing to her private ring, the one she could use to communicate with only Ryan.

"I can't confess to him through the ring! I need to *see* him." She smiled. "Actually, I have an idea."

"As long as it's safe. And remember, it's very bad luck to see your betrothed the week before the ceremony."

Arabelle fidgeted with excitement. "Then I guess I'd better tell him to hurry."

She tapped a message into her ring. Whatever Ryan was doing, he'd immediately feel the vibrations in his own ring and translate the message.

Ryan, she began, *We need to talk...*

<hr>

As soon as Ryan received the urgent but mysterious request from his soon-to-be wife, he set about rushing to quickly complete all the things he needed to do in the elven city of Eluanethra. And he wasn't the only one rushing; the scribes working with him in Eluanethra's library were fluttering back and forth among the rows of books, tracking down the titles he'd listed for them, while others were already hard at work on the painstaking process of copying each and every page of the selected tomes.

When Xinthian entered, he chuckled at the sight. "Young man, I haven't seen my scribes run around like this in years."

"They're a great help. I must apologize for cutting my visit short, but Arabelle would never have summoned me if it weren't critical."

Xinthian held out a hand. "Give me your list of needs. You shouldn't keep your bride-to-be waiting."

Ryan looked uncertainly at the town elder, then nodded and placed the list in his outstretched hand.

"Jelian," said Xinthian, passing the parchment to one of the scribes. "Make sure everything on this list gets delivered to the Riverton Castle library as soon as the copies are complete."

Xinthian then put his arm around Ryan's shoulder and escorted him from the room.

"Thank you, my friend," Ryan said when they were outside.

The town elder laughed. "And I must thank *you* for the wedding invitation! I look forward to attending. Though I can't say I reacted with quite as much excitement as did Queen Labriuteleanan. She said that these days you seem altogether too sure of yourself, and that she very much looks forward to seeing you nervous and uncertain like you were when she first met you."

Ryan gave an uneasy laugh. When he first began his training in the elf city, he and the yet-to-be crowned elf queen were the only two students of Eglerion, the elven lore master. And it was Labriuteleanan—Labri—who first made him aware of the elven custom of public bathing in mixed company. And she made him *well* aware. As soon as she realized that Ryan was embarrassed to face her when she joined him to bathe in the local stream, she made it a point to replicate the scenario as often as possible, and to insistently strike up conversations with him while less than clothed.

"You can tell Labri that I look forward to the renewed nervous uncertainty," he said.

When they arrived at the corral that held his mount, Ryan clasped arms with Xinthian. "Thanks again for all your help."

"Farewell, young Archmage, and send my greetings to your parents."

"I will."

After two days on horseback, Ryan spied the ramparts of Castle Riverton rising from the surrounding grasslands. Flying high over the training grounds were the two dragons, Ruby and Pyre, that had become part of his extended family.

And to think that less than three years ago, those two were eggs.

In the castle's shadow stood a small city that had grown up

just as quickly as the dragons. What had only recently been an empty field was now a fortified series of connected buildings occupying many acres of land. And even now there were workmen everywhere, many of them dwarves, crawling over the buildings like ants as they inspected the masonry and metalwork.

But Castle Riverton was not Ryan's destination. Instead he turned his horse toward a vast expanse of wagons and tents camped a couple miles away. The caravan where he would find his betrothed.

At the edge of the caravan, two guards came out to greet him. Both slammed their fists against their chests in salute. Ryan bowed his head in acknowledgment and dismounted.

The older of the two guards stepped forward. "Greetings, young Lord Riverton, Archmage of Trimoria, and betrothed to our princess. Welcome to the domain of Sheikh Honfrion of the Imazighen. I am Tabor, lead guard. Behind me is my second, Khalid."

Ryan handed his reins to a hostler who'd come running over from the nearest stable. "You two resemble each other. Do all of Honfrion's guards hold such a close resemblance?"

Tabor laughed. "No, Archmage. I'm proud to say that Khalid is also my son."

Khalid stepped forward. "If you don't mind, Lord Archmage, my sheikh asked that I bring you to him upon your arrival."

"I was expected?"

"Yes, my lord."

As the two guards led Ryan through the caravan's crowded merchant quarter, Ryan strengthened his shields with the slightest of mental adjustments. He knew that only he could hear the slight buzzing of the shield that clung to him like an invisible second skin.

The people of the caravan—the Imazighen, Arabelle's people—murmured, whispered, and stared openly at him as he passed.

"It's him! He's here!"

"It's the wizard of prophecy!"

"The princess is so lucky."

This last remark came from a girl with bright red hair. Ryan's eyes met with hers, and she quickly pulled a veil across her face—but boldly stared right back at him.

Three dwarves exited a merchant tent with mugs in their hands, and stopped short.

"I dinna believe it!" said one. "Is dat da Archmage? He glows like a lantern bug with his magic."

"Norgeon, shut yer yap!" said another. "He'll turn you into a mountain pony if you aren't respectful."

The third dwarf laughed. "That'll be an improvement, I say. Ponies are handsome creatures. Norgeon's face reminds me of a ogre's hairy rear end…"

They left the merchant's quarter behind, and Tabor and Khalid led Ryan to a large tent with several serious-looking guards posted in front of it, all of whom gave Tabor a brisk salute.

Tabor turned to Ryan. "Archmage, I'm sure that when you and my sheikh are done, you'll want to visit with the princess. I will wait here to act as escort."

"And I expect you'll act as chaperone too, right?"

Tabor failed to hold back a smile. "Archmage, you know our customs. Our princess must be kept under escort whenever feasible. After the marriage ceremony, you too would be of the Imazighen, and deemed an acceptable escort."

Ryan placed his hand on Tabor's shoulder. "I'd expect nothing less. Is the sheikh ready for me?"

Tabor looked to the posted guards, who nodded. Then Tabor opened the flap and announced Ryan's arrival.

From within the tent, a deep voice boomed. "Ryan, come in, come in. Don't stand out there like a stranger, my son."

As Ryan stepped inside, Arabelle's father, Sheikh Honfrion, greeted him with a clasp of arms and a kiss on each cheek. They sat in the middle of the tent and faced each other.

Honfrion tore some flatbread in half and handed Ryan a piece. "Young Ryan, our people have long been awaiting this moment."

Ryan chewed on the freshly baked bread. "Which moment is that?"

Honfrion pushed up his sleeves, revealing heavily muscled arms. With a surprisingly light touch, he took Ryan's hands. "Ryan, my boy. Those in my family have long had visions of the future. Sometimes the events that are seen are wished-for; at other times, they are horrifying. Arabelle's mother was a particularly strong seer, and Arabelle has such abilities too."

He sat back and wiped the sweat from the top of his head with a cloth. "I, too, have visions—though for a long time I willfully blocked them, and only in recent years have they returned."

His eyes darted around, as though looking through every corner of the tent. "Ryan, I saw your arrival moments before it happened, and I sent Tabor and Khalid out to retrieve you. It was because of that vision that I knew that I must bring you to this tent, so that you could meet—"

Honfrion froze in mid-sentence, and his normally dark brown eyes glowed white. Filaments of magic—invisible, Ryan knew, to anyone but him—began swirling around the sheikh's head and sparking throughout the tent. The energy grew, expanding outward from Honfrion, who remained oblivious to the maelstrom.

And then the swirling torrent of energy coalesced into a column two feet to the right of Honfrion. A woman stepped from the column, and the sparking magic vanished.

The woman was ancient. Gray skin, tangled gray hair, growths on her chin. She wore drab gray robes, yet shimmering waves of white magical energy hovered around her.

"Child of destiny," she said, "I am here. For you, I am a messenger."

Ryan pointed at Honfrion, who was still frozen in place. "What did you do to him?"

"Do not worry, for I will give you what you need. Once I am gone, time will continue."

"Time?"

The woman stepped forward. "Enough! Listen and watch."

The woman closed her eyes, and the tent faded from Ryan's vision.

A scene materialized in his mind.

. . .

The night is dark, the only light coming from a campfire in the distance. Four people are gathered around the campfire, all of them wearing modern clothes. Clothes from Ryan's past.

Ryan gasped. "That's my family and me when we first arrived in Trimoria!"

A few hundred yards away, several of Azazel's troops huddle together, studying the campfire from a distance.

"We already know them to be fools, drunk, or unaware of the dangers they face," said one. "Who creates a campfire so close to the swamp? Swamp cat food or slaver fodder. They deserve to be skewered."

"Kirag said we are to try to extract information."

"I don't care what Kirag said—dead is dead. It's too much trouble capturing people and interrogating them."

Though the events of the vision had clearly happened years ago, Ryan's heart raced in his chest. "We had assassins after us even *then*? How could they know we'd be there? *We* didn't even know we'd arrived in Trimoria yet."

Something lands in the midst of the huddled assassins, and a puff of smoke flies into their faces. As one of the men stands, a figure runs by, slashes his throat, and disappears into the night.

The other assassins choke, and moments later, they collapse. The mysterious figure cautiously returns.

A woman.

She glances at the distant campfire, then down at the assassins, and once again at the campfire. She moves quickly, slashing the throats of her victims, their lifeblood forming sticky pools in the grass.

The mysterious figure stares at her blood-soaked hands. Sobs wrack her body, and she looks up at the sky with familiar eyes...

"Arabelle!"

The vision faded, and Ryan's heart pounded faster than he thought possible. He looked up at the old woman, whose face was an emotionless blank. "Arabelle saved us all?"

The woman's glow brightened. "Know that both you and your betrothed are children of destiny. She acts in Seder's interest, and thus she will always act in your interest as well, for you are Seder's champion."

Her shimmering waves of white energy flared, nearly blinding him, and then fell away, leaving the tent in darkness. Ryan tapped into some of his power and made a ball of sparkling light materialize over his head.

The old woman had not departed. But now she held something in her arms. An infant boy, wrapped in a brilliant white swaddling cloth.

She held it out to him. "Seder's champion, a gift from Seder."

Ryan took the child. It had a hint of whiskers and the proportions of a dwarf. "I… I can't take care of a baby. What am I to do with it?"

A brilliant white aura shimmered around the infant, and it grew much heavier and larger. The light dimmed, and the infant had aged into a dwarf boy. The boy wriggled out of Ryan's arms and stomped his hairy feet on the ground.

He had a full beard now, though thin, and wore billowing white robes. After checking through a series of hidden pockets, he laughed and pulled out a handful of amber dice. He looked up at Ryan.

"Do you want to play any games?" he asked.

What in the world is going on?

Ryan turned to the old woman, but she was already fading away, with a hint of a smile.

As the caravan guards escorted the young dwarf toward Castle Riverton, the child whistled merrily while juggling some wooden balls he'd discovered in one of his many pockets. Ryan was still so stunned, all he could do was watch the boy depart.

Honfrion placed his hand on Ryan's shoulder. "My vision told me you were going to meet someone strange within my tent, but I didn't realize he would appear before my eyes in a flash just as I was telling you about him."

Honfrion hadn't even been aware of the time that had passed within the tent. Perhaps because no time *had* passed. What were the woman's words?

When I am gone, time will continue.

He would have to ask Eglerion about this. Perhaps the lore master would be able to explain what had happened.

Honfrion saw his worried look. "You did the right thing sending him off to the castle nursery. Clearly he knows no more about his sudden appearance than we do. In fact, it seems all he's interested in is playing games."

A woman called out. "Ryan!"

As Ryan turned, Arabelle slammed into him in a swirl of flying hair and peals of laughter, knocking him backward. They both fell in the dirt as she placed kisses on his stunned face.

"Not a very dignified greeting, Arabelle," said her father, chuckling. "I thought I taught you better."

Arabelle's smile was infectious, and Ryan grinned like a fool as she pulled him to his feet. "Ryan! You were supposed to tell me when you got here!"

Honfrion cleared his throat. "My flower, that was my fault. I asked the guards to bring him to me so the two of us could speak."

Arabelle pulled Ryan away from the crowd that was forming. As always, a handful of guards trailed behind them, including Tabor. She glanced at him and squeezed his hand, the slightest tinge of red coloring her cheeks. And she looked stunning. Her white, form-fitting dress accentuated her athletic build and curves, and it was a brilliant contrast to her dark hair and eyes.

She pulled him all the way to her tent, but before they could enter, Tabor cleared his throat. "Princess, it wouldn't be proper for the two of you to be alone."

Arabelle huffed. "But I want to speak to Ryan in private. Don't make me leave the caravan to force the issue, Tabor."

The guard scratched at his beard. "I have an idea. Follow me."

Moments later, Ryan found himself in an empty corral sitting cross-legged in front of Arabelle. The corral allowed them to talk face-to-face in private, while the guards were still able to watch them from a distance.

"Well, I suppose this will have to do," Arabelle said.

"It's fine." Ryan gave her hands a squeeze. "I respect your people's customs. I'm just happy to see you. I don't care where we are."

Arabelle's eyes glistened with unshed tears. "Ryan, I have something to confess…"

As Arabelle's tale unfolded, Ryan soon realized that Trimoria's prophecies didn't involve only the Riverton brothers. Apparently Seder, the same spirit that had taken his family from a summer vacation in the state of Arizona, and led him to become the Archmage of a land called Trimoria, had also set events in motion to ensure that Arabelle received training in the use of weapons and poisons by none other than Castien, the elf sword master.

Finally Ryan understood how she'd shown such miraculous abilities in the knife-throwing competition a few years back.

But it was the last part of her tale that was truly difficult for her to reveal. As she related her view of the very same circumstances that Ryan had just now witnessed himself in a vision, her tears flowed freely, and the guilt and shame was plain on her face.

Ryan barely let her finish before blurting out what he'd just seen in her father's tent—and explained that the actions she was confessing to had saved his family's lives. And when he made it clear to her that he felt all of her actions were justified, and that there was no reason why she should feel ashamed, a torrent of emotions erupted from her as she threw her arms around him and wept, years of pent-up guilt and uncertainty draining from her.

The sun had set during her tale, and even as they held each other, Arabelle's handmaiden came walking toward them, torch in hand. No doubt that signaled it was time for Arabelle to go.

Before Ryan could lose his opportunity, he leaned in to Arabelle's ear and whispered, "I love you."

She hooked him by the back of the neck and pulled him in for a kiss.

Miriam cleared her throat. "Princess, it's nightfall. I'm here to remind you that it is *now* seven days before your wedding, and you know that it's bad luck to see your betrothed the week before your wedding."

Ryan stood and pulled Arabelle to her feet. "I'll see you in a week, Mrs. Riverton."

Arabelle stood on the tips of her toes and whispered into his ear, "I can't wait."

A MYSTERIOUS DWARF

The voice that echoed within his head stopped mid-sentence. Malphas looked up at Sammael, his lord and master, and waited. Minor demons flitted in and out of the cavern, on some missions that the demon general couldn't care less about.

Waves of heat shimmered off of the statue-like demon on the throne; Sammael was concentrating on something that agitated him. The demon lord constantly held back a furnace of unimaginable energy that sizzled beneath his scales, and Malphas feared what would happen if his master ever lost control of that immense power. Even with his lord's control, the throne room was thick with heat. Malphas would have preferred the cooler temperatures elsewhere, but when he was called by his master, he obeyed.

Using his powers, Malphas silently asked, "What is wrong, my lord?"

The flames between Sammael's scales pulsed brighter, sending out fresh new waves of impossible heat. The minor demons streaked away, and those who weren't fast enough burst into flame, disappearing into greasy puffs of sulfurous smoke.

Only Malphas was unaffected. After all, he was second in power only to Sammael himself. He wondered if there would ever be a time when his own power could compare to that of his master, the greatest of demons.

The temperature suddenly plummeted, and Sammael stirred. His grating voice sounded once more in Malphas's head.

"I sensed a disturbance in the mist barrier. For the merest moment, I detected my human minion."

"Which minion, my lord?"

"I have seen what the Aboveworlders now call the First Protector. He is dying, and with him dies the barrier that he maintains."

Finally! Revenge is at hand.

To Malphas's surprise, the demon lord actually stood and walked from his throne. The licks of fire that surrounded him ceased, and he underwent a dramatic change. Instead of a forty-foot-tall black-scaled demon lord—the form in which Malphas had always known him—he became instead a muscled twenty-foot-tall human. Gone were the armored scales, replaced with weak human hide and tufts of hair.

The only thing that remained the same was Sammael's flaming eyes.

Seeing a human before him made Malphas itch, his instincts screaming for him to attack. But Malphas hadn't survived as long as he had without learning to control those instincts. Besides, he still detected the immense power hiding within that thin human skin.

Sammael grinned ominously. "Malphas, I am departing to see the barrier for myself. I want to see if I can hasten its deterioration. Go to the hatchery and find a couple of the shadow stalkers before they get themselves killed. Convince them to scan the barrier. They may find an opening small enough for them to sneak through."

"My lord, what should I have them attack? Everything?"

Sammael's fiery eyes flashed brightly. "Have them go to the First Protector's castle and sniff out the spirit that protects it. When they have that scent, they are to cross the barrier, and kill anyone with that bloodline. It is time for the Thariginians to pass into history."

A warm mist hung in the air as Malphas walked through the breeding grounds, or *hatchery* as it was known—a series of connected chambers that spanned many miles. Here he would find what his master requested.

Hatchlings scurried about, and as Malphas looked on, one of the stupider fools stumbled right into a searing jet of steam blasting from a crack in the earth. Screaming in pain, the demon hatchling staggered backward and stumbled into a nest—where it was immediately attacked and consumed by the younger hatchlings already there.

As it should be, Malphas thought. The weak, stupid, or

unlucky were destined to provide nourishment for the stronger, smarter, and more devious.

Malphas was all of those things and more.

A winged demon came flying past. Malphas snatched it from the air and bit the wriggling demon in half. And as he continued on his way, he savored the taste of the marrow as he crunched on the young demon's bones.

Only the strong survive.

Like the shadow stalkers. Unlike normal demons, the stalkers' bodies were practically transparent—except when they were attacked. The only visible portion of these demon assassins was a small dark-colored rock buried in their chest. They were also rare. Very rarely did they hatch, and when they did, they were usually set upon by their nest-mates before they could begin stalking other demons.

I'd never have believed I'd be looking to nurture one of these beasts.

As he continued to scan the path he walked, Malphas saw a nest surrounded by dead and decapitated hatchlings. And within the nest was a screeching battle. They were moving so quickly he couldn't easily discern the combatants, but nevertheless he dove into the melee.

When he stood, it was with a grating laugh. The demons streaked away for fear of their lives, but he had no interest in them. Squirming in his fists were two of the mysterious shadow stalkers.

They sliced and bashed against his claws, their translucent bodies sparking as they impacted against his scales. Their attacks were painful, but he was too powerful for them to do real damage. He squeezed his claws until they touched that rocky object in the middle of the young bodies. And when he put pressure on that tiny rock, the creatures shivered and fell still.

"One more attack on me, and I'll crush you. Pay attention."

The creatures' hides shimmered, and they both stared up at him attentively. When he loosened his grip, they remained motionless.

"I will give you a blood scent to follow. Our lord and master has requested that you follow the scent and destroy all who carry that same blood."

The stalkers quivered with what Malphas took as agreement, and he marched toward the distant castle with his two new weapons.

Ryan slept restlessly in the tent provided by Arabelle's father, his eyes darting back and forth behind closed eyelids.

Gathered in a field is a vast army that includes all manner of soldiers—humans, dwarves, even elven races. Through their midst rides Aaron, Ryan's brother, now a young general on horseback, barking directions to the various platoon leaders. He is handsome, with defined cheekbones and sparkling blue eyes, and his armor and sword glow with a fiery-red glint.

Aaron unsheathes his sword, waves it above his head, and points to the ridge just ahead. Beyond that ridge a black cloud has formed, radiating despair, and beneath that cloud is another army—this one borne of nightmare.

The armies begin to advance on one another.

The vision flashed white.

Ohaobbok walks a natural stone bridge across a chasm, whipped by wind that threatens to pull him into the abyss below. The ogre is equipped in plate armor that glows a pristine white and emits sparks with every movement. His sword, sheathed at his side, is a tremendous greatsword with a pommel of red.

Following behind Ohoabbok is Ryan himself, except older. In one hand he carries a sparking metal staff, and in the other, a brilliant diamond the size of a melon. The diamond pulses with radiant power.

Crossing the bridge from the opposite side of the chasm is a fiend of blackness and fire, reeking of brimstone and emanating waves of heat. The fiend matches Ohaobbok in size, and it, too, wields a giant sword.

As the two great warriors meet at the middle of the bridge, another presence is felt. Behind the fiend, at the edge of the chasm, stands a deeper, darker presence, palpably evil, so enormous that it dwarfs both fiend and ogre.

Swords clash, and Ryan raises the diamond above his head.

. . .

Ryan shivered as he awoke. It never got easier, seeing his future self in these dreams each night. In fact it got harder, because the version of himself he saw in the prophecy more closely matched the man he saw in the mirror every day.

The final confrontation approaches.

It was still early when Ryan departed the caravan for Castle Riverton, but thousands of soldiers were already milling about in the practice fields, now organized into various training camps. He was passing the mustering grounds when the clash of weaponry startled his horse, which pulled hard against the reins. He patted its neck and spoke soothingly. "Calm down. It's all right."

As he arrived at the stables, a stableboy rushed out to meet him. "Archmage, sir! I'll take care of him for you."

Ryan dismounted and handed over the reins. "He isn't a warhorse, so he isn't used to the sound of battle. It seems to be spooking him."

"Yessir, I have some ear muffs in the stables for him. He'll be fine."

As the boy led the horse to the stables, Ryan looked across the practice field—and immediately spotted the man he knew he could always find here: Throll Lancaster, the king of Trimoria himself, descendant of the legendary First Protector, Zenethar Thariginian.

He stood on a platform in the midst of hundreds of fresh recruits, demonstrating the basic forms of swordplay.

Ryan chuckled. Throll didn't need a platform for people to see him. He was an immense man, topping seven feet. He was also one of the best swordsmen in the land. Although Throll had recently admitted that Aaron, his former student, had surpassed even his abilities.

Throll wasn't the only friend of Ryan's who stood above the rest. Ohaobbok, the ogre of the prophecies and a trusted friend of both the Riverton and Lancaster families, was over thirteen feet tall. Ryan easily located him on the grounds, only to realize that Ohaobbok was entering a sparring ring with Ryan's brother.

This should be good, Ryan thought. Despite his size, the ogre was very quick on his feet, and rivaled all but a few in combat. Ryan hurried over to watch.

Aaron wore his light armor and held two swords in his hands. But Ohaobbok's sword was a good eight feet long, making Aaron's weapons look like mere toys.

Ohaobbok swung first, but Aaron ducked under the whistling blade, moving the tips of his swords in a mesmerizing pattern, faster and faster until they buzzed. It was a trick that Castien, the elven sword master, had taught him. Castien trained the most advanced of the Trimorian troops, and the men who managed to complete his training typically became captains within the newly assembled army.

Though you wouldn't know it to look at him, Aaron's strength rivaled Ohaobbok's. Aaron wasn't magical in the conventional sense—or at least, Ryan had never detected an aura of magic surrounding his brother—but he had a type of internal magic that made him not only immensely strong but tough as a rock. As Ryan's father once commented, "It's as if his bones are unbreakable. He shouldn't be able to exert that much strength with the same kind of bones you or I have."

Aaron also had his own sort of magical reservoir, like Ryan did. When Ryan overused magic, he became exhausted, and only great quantities of food would refill that magical reservoir. Aaron's strength was the same; when he over-exerted himself excessively, his hunger knew no bounds.

Aaron yelled and charged. Ohaobbok nimbly dove out of the way, nearly crushing some of the bystanders.

Castien, standing on an observation dais, screamed at the onlookers. "Stand back from the sparring ring, fools! Do you want to be injured?"

Ohaobbok lunged, swinging his sword in a vicious arc, just as Aaron turned to face his opponent again. Ryan was about to place a shield around his brother when Aaron's sword miraculously blocked the swing, the metal blades scraping against each other. Aaron's feet dug two yard-long furrows as he blocked his opponent's assault.

Aaron smiled, dropped his swords, grabbed the flat of Ohaobbok's blade, and pulled with a mighty grunt. A crack echoed across the sparring ring as the blade separated from the hilt.

Aaron then pulled a dagger from his belt and leaped at Ohaobbok. He landed between his friend's legs and tapped Ohaobbok gently with the blade.

"I win!" he declared.

Ohaobbok looked down at the hilt in his hand and frowned. "Poor manufacturing, I say."

The crowd laughed.

Castien stepped into the sparring ring. "Aaron, don't ever do that again or you'll find a demon's horn buried in your gullet. You cannot count on the shoddy workmanship of practice weapons to get by, even in a sparring session."

"Sorry, Castien." He hitched his thumb toward Ryan. "I saw my brother standing there and wanted to end this quickly. I need to talk to him about his child."

The onlookers turned to stare at Ryan.

"I don't have a child!" he said. *Finding a child and having one are* not *the same thing.*

Aaron joined him outside the sparring ring, leaving behind a fuming elf and a bemused ogre. "So what *is* the story with this dwarf?" Aaron asked. "He seems harmless, but my 'something is wrong' senses tingle anytime I'm near him. He isn't just a dwarf kid, is he?"

"He is, and he isn't." Ryan put his arm around his younger brother's shoulder. "Come on. I'll explain as we walk."

Malphas watched the shadow stalkers scurry along the border of the castle grounds, seeking an identifying scent. Malphas despised being this close to the wizard's castle. Though he was still a good half mile away from its main walls, even from here he could feel the strange force that protected Castle Thariginian's grounds from intrusion.

On several occasions over the years, Malphas had tried to cross the invisible boundary. Every attempt had been painfully unsuccessful; it felt like a thousand daggers were being plunged under his scales. No demon was allowed to pass. Even the shadow stalkers instinctively knew where the edge of the castle grounds lay, and they would go no closer.

Both shadow walkers came to an abrupt halt and emitted a sharp keening. Malphas pointed at the tremendous gray mist barrier to the south.

"If you've captured the scent, then go there, and look for an opening."

Deep furrows of dirt flew backward as the near-invisible demons sped toward the mist.

Malphas's barbed tail whipped about in excitement as he watched them go.

If they're successful, I'll finally get to finish what was started.

Ryan paused at a junction. "All these hallways look the same."

Aaron laughed and pointed up at the wall. "Not anymore. See up there? While you were gone, I had the castle stonemasons put markings on the walls to help us find our way around. The dwarves may be great builders, but they don't understand that the rest of us don't have their natural sense of direction." He shook his head. "Can you believe only a few months ago, we were still sharing a bed in Throll's farmhouse? And now we live in a castle that can house the population of a city."

They continued down the halls, Aaron leading the way and explaining the new markings, then stopped at a large door where two soldiers stood guard.

"Henson, are the children in the nursery?"

"Yes, sir. Commander Riverton, young Lady Riverton, and Prince Lancaster have just returned from their weekly visit to the First Protector's fountain in Aubgherle. The children seem to be having a grand time with their new visitor."

"I heard there's an observation room back this way?" Ryan said. "We were hoping to watch them unobserved for a bit."

"Of course, Archmage. It's just past this door on your right. Truly amazing—you can see through the window, but the children see only a reflection!"

Ryan knew this was his father's doing. Dad might be one of the most powerful war wizards around, but he preferred playing at being a blacksmith with the dwarves, or tinkering with one of his science experiments.

Thanking the guards, they continued down the hall to the observation room, where a large window looked into the nursery, just as the guard had described it. In addition to the one-way viewing glass, holes had been drilled into the ceiling from the observation room into the nursery so they could hear what was being said inside.

Currently, the dwarf—who Ryan guessed was about five, though it was hard to know for sure—was in there playing dolls with Ryan's little sister, four-year-old Rebecca. Throll's son, five-year-old Zenethar, was playing with blocks, and two young swamp cats were sleeping in the corner. These were the kittens of Silver, the Rivertons' former housecat who had been transformed into a three-hundred-pound swamp cat upon the family's arrival in Trimoria. The gray kitten was named Cloud, and the black one was Shadow. The cats were still quite young, but they'd already grown very attached to Rebecca and Zenethar.

One of Rebecca's dolls floated through the air as if of its own accord, and when the girl tried to chase it, she lost her balance and fell into a pile of pillows, her brown hair flying in her face. She got back up, laughing.

"How'd you do that, Ramai?" she said to the dwarf. "I didn't know you're a wizard too."

The young dwarf twirled his finger and made the doll spin in circles around the room. "Wizard? No, I just know tricks."

"No tricks!" Rebecca said, chasing her doll again. "My Maggie is getting dizzy!"

"What do you know of his magic powers?" Aaron asked Ryan.

"I know that he transformed from a newborn to a walking and talking kid in seconds. As to what else he's capable of, your guess is as good as mine. In truth, I don't understand what I'm seeing. Normally I see threads of magic around a wizard when he uses his powers. With Ramai, I don't see anything other than an indistinct white haze. I'm hoping Eglerion might know more."

Zenethar held up a wooden block. "Ramai, can you float this around? I wanna do my archery practice."

"Is archery a fun game?" Ramai asked.

Zenethar nodded. "Ryan does this lots! Just float it slowly."

Ramai levitated the block and made it float around the stone chamber. Maggie dropped to the floor, and Rebecca ran over, dusted her doll off, and gave her a hug.

Zenethar watched the block carefully. Then he flicked his finger, and a sparkling bolt of energy flew at the block, sending it spinning.

Rebecca laughed and clapped with glee. "You got it, Zenny! Do it again!"

Ramai continued to move the block around, but faster now. Zenethar fired again and missed, leaving a tiny scorch mark on the wall.

"This *is* a fun game!" said Ramai.

Ryan muttered, "This could get out of hand quickly."

"Oh, let them have fun," said Aaron. "They can't exactly burn down a stone castle."

But Aaron had spoken too soon. The next time Zenethar fired, he accidentally sent a bolt of energy at Ramai. The bolt bounced off the dwarf's white robe and singed his beard. Ramai slapped at his beard and announced, "That is *not* a fun game!"

Rebecca went over to the dwarf, and Ryan saw tiny threads of her healing magic twirl around her head. As she reached out to the dwarf's beard, the collected energy poured through her hands. "Dat better?"

Ramai grinned at the young healer through his scraggly young beard.

Rebecca glared at Zenethar. "You s'posed to be Protector!" She stomped her foot and pointed at the dwarf. "Don't hurt our friend!"

Zenethar bowed his head. "I'm sorry."

But Ramai had already forgotten it. "Want to learn to juggle?" he said. "It's a fun game." He pulled a wooden ball from within his robes and rolled it to Zenethar. Then he pulled out several more.

"Wow," said Rebecca. "You gots lotta stuff in your robes."

Aaron turned to his brother. "That's one unique dwarf you've found."

Ryan shook his head. "Tell me about it."

———

Sammael concentrated on the barrier that shimmered in front of him. Normally he would remain within the cool depths of the abyss, but at a distance, even he found himself lacking a *feel* for the magics employed in the creation of the mist barrier.

Sniffing, he detected the ordered threads of power employed in its construction. It so reminded him of the smell of his brother, Seder, that he shivered with the memories of their arguments.

At the dawn of time, the spirit world had birthed Sammael, lover of chaos, and Seder, lover of order. Rulers of their respective realms, but with opposite goals. Any opportunity Sammael took to influence a world, Seder fought back. It was always a stalemate.

And then there was Lilith.

The Creator made Lilith much later. She came into being only five thousand years ago. It was then that Sammael thought, "With her, I can overcome my brother, and finally own a world for myself."

Lilith seemed to prefer Sammael, and was easily influenced… at first. But soon after her arrival in the spirit world, she disappeared.

For millennia, Sammael puzzled at this. *How did she leave the spirit world?*

Eventually, he discovered that Lilith had fled to one of the

Creator's lower worlds—worlds that held his lesser creations, creatures that were weak but numerous. The world she had entered had named itself Trimoria.

He saw her through the eyes of some of those who she'd interacted with.

She was ruling a world, and I wanted to join her. Seder couldn't overcome us both.

Long ago, he'd found Seder building his influence within certain inanimate objects on various worlds, but only now did Sammael understood the wisdom of such activity. That was how he could escape the spirit world and follow Lilith.

While still in the spirit world, Sammael had reached out to this world, using all of his power. He'd latched on to a demon who held in its grasp a large crystal, one that he was able to infuse with a piece of himself. It was a moment of excruciating pain, a sensation he'd never before experienced. Once the process had begun, he couldn't stop it, and he felt his essence stretched to the breaking point.

For the first time since he'd become self-aware, he wondered if he could cease to exist.

And then he woke in a new world. Trimoria.

He was filled with euphoria as he realized that Seder's influence was almost non-existent in this world. But it was then that he felt his weakness. No longer was he omnipotent. He had at his disposal only a fraction of the powers he'd enjoyed in the spirit world. Still, even a fraction of his powers made him far more powerful than any of the creatures of Trimoria.

Now, as he stood in front of the barrier, he exerted all this fractional power against it. He mentally pushed against the mist, feeling for a weakness. The magical threads bent, but with no effect. He stretched his senses even further. *There must be...*

For the briefest of moments the threads parted, and he sensed life across the barrier. And not just life—points of Seder's influence.

In that split second between the beats of a heart, he sent his powers rushing through. He pushed against those white balls of Seder's power. But his authority was deflected. He couldn't see into their minds. Except in the case of one.

He found a wizard of great strength who didn't have Seder's protection. And then the barrier closed like a trap.

He laughed when he saw that the shadow stalkers were no longer on this side of the barrier.

Sow chaos, my little creations.

As Sammael walked back to the comfort of the Abyss, he had only one thing on his mind.

Who is Ryan Riverton?

TWO BECOME ONE

"Mom," said Ryan, "why don't you have one of the seamstresses do that?"

His mother sat on her padded chair, using a gossamer gold thread to embroider the new family symbol along the fringe of Ryan's wedding robe. He didn't have the heart to point out that the seamstresses would do a better job.

She worked on evenly spacing her stitches. "I have helpers taking care of so much as it is. The very least I can do is this."

Honestly, Ryan wasn't really happy about the robe in the first place. He preferred his regular robe—durable, comfortable, and plain. His wedding robe was white silk with a red fringe, and now it would be adorned with golden dragons and triple lightning bolts. But knew better than to argue. She'd made up her mind on what he was wearing.

That same image—the dragons—had been appearing all over the castle in recent days, hung from banners, even engraved into the very stones of the castle itself. It was all part of readying the castle for the day of celebration. Ryan's wedding day.

Tomorrow.

"Mom…" Ryan said hesitantly. "Honestly… I'm nervous. Do you have any advice for me?"

She chuckled as she continued her needlework. "Just do whatever Arabelle asks you to. She's a good girl, very smart, and a gentle soul. When you two are married, she should be the first and last person you listen to."

If only she knew, Ryan thought. *Arabelle isn't nearly as gentle as she thinks she is.*

"But for right now," Mom added, "I advise you to go find your father, and the two of you go greet your guests. Many are already here, and the elves are due to arrive at any moment. This is your wedding, so it's your responsibility to welcome them."

Ryan bent and kissed his mother on the cheek. "Yes, milady."

Ryan found his father in the castle smithy, working with his growing entourage of dwarven helpers. He agreed that the two of them should go meet the guests, and he was ready to head straight off and begin. But there was one problem.

"Dad," said Ryan, "maybe you should go shower first."

"His father was a mess. Soot covered his face, and he wore a filthy apron, singed from the constant contact with burning embers. Even his beard, which he'd grown over the last year despite his wife's protestations, had streaks of soot to match the increasingly present streaks of gray.

Dad looked down at himself and shrugged. He hung up his singed apron, rolled up his sleeves, and dunked his head into a water barrel. Then he began scrubbing his face and arms. When he was done, he stood, water streaming from his beard, and a dwarf threw him a towel.

The dwarf laughed and elbowed some of the other blacksmiths. "I be tellin' you boys. Our Lord Riverton be just like one of us. Hard worker, and don't be carin' about nonsense like showers. I tells ya, a good dunk in a barrel's all a dwarf be needin' to be presentable."

Dad laughed. "Speaking of that, Bintas, when the rest of you soot-covered anvil bangers join me in celebrating my boy's wedding tomorrow… you're going to have to clean up. Lady Riverton would have words for me if you showed up in your work clothes."

Bintas frowned under his dark beard, but with a glare at the other dwarves, he said, "Have you no worries, milord. Even if I have to chase these filthy ale-guzzlers into a river, I'll make sure the crew is all presentable for tomorrow's fun."

"I promise you it'll be worth it. I've ordered fifty barrels of the good ale from the Bloated Buzzard in Aubgherle. Nothing but the best for my guests."

That pronouncement was met with a big huzzah. The dwarves would clean themselves up all right, if that's what it took to partake in several fine mugs of ale.

<hr>

Ryan's face burned with embarrassment as Silas, the head of the Redbeard clan, told him stories about his own wedding day—*and* the night that followed. He extracted himself from the conversation as quickly as he could.

They were in the castle's main hall, where several hundred guests from throughout Trimoria were talking, drinking, and having a good time. Ryan didn't even know who most of these people were, but he'd dutifully bowed to and made pleasantries with dozens upon dozens of them already.

So he was relieved when someone he actually knew came over to join him and his father. Throll walked right up to him and raised his mug in salute. "Ryan Riverton, for the sake of your parents and bride, I order you to relinquish that somber demeanor! Smile, young man. For tomorrow, you will be married, and your life will forever be changed."

Those standing nearby cheered at their king's words, and soon most of the hall was banging their mugs on the banquet tables.

"Hear hear!"

"Drink up!"

His father yelled over the din. "Well, Ryan? Drink up! It's a moment to celebrate!"

Ryan drank the cool yeasty beverage and felt the heat spread through his limbs. When he'd drained the mug, someone thrust another tankard in his hand, and the party began in earnest.

Ryan woke the next morning on a cot in his parents' bedroom. He didn't remember how he got here, or why, but here he was. His parents were here, too, and they were arguing. Apparently, about him.

"What were you thinking, Jared? Drinking like a sailor and getting our son drunk the night before his wedding."

"Ryan needed to loosen up, Aubrey. He had a lot of fun last night. He was actually dancing with the queen and having a blast."

Ryan sat up, and the room tilted unexpectedly. He had to grab the edge of the cot to keep from falling back down. His temples throbbed, and his mouth was impossibly dry.

"I don't remember dancing with Gwen," he said. *Although it seems there's a lot I don't remember.*

Jared laughed. "Not *that* queen. You were dancing with Labri."

Ryan groaned. "Don't tell me I made a fool of myself in front of the queen of the elves."

"No, you were fine. Throll and I kept an eye on you. You just danced, laughed, and sang kid songs at the top of your lungs." He chuckled and sang, "If you're happy and you know it clap your hands…"

Ryan couldn't tell if his Dad was joking. "No. I didn't. Did I?"

"You did. But it was great. The dwarves were banging mugs on the tables as they joined in, and soon the words turned into the perfect barroom chant as you led the partygoers into things like 'drink your ale' and the like."

Ryan smiled weakly at the thought of the entire hall singing nursery songs from another world. He stood, slowly, and winced.

"My head is killing me."

Aubrey grabbed his elbow and placed her other hand on his forehead. "I can't take all of the symptoms away, but I can remove some of the pain. Trust me, I just had to do it for your father. He seems spry now, but you should have seen him a few minutes ago."

Shimmering threads of magic pooled around her head, and Ryan felt a sudden release of tension.

"Thanks, Mom."

"You still need to take care of yourself," she said. "In particular, you to drink some water. *Lots* of water. You're dehydrated, and there's nothing magical I can do about that. You have a big day ahead of you." She shook her head at her husband. "And this was not the way to start it off."

Behind her back, Dad gave Ryan a sheepish shrug and a wink.

A two-man patrol walked the perimeter of the central marketplace within the Imaghizen caravan. Now that the morning mist had been burnt away by the midday sun, the market was bustling with activity. The caravan included over a thousand wagons, and it seemed today every one of its people was out, either selling or buying.

But the soldiers were always on watch, even on a bright day such as this one, as every now and then the caravan was struck by roving bands of thieves, or, occasionally, slavers.

One of the patrolmen shook his head. "We should be sampling some of the fresh breads rather than walking patrol. On a bright day like this, can you imagine a band of thieves daring to even come close?"

His partner shrugged. "It's easy work. Better than night duty. Besides, you don't want to go filling up on bread. Didn't Miranda promise you a hearty stew after your shift?" he chuckled "In fact, I bet that's not the *only* thing she promised to give you."

The first soldier blushed, but before he could reply, plumes of blood jetted from both men's necks as they were attacked by something they could barely see.

***

"It's my pleasure to announce the arrival of the lord and lady of the castle. Headmaster and headmistress of the Riverton Academy of Magic. The greatest war wizard of our time and the greatest healer to ever grace our people…"

Aaron leaned over to his brother. "How long is this introduction going to take?"

Ryan stifled a laugh. "Grendel's always been a blowhard."

The introductions continued, with Aaron coming next, and then it was Ryan's turn.

"And finally," said Grendel, "let me introduce one of the two people responsible for our gathering today. Despite his young age, this scion of the house of Riverton is partially responsible for freeing us from Azazel's chains of servitude. He is charged by prophecy, along with his brother, with leading our fight against the maw of darkness beyond the barrier. To everyone gathered here today, allow me to introduce the Archmage of Trimoria, and today's groom… Ryan Riverton!"

Ryan walked into the long stone chamber to the sound of the crowd's stomping feet. The hall was set up with row upon row of benches, and they were all packed—hundreds of people who had come to witness this, his wedding.

Ryan walked down the center corridor to the dais at the far end. His family had preceded him, and looked back from the bench in the front row. Ryan returned their nods and smiles as he passed, and stepped up to the dais, where Throll was waiting.

The king patted Ryan on the shoulder. "Feeling all right?"

"Other than being more nervous than I've ever been in my life, sure. I'm fine."

Throll chuckled.

As Grendel launched into his final introduction—this one for the bride—Ryan double-checked his robes, making sure every-thing was in order. Throll put a hand on his shoulder and whispered.

"Stop fidgeting. You look fine. And even if you didn't, it's too late to do anything about it now. Just smile and relax."

Grendel's voice continued to boom through the hall. "… princess of the Imazighen, great healer of her people, and the lady of today's ceremony… Arabelle Riverton!"

That was one thing Ryan had thankfully gotten used to in advance. In accordance with the customs of the Imaghizen, Arabelle had taken Ryan's last name as soon as they were betrothed.

Ryan suddenly felt a moment of panic. He turned to Throll.

"You have the white ribbon?"

Throll patted his shoulder. "Shh… look…"

Ryan turned to face the hall and saw Arabelle floating toward him, escorted by her father. She looked radiant, her multi-layered black silk dress billowing as she walked. A traditional veil was draped across the lower half of her heart-shaped face, leaving only her soulful eyes uncovered—eyes that were only for him. Once again he was convinced that he was the luckiest man in Trimoria to have her in his life.

Honfrion kissed his daughter on both cheeks, and she gave him a hug. As he joined Ryan's family on the front bench, tears glistened in his eyes. And it wasn't just him. Ryan's mother was dabbing away her own tears, and even Dad looked choked up.

Arabelle stepped up beside him and gingerly took his hand. He stared down into her dark eyes and smiled.

"You two ready?" Throll asked quietly.

Ryan and Arabelle both nodded, not taking their eyes off one another.

Throll projected his voice across the chamber.

"Arabelle Riverton, do you vow to be matched from this day forward to Ryan Riverton, to have and to hold, for better or for worse, in sickness and in health? To love and cherish him, to keep no secrets from him, to bear him no ill will? Under the Creator's witness, do you vow this?"

Arabelle squeezed Ryan's fingers and spoke in a strong, unwavering voice. "I do."

To Ryan's dismay, tears blurred his vision, and Arabelle matched him tear for tear.

"Ryan Riverton, do you vow to be matched from this day

forward to Arabelle Riverton, to have and to hold, for better or for worse, in sickness and in health? To love and cherish her, to keep no secrets from her, to bear her no ill will? Under the Creator's witness, do you vow this?"

"I do."

Throll pulled out a long white silk ribbon. The couple held their arms out, and the king looped the silk around their arms, loosely binding them together.

"With this ribbon, I bind you. Let this ribbon symbolize the binding of two lives as one. Just as two trees can be grafted together, I now bind you both. May the roots of your shared life and the strength of your love bring you happiness and prosperity. Let nothing in this world tear this binding asunder. I call upon the blessings of the Creator to sanctify this pairing, and to show his pleasure by giving them a long and productive life together—"

The torches that lined the walls suddenly flared with a brilliant white light, and just as quickly, they dimmed again. A quiet murmur ran through the crowd.

Throll cleared his throat loudly and continued.

"As the Protector-General and King of Trimoria, I pronounce you husband and wife. Ryan, you may kiss—"

Arabelle flipped away her veil, leaped into Ryan's arms, and kissed him deeply. The audience burst into laughter.

When the two broke apart, both breathless and red-faced, Throll put his hands on the married couple's shoulders and presented them to the audience. "May I be the first to introduce you to the newest Lord and Lady Riverton. Come, greet the happy couple, for it is a joyous occasion. "May all within these halls be of good cheer and celebrate!"

Throll raised a mug to his friends. "Aubrey, be strong. You knew this was going to happen."

It was very late at night—or more accurately, very early in the morning—and the guests had staggered to their accommodations, leaving only Throll, his lovely wife Gwen, Honfrion, and Jared and Aubrey to watch as the servants cleared away the last of the celebration.

Aubrey wiped a tear from her cheek. "I know, but soon Aaron will be marrying Sloane, and my babies will be someone else's responsibility."

Gwen took Aubrey's hand in her own. "Trust me, I know how you feel. It was only moments ago that Sloane was bouncing on my lap and the only one she wanted to talk to was me. Now, she only wants to talk to Aaron—or perhaps use her magic to talk with all the animals on the farm. Even Zenethar is pulling away now. He always wants to be off practicing his magic. I sometimes feel like I'm not needed anymore."

Throll looked at Jared. "Is this the kind of somber conversation we have to look forward to from now on?"

Jared laughed and changed the topic. "Honfrion, do you have any insight into where the new couple is off to on their honeymoon? I have to say, I'm still not comfortable with all the secrecy."

Honfrion shrugged. "I don't know for certain, but my Arabelle said she wanted to visit the elves. I wouldn't be surprised if they're halfway to Eluanethra by now."

Aubrey smiled. "I think you're right about that. I ran into Arabelle's maidservant a few days ago, and she hinted that Arabelle had arranged something with Labri."

Throll bowed his head. "Well, wherever they're off to, I just pray they find some moments of happiness together. I have a bad feeling that times will be changing soon."

When Arabelle and Ryan arrived at Eluanethra, they were escorted to a cozy cabin on the edge of the town hidden deep in the forest. Miriam and Labri had specially prepared it for them with everything the newly married couple needed: fresh fruit and wine, a comfortable bed, and all the privacy they wanted.

Now, as Arabelle lay next to her sleeping husband, she smiled.

Husband. She liked the word. It felt new, but natural.

She trailed her fingers through his dark brown hair, and his eyebrows furrowed. He was dreaming. She wished she had Sloane's gift of reading minds.

Then he kicked his feet, tossed his head back and forth, and whimpered. She quickly soothed him.

"Shh, my love. It's only a nightmare."

On a hunch, she pulled healing energy from deep within her body and pushed it into him. Normally, if she transferred healing energy into someone who wasn't sick or injured, it would bounce back at her, as it had no place to go. But Ryan's body accepted her energy, and his restlessness abated.

She wondered: *Was he sick and I didn't know it?*

Rebecca and Zenethar watched as Ramai taught them a new game they could play with dice.

"We'll start with something simple. You can count, right?"

Rebecca nodded confidently. "I can count to ahunrid. Is that enough?"

Zenethar laughed. "It's called one-hun-red." To Ramai he added, "I can count to a quizillion!"

"All right, that's good enough," said Ramai. "The object of this game is to—"

A yell sounded just outside the nursery, cutting him off. The two swamp cats leapt to their feet growling, their fur standing on end.

Ramai ripped off his billowing white cloak. "Hide under this. And stay still." He threw the cape over them both, and the two children disappeared.

The door smashed open, and a nearly invisible blood-covered figure appeared in the doorway. The cats both leapt at it, but with a crack of bone they were flung backward. They landed hard on the floor, broken and twitching.

Ramai quickly realized what he was facing. The creature would have been invisible were it not for the blood that covered it… and the stone mass at its center. This was a shadow stalker.

He strengthened his shield of obscurement around the children, then concentrated on his dice. They glowed with a white aura, then flattened and expanded into sharpened throwing stars. One right after the next, he flung them all directly at the mass at the demon's center.

The shadow stalker staggered back only momentary as the stars penetrated its chest. Then it continued to move forward, unfazed, sniffing the ground for its unseen prey.

Ramai focused on the stars now embedded in the demon's chest. He chose the one closest to the creature's central mass, and transformed it again—this time making it form a solid ball around that fist-sized rock.

The stalker gasped, flailed—and then collapsed, dead, its translucent body bursting into flame. Ramai had suffocated it.

Aaron raced into the nursery just as the remnants of the demon's body turned to ashes. Several soldiers were on his heels.

"Where's my sister?" he demanded.

Rebecca and Zenethar slipped from underneath the cloak, reappearing as if from thin air. But instead of running to her brother, Rebecca ran to the injured cats. "Shadow! Cloud!" She laid her hands on the animals, using the healing powers she'd inherited.

Ramai gathered his throwing stars—now transformed back into ordinary dice—from the pile of ashes, then sniffed the air. With alarm, he grabbed his cloak and raced past the bewildered soldiers and out the door.

Castien sprinted down the long corridor, chasing the echoing sound of a soldier's scream. When he saw the blood-soaked walls and bodies ahead, he drew both of his swords.

He sprinted through the doorway into the throne room, only to find a nearly transparent creature, spattered in blood, hovering over the unconscious king of Trimoria.

The elf launched himself across the room, but the creature moved with blinding speed, lashing out with a rope-like appendage. Castien's blade blocked the attack, but the strength behind the blow was incredible, and his arm twisted violently upon impact.

Despite the pain in his right arm, the sword master quickly wove a pattern in the air with his swords and moved between the demon and the king. The beast seemed to have no real interest in Castien, but only wanted to get back to the king. And it was so fast—it was all Castien could do to stay between the monster and its desired prey.

A young dwarf came barreling into the room, glowing with an eerie white aura.

"Careful, dwarf," Castien cried. "Call for help—lots of it!"

The demon slammed into Castien. Again he deflected the

attack with his swords, but this time he felt his muscles tear, and he staggered backwards.

It was coming at him again when the dwarf threw several projectiles that made the creature pause.

Castien took the opportunity to crouch over the king in a defensive position. But the pain in his arms and shoulders was intense.

I'll not survive another assault.

The dwarf stepped closer to the demon and made an intricate motion with his hands. The white glow around him dimmed, and the projectiles lodged in the monster's body glowed white.

With a clap of the dwarf's hands, the discs transformed themselves into yellow cubes.

Dice?

The creature collapsed, thrashed about, then crackled with fiery energy. Within moments it was nothing but ashes.

Castien sat up groggily. He must have passed out, because a student healer was hovering over him.

The student handed him a flask. "Drink this, sword master. Headmistress Riverton charged it herself."

Castien unstopped the flask and drank deeply, feeling the potion's healing properties knit the fibers of his muscles back together.

Then he remembered. "The king!"

"He is being cared for. See for yourself."

The student stepped aside, and Castien saw the king was now

sitting upright, pushing away a flask being offered to him by Aubrey. Aaron Riverton was kneeling at the king's side.

"Two mugs full is more than enough!" Throll cried. "You're worse than my mother."

"A little extra healing won't hurt, Throll. You very nearly died."

Castien rose and went to his side. "Are you sure you're all right, Your Highness?"

"I'm perfectly fine now, thanks to Aubrey. And to you. If you hadn't arrived when you did... How did you stop that thing?"

"I didn't, Your Highness. At best I delayed it a few seconds." He shook his head. "It was defeated by a dwarf."

"What dwarf?"

It was Aaron who answered. "Ramai. Ryan's mysterious... 'child.' It seems he alone dispatched both of those creatures."

"There was more than one?"

"Yes, but only the two, both of which, as I have said, are now dead. Dad has scanned the area to confirm no other sightings, and he's had the war wizards pair off and set up a constant patrol."

At that moment Jared and Ramai came into the room, with Rebecca and Zenethar following.

Aaron gestured to Ramai. "Your Highness, this is the dwarf who saved your life."

Throll rose to his feet, only to kneel and bow his head. "Ramai. We have much to be thankful to you for."

Ramai seemed merely amused. He took some balls from a pocket of his cloak and began juggling.

Dad looked down at him. "Ramai, do you know what those things were?"

Ramai shrugged. "Those were shadow stalkers. A demon hatched from the abyss. They are rare. But they don't like to play games. I've tried to play with them many times over the centuries. They don't like games at all."

"O-over the centries?" said Zenethar. "Ramai, how old are you?"

As if in answer, a white glow bloomed around the dwarf, and he rose into the air. He turned to face Jared, and though his lips did not move, an otherworldly voice emanated from him.

"Charged you are with bringing life to this castle. A Dedicate will you need to find, and nearby will they be."

His eyes closed, and the voice spoke again.

"In this time and place, the games I wanted to play are complete."

When the dwarf opened his eyes again, a white light shone from them. With an impish grin, he waved at everyone and began to slowly fade from sight.

But before he completely disappeared, he winked. "Farewell. There are others who need to learn some new games."

A SACRIFICE IS NEEDED

Through weary eyelids, Ryan awoke to see something he'd never expected to see in the middle of the night. A sweat-covered woman with daggers in each hand, viciously lunging at an unseen opponent.

He couldn't help but smile. *She's my wife.*

She continued her nighttime exercise, slashing at imaginary targets, then spun, her damp hair whipping across her face, and saw Ryan watching.

"Sorry," she said. "I didn't mean to wake you."

Ryan gave her a mischievous smile. "I'd have thought you'd be tired after…"

Arabelle grabbed a towel and dried herself. "I'm quite ready for more if you are."

Ryan blushed. "No—I mean, yes. I mean… don't you sleep?"

Arabelle put her daggers away, then bounced into bed and ran her fingers through Ryan's hair. "I told you about the time I was poisoned, and the nighttime training that helped me survive it."

"Yes, I just… I didn't realize you still did that. The poison has been gone for years."

"Well, now it's a habit. I very rarely sleep for more than an hour or two at a time, and vigorous exercise is the only thing that can get me back to sleep again. But now that we're married…" She burrowed under the covers, pressed her body against his, and put her lips to his ear. "Perhaps my nighttime exercise is something you could help me with."

As Ryan and Arabelle walked hand in hand through the forest city of Eluanethra, he couldn't help but notice the wide smile on Arabelle's face.

"I see that you like Eluanethra," he said, reaching around her waist and giving her a squeeze.

Her grin widened. "I do. Since I was a little girl, I dreamed of being here."

Just then a woman shouted and came running toward them. Arabelle smiled and shouted back a greeting, and Ryan realized with surprise that this was Arabelle's handmaiden, Miriam.

"Oh, Princess, I can't tell you how exciting it is to be here! Elder Xinthian allowed me to visit and… they took me seriously and… astronomy projections as precise… need proper aperture…" She was so out of breath she could barely string her words together.

Xinthian came walking up behind her, at a much more sedate

pace. He placed a wrinkled hand on her shoulder, and she jumped, startled.

"Oh, Elder, I didn't see you. I was just telling my princess about all that we've talked about..."

"Yes, my dear, I heard." Xinthian normally didn't show much emotion on his face, but he smiled fondly at Miriam. "Arabelle," he asked, "did you know she had such a gift?"

"A gift?"

"Oh, yes. This girl has a real aptitude for calculations. Especially as it pertains to the study of stars and what we see above us."

"Uhh... no, I didn't realize that."

Miriam blurted, "I'm sorry, Princess, but I didn't think you had interest in such, so I never spoke much of it."

"Well," said Xinthian, "Have you two lovebirds broken your fast yet?"

Ryan and Arabelle shook their heads.

"Good! Neither have I. Come. Let's eat together, and we can talk."

Malphas approached the castle once more. He knew of only one way to tell if the shadow stalkers had done their job. If the protection around the Thariginian castle had abated, he would know they had succeeded.

As he came nearer, he saw the cursed elf that haunted the castle's ramparts. Without thinking, he launched himself forward

—right into the searing power of the castle's protection. It hadn't lessened in the slightest.

The shadow stalkers had failed.

Malphas's scales cracked, and the exposed flesh underneath burned as he staggered back out of range of the spirit's damaging assault. Had he been a lesser demon, he'd have been killed.

And I may still be killed. Once Sammael hears of this failure.

As Malphas entered the throne room, sheets of flames shot through the cavern, and Sammael roared with frustration.

Malphas reached out with his mind. "My lord, what is the matter?"

Instead of using telepathy, Sammael growled across the cavern. "The shadow stalkers have failed in their mission."

Malphas rubbed at his cracked scales. *At least I don't have to break the news myself.*

"Lord," he asked, "what about the mage you detected?"

The ball of fire that had been Sammael slowly condensed into the familiar forty-foot-tall demon, and Sammael's response appeared in Malphas's mind.

"He remains vulnerable. Time is all I need. He will be mine."

Bintas turned the elven sword over in his hand while Castien looked on. On Castien's collar was a dragon followed by three golden swords. Bintas knew that a single sword was for a soldier in the army, and two swords crossed over each other signified a captain in the army, whereas the triple sword was reserved for a general of the armies, of which there were only three. And the *golden* triple sword… that was for the sword master of *all* the armies.

Even Bintas knew of Castien's deadly reputation.

"Sword master, I've never seen such stress fractures in elven steel before. Honestly, I'd not be tinking it be possible. What would you have us do?"

Castien walked to a pile of damantite ore, picked up a piece, and tossed it to Bintas. "Lord Riverton said his smiths are the best in Trimoria. I'd like you to make me a new pair of swords with the same design—similar weight, similar balance. But I want it made from *that* ore."

"Of course, sword master. But for us to do it proper, it may take us some time. Especially with Lord Riverton having us busy pushing out armor for da troops."

The door opened, and Lord Riverton entered. He wore his wizard's robes, and on his collar was a dragon along with a shimmering golden crown, signifying him to be a ruling lord.

He clasped arms with the sword master. "How goes it, my friend?"

"Your timing is excellent. I was just trying to convince your crew that I need some improved swords made of damantite. Seeing as the last demon I faced damaged my elven blades."

Lord Riverton held out his hand, and a sparking blue ball of energy materialized above it. "Now that I have your attention," he said to the dwarves, "I want to be very clear. We're going to be much busier than we have been, starting now. I'll need you to start with Castien's swords, but I'll be here to help you with the damantite. I have some ideas on how to speed things up." He smacked his hands together and grabbed an apron, then turned to Castien. "Leave your swords so we can make forms from them. I'll bring you the completed replacements when they're ready."

"Thank you, Headmaster." Castien turned and left the smithy.

Jared addressed the smiths once more. "We have all sorts of armor and swords to make from this stuff, and today is the day. You folks, get the largest crucible we have. The rest of you, get shovels and forms ready. We have a lot to do."

As the last bits of damantite ore were dumped into the crucible, Jared sent fountains of energy into the already white-hot mound. Sweat dripped from his brow from both the heat and the effort.

"Bintas, and the rest of you," he said. "Get the forms ready. We'll only get one chance at this, and I'll skin you all if we make a mess of it!"

Bintas turned to his fellow dwarves. "You heard 'im, boys, let's show dem demons we know how to be workin' da metal! Give me yer sign when you be ready with yer forms."

Within minutes, the floor of the entire smithy was filled with interconnecting forms for all sorts of armor and weaponry.

Just as the last of the forms were snapped into place, Bintas got a thumbs-up from the workers and he yelled over the din.

"Sir, the forms be ready for da pour. And everyone else, hold steady! We don't want dem shiftin' about. And once the pour is flowing in da forms, step back—or you'll be gettin' blasted by Lord Riverton!"

Jared focused on the content of the nearly-overflowing crucible, and just as the metal's color changed to the right hue, indicating it had reached the right temperature, he nodded to his head of the smithy.

Bintas quickly scraped any hints of the floating slag away and yelled, "Brace yerselves, boys!" He pulled a lever, and with a creaking sound, the crucible slowly tipped its white-hot contents into the first form. And as instructed, as the molten metal spread from one form into the next, the dwarves that had been holding the forms in place scrambled backward.

Normally, a pouring of metal for large armor pieces could only be done across a few forms, because by the time you got to the second or third form, the metal was already cooling, and its movement slowed. This caused the metal behind it to bunch up and spill out of the forms, ruining the project. But Jared got around that by continuously pushing more energy into the flowing metal, to ensure it stayed at the right temperature as they moved through all the forms that had been connected throughout the smithy.

When the last remnants of the molten damantite were poured from the crucible, Jared let his magic sputter and stop. He was glad when Bintas took over.

"Remember boys, as the metal turns to red, slowly pour water on it and watch for da steam! That stuff will cook ya just as sure as dem dragons flyin' about da castle will."

One of the dwarves yelled back, "Bintas, I been doing dis for forty years, don'tcha tink I knows about steam burns?"

As the dwarves ran around studying the metal and methodically pouring water on the cooling forms, the smithy turned into a steam room. But soon dozens of forms were ready for the anvil.

Jared set aside the healing potion he'd been drinking to replenish his strength. "Bintas, tell me what we've got."

The smith grabbed a hammer and banged at one of the forms. After ladling water on top, and getting no steam, he picked up a very roughly formed chest plate. He banged his hammer on the armor again, listening closely to the sound. Several bangs later, he smiled and moved on to the next form.

As if that was a signal, the other smiths mimicked the process on other forms—testing, banging, listening.

"Well, you good-fer-nuttin', ale-swilling mutton-riders, what be the results?" Bintas shouted. He went around, gathering the reports from all the smiths, then returned to Jared and read from his chalkboard with a smile.

"Sir, we have one hundred and nineteen pieces ringin' true, and only eleven pieces dat have flaws and will need to be melted and recast."

Jared scratched at his beard. "How long does it normally take for us to create a dozen pieces of armor from damantite?"

"Depending on da size, normally we be capable of doin' four pieces a day. But dat's if'n us dwarves gotta heat the ore ourselves in the forge. Keepin' in mind we can't wiggle up magic heat."

"So we just managed to create a month's worth of armor in a day?"

Bintas pulled at his beard and smiled. "Yes, milord. A very good day's work, I'd say. Time for ale, don'tcha tink?"

"We still have lots of work ahead of us," Jared said, then smiled and added, "which is all the more reason for a drink!"

Wat shook his head as he looked over the remains of the once-proud town of Ilonia. There was a time when it was renowned for having some of the best wine in all of Trimoria, but that was long ago. It had now been nearly a century since Azazel had burned the entire place to the ground. Now only the fountain remained. Everything else was charred, broken, and overgrown, but the fountain itself was somehow untouched by the ravages of time.

Ignoring the men and dwarves who were digging all around it, he stepped forward and studied the inscription.

Bring to me your children for testing as they are newly born. For the waters declare them wizard, and our hope abides with them. A weekly bath will inoculate the wizard from the sway of evil.

Wat dipped his hands in the fountain's waters. The orb in the hands of the fountain's statue—a statue of the First Protector—glowed with a white intensity, identifying Wat as wizardborn.

One of the nearby workers whispered to his friend, "A damned powerful wizard *he* be."

"'Course he is," the friend replied. "Don'tcha see da dragon on his collar? He be one of our war wizards, and a dwarf too."

Wat prayed silently as he washed his face in the cool waters of the fountain. Then he stepped back, and a tall human stepped toward him hesitantly.

"Sir wizard, sir? I'm the foreman of this crew, and I'll be taking good care. But if you have any additional instructions, sir…?"

Wat shook his head. "Just do as the Archmage said. Dig four feet below it and raise it as one solid object. You cannot allow it to break."

The man nodded firmly. "Yes, sir, you can count on us, sir. It might take a bit, but I swear we'll bring it whole to yon Castle Riverton."

"And I have faith in your efforts. Don't worry about me. I'm not here to oversee your work, just to help protect you from that which creeps in the night."

The foreman looked nervously at the dead city around him. "And we be ever so thankful, sir."

"Ryan," said Arabelle, "I'm going with a group of the RAM students to visit the fountain in Aubgherle. Why don't you come with us?"

Ryan looked up from his desk, which was stacked high with books. "Arabelle, you know I can't go anywhere. Not until I figure out this puzzle of breathing life into the castle."

Arabelle put her hands on his shoulders and kneaded his muscles. Even with his eyes closed, he sensed the white threads of healing energy she poured into him. He wasn't sure why, but he'd frequently found Arabelle healing him when he wasn't aware of any injury he'd sustained.

She kissed the top of his head and poured more energy into him. "You need to get out of this dusty library sometimes. I'm worried for you."

Ryan took her hand and gave it a kiss. "I know. And you're right. I just—I feel like I should be doing more somehow. And I don't even know what to focus on first."

The truth was, he was starting to feel lost. And he didn't like the feeling. So as soon as Arabelle had departed, he went right back to work.

He recalled Ramai's words: *"Charged you are with bringing life to this castle. A Dedicate will you need to find, and nearby will they be."*

He growled and muttered aloud, "But what the hell is a Dedicate?"

It wasn't until hours later that he finally had an answer. He was looking through a shipment of books that Xinthian had sent from Eluanethra, many of which talked about the dedication of Castle Thariginian, when he found what he was looking for.

He smiled as he read the page header aloud: "Selecting a Dedicate."

Aaron knelt by his sister's bed and shook her gently. "Rebecca, wake up. We have to go to the library."

Shadow lifted his head from the foot of the bed, blinked once at Aaron, then lay his head back down across Rebecca's legs.

Rebecca opened her eyes. "Can Maggie come? She's scared to be alone." Her doll, as always, was on the pillow beside her.

"Of course she can."

Soon they were walking hand in hand down the castle corridors, Maggie in Rebecca's free hand, Shadow following silently behind.

"Are we reading stories? Is dat why we're going to the libary?"

Aaron laughed. "No, Rebecca. Remember how we're supposed to wake up the castle?"

"Yup."

"Well, Ryan found the secret to how it's done, and we're going to find out now."

They found Ryan, along with Mom and Dad, waiting for them in the castle library. Ryan was pacing back and forth in front of a table stacked with books, while Mom and Dad sat comfortably in padded chairs. Dad motioned for Aaron to take a seat, and Rebecca climbed into her mother's lap.

Ryan finally stopped pacing and looked up. "I'm sorry I called you at such a late time, but when I found out, I couldn't wait." He looked tormented, and the dark circles under his eyes showed how little sleep he'd been getting. "Ramai hinted that we'd need to find something called a Dedicate. Nobody I knew had a clue what that meant, nor did any of the books I'd ever read say anything about it. Until I found these." He lifted three tomes from the table. "Xinthian sent me the records of the dedication of Castle Thariginian, and these three volumes describe exactly what's needed to connect this castle with the world of the spirit."

"Is that what a 'dedication' really is?" Jared asked. "The castle and the spirit world are linked? And that creates the benefits that are present in Castle Thariginian?"

"Well, I'm not sure. I mean, I'm not sure whether our link will have the precise same results. Mostly I've been concentrating on just establishing the link in the first place. But one benefit I know of for sure: the spirit link *will* protect those within the castle from the demons. So it's definitely worth it."

"So what do we need to do?" Mom asked.

"First we need to gather the Conclave of Wizards. The strength of all of the wizards will be needed to pierce the veil between the worlds."

Dad snapped his fingers. "Done. I'll make the arrangements right away. What else?"

"Well, as Ramai said, we must have a Dedicate. And that's the hard part. Let me read you a couple of passages."

Ryan opened one of the three books and read aloud.

"Choosing the Dedicate for the ceremony was simple, for amongst the Thariginians was a child with magic most profound, yet uncontrollable. The child was a seer and a wizard. Unfortunately, the nightmares that plagued the child resulted in fires and injuries to all who were unshielded from the child's torrents of uncontrolled magic.

"It was appropriate that the child dedicate his uncontrolled magic to the link, for the magic of foretelling was rare indeed and deemed more valuable for the people."

Ryan flipped forward several pages and read again.

"Upon completion of the seal between the worlds, the Dedicate successfully retained his foretelling ability, and the

Archmage detected that no other abilities remained to the child."

The worried looks on Mom and Dad's faces indicated they understood the implications, but Aaron felt he needed to ask.

"Does that mean one of us needs to give up our powers in order to perform this ceremony?"

Ryan nodded somberly. "I'm afraid so. To do this, one of us is going to have to sacrifice our abilities. Either me, Mom, Dad, or Rebecca."

"Or me," Aaron said.

Ryan shook his head. "No. You're clearly magic in some way, but you're an enigma. You have no aura of magic around you. So I wouldn't know how to pull a thread from you and wrap it in the seal for the ceremony. So it's got to be one of us other four."

He looked around at everyone. "I'm sorry. I don't know what to do."

Dad took a deep breath. "I know what to do. I'll do it. I'll be the Dedicate."

BREATHING LIFE INTO A CASTLE

Sammael projected his senses past his throne room, probing at the magical mist that separated his minions from the remnants of Trimoria. He'd been testing the barrier repeatedly over the last several weeks, and had been pleased to detect moments of weakness—moments when the barrier's strength waned and it was held together by only a gossamer weaving of magic.

It was at these moments when Sammael was able to penetrate the barrier with his mind, and exert his influence on those creatures that carried strands of the spirit plane with them—or what the Trimorians called "wizards." In his mind's eye, these children of the spirit world pulsed like tiny beacons of light.

Now he stretched his mind toward one of those points of light. Most of these so-called wizards were weak and practically useless, and few could resist his influence. This one seemed no different. But as he burrowed into the creature's mind, he was expelled with a flash of white light.

He let out a string of curses. This wizard, like so many others, was under his brother's protection. But how? How had Seder touched so many in this world when he remained in the spirit plane?

In frustration, Sammael tried a different approach. He scanned for the familiar mind of Zenethar, the Archmage responsible for the barrier's existence. This one was easy to find—unlike the points of light that dotted the landscape, this wizard's mind shone like a beacon.

He touched the wizard's mind. As expected, the wizard's defenses flared against him. But Sammael chuckled.

The Archmage's defenses were weakening.

It is only a matter of time.

In response to Dad's pronouncement, Mom shook her head, her eyes glistening. "No, Jared! I won't let you."

Dad gently put his hand on her arm. "Honey, it's the way it needs to be. We have too few healers as it is. Your skills will be desperately needed in the upcoming war."

"Are you listening to yourself, Jared? It's going to be a war. And you're a *war wizard*. You think your skills won't be needed?"

Before the argument could escalate further, Rebecca shouted, "Get away from Maggie, you bug!"

Ryan turned and saw his little sister tossing a spark at a

spider that had been approaching her doll. The creature scurried away, unharmed.

A spark? But Rebecca was a healer…

"Rebecca," Ryan said softly, "can you show me how you scared that spider again?"

Rebecca hugged her doll tightly and pointed. "Bad spider!"

The tiniest glimmer of a spark flashed from her finger, traveling less than a foot before fading from existence. And Ryan detected something he'd never seen in his sister before. Buried deep within the pulsing threads of her innate healing power was the most ephemeral of magical threads. The thread dedicated to producing the weak sparks.

"Rebecca," he said, "did you know you had the ability to send sparks at things?"

Her lower lip quivered. "I hate it! I'm a healer, not a sparkler. It's too scary."

Ryan rubbed her back and smiled. "Rebecca, would you like to be the one to wake the castle up? The thing is, you'd have to give up your sparking ability."

"For real? I can wake the castle?"

Mom knelt down beside her. "But you wouldn't be able to spark anymore. You understand?"

"I don't want to spark anymore." Rebecca clapped her hands. "Can we do it now? I've never seen a castle wake before!"

The Conclave of Wizards had congregated in the room at the very heart of the castle. In fact, it *was* the heart of the castle. It was a plain room, adorned with nothing more than the sconces on the walls, and barely large enough to contain the assemblage, but it was remarkable in two ways. First was the door—a slab of petrified oak, hung on damantite hinges, practically impervious to damage. And second was the matching set of damantite squares, one in the center of the floor, the other directly above it in the ceiling.

Ryan looked over the assembled wizards. His parents were there, of course, both of them holding Rebecca's hands. Arabelle gave him a smile and a wink, and beside her stood the dwarf wizard Wat and Labriuteleanan, queen of the elves. There were also five students there, the strongest magic users from the academy—three war wizards and two healers. It was strange to realize that this was almost certainly the most powerful collection of wizards gathered all together in one place in centuries.

When he was satisfied that everyone was ready, Ryan began.

"Welcome, everyone, and thank you all for joining in this dedication of Castle Riverton. The room in which we are now gathered is modeled after a similar room in Castle Thariginian, right down to its precise placement within the castle. This is the heart of Castle Riverton. The life and awareness of the castle will begin in this room, and from here it will infuse itself throughout not only the rest of the structure, but all of the castle's domain."

He pointed to the damantite square in the floor. "That square is the top of a very long beam, buried deep within the land. This is how the power of the spirit world will enter the castle. It will… make the heart beat."

He then pointed to the square in the ceiling. "And that is the end of a metal beam that stretches toward the sky, right through the highest spire in the castle. It's what in my old world would have been called an antenna, but here… we can call it a spirit beacon."

Ryan turned slowly, meeting everyone's eye. "To begin this awakening, I will start by linking our powers together. It will require all our strength to be able to pierce the veil to the spirit world. I will then siphon the power our group generates, and launch it through the damantite above us."

Finally, he smiled at Rebecca. "My sister has bravely volunteered to be the Dedicate for this process. In so doing, some of her power will forever be dedicated to the life of this castle and will maintain the connection to the spirit world. I'll tie the threads of that power to both of the beams, linking the sky and the land."

Rebecca grinned. "I wake the castle."

Ryan chuckled despite the seriousness of the moment. "That's right." Then he looked once more around the circle of wizards. "Are we ready?"

Everyone nodded.

"Okay, then let's begin. Form a circle and link hands. Push your energy into the ring, pushing to your right. Build up slowly, but ultimately we want all the energy you can manage. Then try to loosen your control of your magic. I'll shape the threads of magic as required."

The Conclave linked hands, and Ryan felt a steady flow of magic running through the circle.

As the flow's pace increased, he nodded to Rebecca, who closed her eyes. He sorted through the threads of her magic and found the one dim thread responsible for her feeble sparking ability. Concentrating, he stretched the thread, then tied one end to the damantite beam above him, and the other to the beam below him.

The power racing through the circle of wizards accelerated, and the room shook. Then Ryan pulled deeply from his reserves and contributed a torrent of his own power into the blazing ring. Finally, when he felt the energy level was at its peak, he diverted the rotating stream into the beam above.

Light exploded within the room, and the entire castle trembled. Though only Ryan could see it, a fountain of multi-colored wizard energy had just sheared right through the thread of power from Rebecca, and had replaced it with a pure white light that connected the damantite beams above and below.

But what happened next, everyone could see. A purple globe of light appeared just beneath the ceiling, and began a rhythmic pulse.

They'd done it.

It was Rebecca who announced the achievement. She pointed up at the pulsing orb. "It worked! That's our castle's heartbeat. It's alive."

As Ryan walked through the castle with his wife, she leaned her head against his shoulder. "The castle is so different now. This corridor was always cold, but now it's the perfect temperature."

That was only one of many changes people had noticed in the days since the dedication. The most obvious one was the light that emanated from the walls—but only when needed. The castle somehow recognized which corridors and rooms needed light, and which didn't. It was now commonplace to walk down a hallway and watch it light up ahead of you and darken behind you. And there was no longer any need to light the torches in the sconces.

Ryan kissed the top of Arabelle's head. "Rebecca even says the castle talks to her. That's something I have to study."

They arrived at their rooms, and Arabelle pulled him inside. "Study later. You promised you'd spar with me."

Ryan chuckled. Until they were married, he'd never realized just how dedicated Arabelle was to exercise. She'd even transformed an entire room in their quarters into a workout room. And now she wanted to get him involved.

She stripped off her jacket and tossed it in a corner. Ryan removed his robe and changed into a tunic and pants. "Are you sure?" he said. "I was a second-degree black belt in karate, and I'm a guy. I'm stronger and bigger. This isn't exactly fair."

Arabelle laughed. "I don't care what color belt you wear. You laughed when I said that women could fight in this war if they were properly trained. I'll show you what my training has given me."

Ryan decided to humor her. "All right, but don't hurt me."

She gave him a devilish smile. "Don't worry. I'll repair anything I break."

Ryan assumed his ready stance. "All right, let's—"

Before he could finish his sentence, Arabelle leaped toward Ryan's side and pivoted. Her leg shot out, connecting with the back of Ryan's knees. As his legs buckled, she spun and grabbed his hair, pulled his head back, exposing his neck, and produced a dagger from somewhere in her tunic, which she held against his neck.

Ryan's only reaction was stunned shock.

Arabelle grinned. With the dagger still held against his neck, she pressed her lips against his and followed him as he fell backward. She straddled his belly, keeping the dagger against his neck. "And now you're going to do whatever I want."

Sloane was still rubbing the sleep from her eyes as she followed Arabelle through the corridors. Arabelle had woken her to tell her about Ryan's nightmares, and her hope that with Sloane's ability to touch minds, she could determine what was troubling him.

They walked quietly into Arabelle's bedroom, where Ryan was soundly asleep in bed. Sloane knelt beside him and dove into his mind.

Instantly, the smell of rotten eggs filled her nose—but she received no images, no other sensations. Patiently, she waited.

A sound—children screaming. Part of his dream?

Then the screams stopped, and she tasted the coppery tang of blood. It was so strong, she was barely able to control her gag reflex. The temperature plummeted, and she shivered uncontrollably—yet before her, Ryan's body broke into a sweat.

It was then that Sloane received her first visual image, and it was so alarming, so intense, that she involuntarily rose and stepped back, breaking the connection.

She'd seen a pair of flaming eyes, staring right into her.

Arabelle caught her by the shoulders and pushed healing energy into her until her anxiety abated. Then she turned Sloane to face her.

"Please, Sloane," she said quietly. "What did you see?"

In a corner of the castle's library, Ryan studied one of the new books from Eluanethra—a book called *Vectoring Energy*. The book explained how it was possible to link two objects to allow the transfer of magical energy from one to another. When power was infused into one object, the other object would receive the energy. Essentially, the first object wasn't a container for the energy, it was a gate for it.

But this linking could only be done by someone with his special gifts of insight into how magic worked. Ryan felt a tingle of excitement when he realized that he was reading a book written specifically for Archmages.

Footsteps approached, and he looked up to find his friend Wat Crazybeard standing before him. Wat was a powerful war wizard, and a graduate of RAM. He was of average height for a dwarf, a bit under four feet, but he wasn't nearly as thickly built as others of his race. Most notable about him was his that he kept his long beard tied in braids; they reminded Ryan of a bunch of brown snakes hanging from his face.

"Greetings, Archmage. May I sit and report to you my findings?" Wat asked.

"Please." Ryan nodded to a seat.

Wat sat, a leather-wrapped manual on his lap. "What would you like to hear about first, Archmage?"

"Wat, we're alone—just call me Ryan. And tell me your news in whatever order makes sense."

"Okay… Ryan. I'll start with Ilonia. We found the fountain intact and in perfect condition, and the men were able to free it from the ground. But it was too heavy for wagon transport, so we had to get clever. We're moving it by rolling it over a series of logs. It's slow going, but I'm happy to report that the fountain now lies only a few days' distance from the castle."

"Does the statue's orb still work?"

"Works perfectly. Whatever strange properties are contained within the fountain, they were not bound to the land the fountain rested in."

"Good. What else?"

Wat raked his fingers through the braids that hung from his chin. "You'll recall that I reported to you earlier on a previously unknown fountain discovered by the Rockfist clan, near the First Protector's ancient residence in the mountains west of here. I traveled to see it for myself. Unfortunately, at first the dwarves there wouldn't even speak to me. Seeing as I have no clan."

Ryan felt a pang of sympathy. Wat was an orphan, raised in a human orphanage in Cammoria, and as such had never been part of a clan. And in dwarven society, that made one a pariah.

"But," Wat continued, "I finally found a kind soul in old Donlas Harbinger. He's the dwarven keeper of histories—the closest thing to a librarian that the dwarves have—and it was his support that convinced the Redbeard and Rockfist clans to lead me to the fountain. It's hidden deep within a very narrow mountain crevice, on a path that isn't even navigable by horse. I see no way we could manage to transport it."

"But you saw it? It's really a fountain from the First Protector?"

"Oh, yes, it's one of the fountains. And I tested the orb—it still works."

"And you're sure there's no way to move it?"

"Well… pretty sure. There *was* a second path leading to the fountain, coming from the opposite direction. Unfortunately, the fountain is deep within ogre territory, and that path would have only taken us in even further. In fact, when I lit the orb, it drew some attention. A rumbling came from down that path, as if something large and ogre-like was approaching. The other dwarves and I didn't stick around to investigate further."

"I understand. There's no need to go around picking fights with ogres. Do you have anything else to report?"

"No, but… I do have a favor to ask. While I was in the mountains, Donlas and I got to talking, and I guess he appreciated my interest in books, because he gave me a few volumes to take with me. And this one…" he lifted the book in his lap, "well, it's fascinating. It speaks of the clan that is no longer spoken of in dwarf society. In modern language, they'd be known as the wanderers. In the old language, they were known as the Ta'ah."

Wat leaned forward with excitement. "According to this, the Ta'ah are rumored to be the only dwarf clan to count mages among their members. I'd like to spend time with Eglerion and possibly travel to Eluanethra to research this. If there is one thing I'm good at, it's teasing information from the pages of a book."

"Of course, my friend. Do you think you might be descended from that clan? Does the clan still exist somewhere?"

Wat shrugged. "That's what I hope to find out."

Ryan nodded. "Well, I'll contact Xinthian and Eglerion. I'm sure they'll be happy to help." He tapped at one of the rings on his fingers. "Also make sure you take one of the communication rings with you. There's no telling when we'll all be needed, and I suspect we'll have little warning."

"Thank you, Ryan."

They stood and clasped arms, and Wat left, clearly excited about his new research project.

As Ryan was taking a seat again, he accidentally bumped against his damantite staff. He grabbed it quickly before it fell on the ground. But just before he leaned it against the chair again, he noticed something unusual.

I could have sworn...

On the end of the staff, he'd embedded a diamond that had once belonged to the First Protector. Diamonds were capable of holding vast amounts of energy, and so of course Ryan kept a magical charge in the one attached to his staff, just in case he ever needed to draw upon it. That charge made the diamond glow, but...

Is the diamond glowing brighter than before?

How can that be?

GENERAL OF THE FOUR-LEGGED ARMY

Sloane studied the uncertain looks on the soldiers gathered in the hall. None of them were officers, yet they'd been ordered to gather in the officers' assembly, a building they'd never even set foot in before. To add to the tension, the men's commanding officers were standing along one side of the room, silently observing them.

Aaron's arm snaked around her waist, and he gently pulled her to him and inhaled the scent of her hair. She read his thoughts, and shoved a sharp elbow into his ribs.

"Stop it, Aaron. We're in public. Stop thinking like that."

Aaron sighed. "I can't help it. Is there any reason why we can't get married yet? What's the point of waiting? I'm twenty, you're nineteen. We're only two years younger than Ryan and Arabelle."

Sloane dragged her fingernails lightly over Aaron's muscular forearm. "I think my father wanted us to wait until this… this upcoming war is over."

"But—"

She tilted her head toward the door as Castien entered the hall. "Time for the ceremony."

Aaron whispered, "We aren't done with this conversation."

"Take it up with my father," she said with a smile. "You know *I'm* ready."

She dropped Aaron's hand and strode toward Castien. The stoic elf nodded respectfully.

"I'm glad to see you're on time, Princess."

At Castien's command, the soldiers formed a perfectly straight line, standing at attention. Castien walked slowly down the line, inspecting them.

Meanwhile, Sloane stood several feet back, using her power to peer into the men's minds. She sensed emotions ranging from confidence and arrogance, to uncertainty and fear of failure. One common thread among them was a healthy wariness about what lay on the other side of the magic barrier.

It was Sloane's job to find deception or signs of weakness. The armies couldn't afford rogue or cowardly officers in their midst. Unfortunately, there'd been a few recent desertions—and to the great shame of those involved with RAM, the deserters had all been students of the academy.

Castien finished his inspection and looked surreptitiously to Sloane. She projected her thoughts into the mind of the sword master. None of the soldiers had any intent to deceive or abuse their role in the army.

Aaron then stepped forward to take the men's oaths. He

pulled a small leather bag from his belt and gave each soldier a damantite ring with a golden dragon insignia emblazoned on it—a sign of their new rank and responsibilities. When he'd awarded a ring to the last soldier in line, he stepped back and stood before them all.

"Do you all swear to lead your men faithfully in their duties and to set an example for them?"

The man answered in the affirmative.

"Then put on your rings of office."

Sloane felt the soldiers' burning pride as they put on their rings. They were now officers.

Aaron continued. "The rings you wear are not only a symbol of your rank, they are a magical tool that can be used to communicate across great distances. This invention of my father's will allow us to coordinate troop movements and strategies without having to depend on messengers."

Aaron nodded to Oda, a heavily muscled dwarf, who stepped forward. "All right men, everyone take a seat. My name is Oda, and we be expectin' that what you learn in these here halls, you'll be keepin' secret. Understood?"

The men again replied in the affirmative. Sloane projected into Oda's mind that she detected no deception.

Oda gave her a quick wink before turning back to the soldiers. "Men, you're about to learn something called Morse code…"

"Princess, dem animals make me nervous. They're so… big."

The speaker was a dwarf with a large rounded belly and a brown beard that scraped the grass. Glennock Alebelly.

"Listen to me, Alebelly," said Sloane. "My troops may be animals, but they're intelligent in their own way. They understand the visions I've placed in their minds of the demons that we'll face, and they're devoted to fighting at our side to repel this force. So—for now at least—" she gave the dwarf a brilliant smile, "they're willing to forgo snacking on the occasional dwarf."

One of the elves walking beside her barely hid a grin. "Though if you act like prey, they might try for a little nibble."

The dwarf grumbled. "I'm not afeared of the swamp cats, and if you say I can trust da wolves… then I'm supposin' I do. But Princess, it's those dragons. I know you claim they're good and harmless…"

Sloane shook her head. "I never said Ruby and Pyre were *harmless*. But don't think of them as animals; they're much smarter than you imagine. They're a race of good creatures with honor running through their veins. Anyway, the dragons won't be training with us; they'll be practicing with the wizards. I've asked them to come visit our training areas only so that our four-legged troops get used to them flying overhead and aren't frightened in battle."

The dwarf shrugged. "Good and honorable they might be, but when I see them, my mind still yells, 'Run, dwarf, run.'"

A shadow flew above the clouds, and Sloane smiled as she detected the thoughts of the two dragons. The brother and sister were arguing—as they so often did. Ruby's mind growled with frustration as Pyre insisted on making his own impulsive decision.

Moments later, a member of her elven escort yelped a warning as he spied Pyre diving—and aiming directly for the group. The soldiers ducked, but Sloane knew there was nothing to fear. Sure enough, Pyre skimmed right over their heads and struck the ground twenty feet behind them, landing hard and creating an unnecessarily grand explosion of grass and dirt.

He's such a show-off.

Pyre was a black-scaled dragon, and now that he was fully grown, he measured sixty feet from his snout to the tip of his tail. Tendrils of smoke rose from his nostrils as he bent forward toward Alebelly, speaking with a deep, rumbling voice.

"Don't run, little dwarf. It would be that much harder for me to take a little taste. I've always heard dwarf tastes like mutton..."

Pyre was suddenly knocked over by a smaller version of himself—his sister, Ruby. She had plummeted earthward from another direction, and the two Riverton dragons roared and wrestled, gouts of flame erupting as they argued in the old tongue. Sloane didn't understand the old language the dragons were born with, but her mind could understand the thoughts behind the words.

"Crimsonpyre, you promised me you wouldn't try to scare the little people anymore."

"Bah! The dwarf started it, Rubyrend. I heard him say he was scared of me and I've never done anything to make him scared. Until now." He gave a toothy grin.

Sloane projected a message into the dragons' minds. "Please

settle down. The two of you fighting is only making everyone more frightened. The poor dwarf is likely going to have nightmares now."

Ruby gave one last nip to her brother's tail, and he hopped away with a yip of pain.

Sloane walked over and patted Ruby's haunch. "I still can't believe how big you two are."

Ruby leaned her giant head gently against Sloane with a grumbling noise that resembled purring.

Sloane turned to the soldiers and made introductions. "This beautiful dragon is Rubyrend—but I usually just call her Ruby. She's the sensible one."

Ruby blinked with her large amber eyes. "Girls are always more sensible." She snorted, and a stream of white smoke shot at her brother.

Sloane then walked over to Pyre and scratched vigorously at his chin. "This big boy is Crimsonpyre, but I call him Pyre. He's a bit brash and playful." She nodded to Alebelly. "He heard you talk about being scared of him, and believe it or not, that hurt his feelings. That's why he came swooping in like he did."

The dragon looked sulkily at the dwarf, whose knees were shaking. "I'm sorry, tiny dwarf. You can run if you like."

Ruby growled in the old language, her snout shooting steam. "Promise him you won't eat him!"

Pyre looked down at the ground and sighed. "Don't worry, dwarf. I won't eat you. I'm sure you taste bad."

Alebelly stepped uncertainly forward. "Pyre, I didn't be meanin' to upset you. It's not sensible to be a-scared of sumthin' that others be telling you is... uhh..."

Ruby shook her head and turned to Sloane. "Are all boys so ill-equipped in speaking their minds?" She turned to the dwarf. "My brother accepts your apology."

Ruby gave her a brother a nudge with her head. "And I just have to accept you're all muscle—and being a boy, you're just stupid sometimes."

Pyre raised his head and gave his sister a big grin.

"All right, folks," said Sloane. "Let's keep moving to the training camps. We have a lot of tactics to work out, and a lot of practice."

One of the human soldiers grumbled, "And we have to figure out how to keep the swamp cats and wolves from killing each other."

TROUBLE WITH THE FIRST PROTECTOR

Malphas hefted a large bag over his shoulder and grinned as he climbed down the trail that led to the next breeding pit. He'd just been told by his lord that the barrier was weakening, and soon he'd be able to destroy the remnants of the Aboveworlders.

He scanned the pit below him, looking for the breeding mistress. The darkness of the Underworld was never complete. On the walls of the caverns grew a glowing white lichen, and the steam that bubbled from some of the hot springs carried a natural light as well. But even without these sources, Malphas would be able to see the heat signatures of all the life-forms crawling through the caverns.

From his bag, he pulled out one of the demons he'd knocked unconscious on the way. With a quick slash of a claw, Malphas sliced open the neck of his helpless victim and tossed it into the pit. The demon's ichor spilled on the ground.

After a moment, the sound of rocks shifting and the tremor in the earth confirmed what Malphas couldn't see. The breeder had awakened.

Then the ground in the pit opened, and from the depths crawled a giant worm-like creature. It was six feet thick, a hundred feet long, and covered in mucous. On its head was a circle of tiny horned projections that it used to chew through the ground.

Its undulating muscles carried it with surprising speed toward the bleeding demon. The creature's front end expanded, a long, tube-like projection emerged, and with a sudden inhalation, the dead demon disappeared into the giant worm. The creature's slimy skin changed from a grayish to a yellowish-white. Its muscles flexed, and its rear dragged closer to its front until it was only about twenty feet long.

And as it constricted, it left a trail of leathery eggs behind.

The breeder-worm then burrowed once more into the ground, leaving behind a smell of ammoniated sulfur.

Malphas growled at the demons that he'd ordered to follow him. "Gather the eggs and bring them to the hatchery." A dozen demons scurried past him and climbed down the walls of the pit. "And if I catch any of you eating these eggs, I'll be sure you're fed to the next breeder."

Malphas grinned.

My troops will soon be more than sufficient for what's to come.

Sloane breathed in deeply and let the smells of the Aubgherle market fill her. The aromas of freshly baked bread and spice carts always brought back fond childhood memories.

But this was not a day for shopping. This was training—training her animals to restrain themselves among humans.

Silver, her most trusted swamp cat, nudged her hip and made a guttural noise from deep within his chest. *"The swamp cats are well-behaved. But the wolves are getting distracted."*

Sloane rubbed behind Silver's ears and looked toward the half dozen wolves veering toward the cooking stands. The scent of roasted meat was one that even she had difficulty ignoring, yet she sent a mental reminder to them. *"Grey Wind! Keep your pack in order. The citizens know you're in our armies now, but not everyone may accept the fact yet. I don't want any misunderstandings."*

The leader of the pack yipped at his companions. *"Get away from the no-tails' food. We can't let those cats make fools of us. Ignore your noses for now."*

One of his pack-mates growled. *"We'd be fools not to taste the food the no-tails have available. I'm not finicky like those black-furred hissers."*

The shoppers and vendors eyed the wolves warily as they meandered through the stalls. But only Sloane could hear the animals' conversation. To everyone else, the pack's discussion was merely a series of growls, yips, and the occasional whine.

One of the wolves sidestepped a rolling cart and bumped into an adjacent swamp cat, who hissed in reply. Sloane reminded them all again that they were to tolerate each other. That was perhaps her greatest challenge. She had to make sure large groups of different species could get along and coordinate, so they would be effective against a common enemy.

One of Sloane's rings vibrated with a message from her father.

Throll. Sloane, you're in Aubgherle, correct?

She tapped out a reply. *Yes, I'm in town.*

Come to our old farmhouse now. We need your skills.

Be right there.

Sloane then projected a mental message to her animal companions. *"Let's jog for a bit. Follow me—and don't get distracted."*

With the animals being fed outside by some very nervous farmhands, Sloane took a seat in her former living room with her father and Aubgherle's new Protector, a man named Yakov.

"Tell her what happened," Father said to Yakov.

The man nodded. "It seems that one of the RAM's missing hedge wizards, a human named Garth, returned to his family a couple of days ago. Now that your family has moved into Castle Riverton, the family had begun maintaining this farm—"

A muffled cry and a thumping came from one of the bedrooms.

Yakov waved dismissively. "I have the criminal tied up in the other room. Your father wanted you present before I questioned him further."

"What did he do?"

The Protector pursed his lips. "Yesterday, in the middle of the day, Garth killed his youngest brother, and tried to kill his own father. Luckily, the farmhands were able to wrestle the miscreant to the ground. That was when they called me. As you probably know, Lord Riverton has asked that if any of the missing wizards are found, we are to return them to Castle Riverton."

Father's knuckles made popping noises as he clenched his fists. "But first we're going to question him. And that's why you're here, Sloane." He turned to Yakov. "Bring him in. Let's get this over with."

For the third time, Father asked, "Why did you attack your own family, Garth?"

The disheveled hedge wizard stared blankly ahead, not even acknowledging the question. Perhaps he wasn't even aware of it. For even as Sloane peered into his mind, she found nothing but deep pools of blackness.

She telepathically sent her father a suggestion that might help loosen the control Garth had on his thoughts.

Father's open hand whistled through the air and struck Garth's cheek, sending the man and his chair to the floor.

For an instant, a flood of images escaped from the tight control of the man's mind. Sloane took them in with a horrified gasp. But then the darkness of his mind clamped shut and the flow of his thoughts ceased.

"What?" said her father, looking at her with concern. "Did you get something?"

Sloane looked up at him, tears blurring her vision. "There is something very wrong with that man. He… he isn't what he seems."

Father knelt in front of her. "Tell me. What did you see? I need to know."

Sloane took a deep breath, but the knot of fear in the pit of her stomach refused to loosen. "It was for only a second. There were screams of torture. I felt the nails of creatures ripping me apart. And then I saw—I saw what he intended. I saw you, Father. And Mother, and Zenethar, and me, all of us lying on this floor, our entrails spread everywhere, and this… this beast was bathing in our blood."

Sloane's father bent down and gave her a kiss on the forehead. "Go outside. You don't want to witness what I'm about to do. But hopefully, before this man dies, he will divulge who set him on this path."

Sloane nodded and left the farmhouse. Before the door closed behind her, she heard her father say, "Yakov, get me a hammer."

***

Ryan rested his head on the pillow, but though he was thoroughly exhausted, sleep had been elusive lately. And when he *did* sleep… well, though he didn't remember his dreams, Arabelle had told him about them, and about the troubles they were causing him. Even with her nightly healing, the stresses were wearing on him. He was losing weight, and he always had a headache.

He rolled over to face her. She was sleeping peacefully, her chest rising and falling in a slow, steady rhythm. He noticed a faint freckle on her nose, and smiled. Even her slight imperfections were beautiful to him. He had just reached out to move a stray lock of her dark-brown hair when her eyes snapped open, and he yanked his hand back in surprise.

Instead of the warm soul-filled eyes he loved, her eyes had transformed into white orbs, and her entire body began to glow, tendrils of white energy forking across her like lightning.

Just when he was about to call for help, the magic subsided, and Arabelle grabbed Ryan's hand.

She fixed him with a look of alarm. "We must save the First Protector!"

***

"Arabelle," said Aaron, "are you sure you can't give us more specifics?"

Arabelle held tightly to her reins as their horses threaded through the mountain pass. As her visions always did, this latest one had left her feeling anxious and uncertain. Even now, two days later, it still weighed on her. Her power of sight was a gift, but also a curse.

Her people, the Imazighen, had a history of producing seers—people who could see what was happening in faraway places. Usually the visions were a prediction of what was to come, but she rarely found them useful. They had a tendency to be incomplete and cryptic.

"I wish I could tell you more, but it was hazy. It was more… *knowledge* than it was sight. All I know is that the First Protector was being attacked. And it felt like it was happening right now, or almost right away."

One of their dwarven escorts nudged his mountain pony to her side. "Lady Healer, I dinna mean no disrespect, but don'tcha tink you might have been seein' the tale from centuries ago? You know—whens he was fightin' the demons and such. The Protector, he be safe and sound in the same cave for a long, long time."

Arabelle shook her head. "No, it isn't like that. I saw him in the cave, and he was being attacked. And I know it was now, or soon. I just… know."

Aaron opened his mouth to speak again, but Sloane held up a hand. "Sorry, Arabelle, it seems my fiancé plans to ask you a bunch of questions one at a time. If you'll allow me, I'll address the one that seems most pressing." She twisted in her saddle and faced Aaron. "Yes, I did bring some chicken if you're hungry."

As their horses picked up the pace on a wide downward slope, Ryan pulled alongside Arabelle. "Did you bring *me* any chicken?"

She grinned. "You'll have to be happy with mutton."

Ryan sat cross-legged inside the First Protector's cave, studying the shimmering cocoon of energy that surrounded the famous wizard. Thanks to his unique vision, he could see the invisible threads of magic around the First Protector. It was a complex construction, the knots of energy tied so deftly as to prevent any external tampering, each thread forming a symbiotic relationship with the threads around it. But as Ryan followed the pulsing threads, he deduced the purpose of each one, and his understanding of the cocoon's construction slowly took shape.

Aaron and the dwarves stood watch outside, but Arabelle and Sloane were in the cave with him. Arabelle was there in case any form of healing was needed, and Sloane was performing her own examination of the Protector's body, applying her special skill.

Sloane gasped suddenly. "I heard him! He... he's feeling a tremendous amount of pain."

"Do you think I can help?" Arabelle asked.

"It's worth a try."

Arabelle stepped forward, and her healing energy pooled all about her in a white cloud that only Ryan could see. She reached out, letting her palm hover inches above the First Protector, and a trickle of energy poured from her splayed fingers. But though it entirely enveloped the shimmering cocoon that protected the ancient wizard, it was unable to penetrate the magical shield.

Ryan was about to advise Arabelle to stop when the shield flickered for the tiniest fraction of a second—and all of the healing energy instantly disappeared within the cocoon.

Arabelle staggered backward, almost falling over. Eyes wide, she looked at Ryan with a wan smile. "I've never felt anything like that. It was as though all of my healing energy was held in check—and then instantly absorbed all at once."

Ryan turned to Sloane. "Do—"

"Shh!" Sloane held up a hand, silencing him.

With a shrug, Ryan turned his attention to the cocoon of energy once more. This time he noticed sections of the construction that looked... damaged. He moved closer, and sure enough...

There. A frayed edge.

And there. Another.

The magical streams of energy were thinning. They were starting to unravel.

Ryan closed his eyes and used only his magical senses. Without the scintillating lights obscuring his vision, he could more clearly see the tightly woven shield of magical threads, pulsing with the heartbeat that lay within, as if they gathered their strength from the Protector himself. His eyes still closed, Ryan moved around the cocoon, examining every square inch.

And he found one stray thread. A thick, pulsing gray thread that went deep into the earth. He couldn't guess its purpose.

He opened his eyes to find Sloane staring at him.

"What is it?" he asked.

"He spoke to me. He thanks 'the healer' for her efforts, but he says the healing will only put off for a short time what is inevitable." Her expression turned grim. "He claims to be on a precipice. He's being assaulted by the same nightmares I've seen within you.

"He also says that 'Seder's Archmage'—that's you—will need guidance, but that he himself cannot provide that guidance. He says that you must seek out someone named Nicnevin. You must seek him out 'past the end of the world.'"

Ryan scratched his chin. "Did he tell you who this Nicnevin is, and why I must seek him?"

But it was Arabelle who answered. "Nicnevin is a she, not a he. She's an ancient elf queen."

Ryan raised his eyebrows. "How do you know that?"

Sloane laughed. "Years ago, she had a book titled *Nicnevin.*

An ancient tome that predicted the coming of the demons, and other things."

Arabelle turned to Sloane with a look of surprise. "I've never told you about—oh! You read my mind again, didn't you?"

"Whoops." Sloane's cheeks reddened. "I—" She cocked her head and turned back to the dais. "Quiet, everyone."

Ryan followed her gaze and saw a tendril of magic escape from deep within the cocoon. The light in the cave dimmed, and a grainy voice echoed through the small cavern.

"Greetings, my granddaughter. I wish that I could see you with my own eyes, but I'm blessed by your presence, and I thank you for it. Tell your father that it would please me if he would honor a dying man's last wish and restore my family name to the son he named after me. You may also tell him that I give my blessing to your own intended union, and would be very glad if I could hear of it from you before I pass."

Sloane listened silently, tears streaming down her cheeks.

"Archmage of Seder. I saw a vision of you over five centuries ago, and I'm glad to finally feel your presence as well. Though I can taste the malignancy that seeks you out. Don't make the same foolish mistakes of pride that I made.

"My granddaughter spoke for me truthfully. Seek Nicnevin. You must reach her and learn from that crazy elf. I can detect in this room another minion of Seder. Take her with you, for it is she who will convince Nicnevin. Without her, your confusing aura will likely be your downfall."

Ryan looked at Arabelle, who nodded grimly.

"Don't underestimate the danger the elf poses. She is likely the most powerful wizard to have ever walked the lands of Trimo-

ria. If even half of what she's rumored to have done is true, she is dangerous beyond measure. And if the rumors are to be believed, her power was turned against her by one of the great spirits, and it drove her mad.

"None of you have the luxury of time. The threads of all of Trimoria's fate lie within your grasp. Delaying the inevitable will cause them all to unravel. Now go!"

LILITH

Seated on a carved throne of polished granite, Lilith closed her eyes and reached her mind to the world above. She felt the magical barrier pulse with energy, and she tasted the powers that were involved during its creation. It still carried the power of Seder within.

Thoughts of Seder reminded her of how different her life had once been. It had been thousands of years since Lilith had last interacted with either of her brothers, but the memories flooded back as though it were only yesterday…

"Seder, I don't understand you. You spend so much time observing insignificant creatures in other worlds, whereas I can hardly gather your attention long enough to have a conversation with you."

The unfocused look on her brother's face faded, and he

turned to her with a smile. "Dear Lilith, it is within your nature to care for others. You should try and reach beyond our realm. There are so many who need our help. I've shown you how to reach out and make them aware of you. Influence and teach, my young sister. It is our way."

Then he turned away from her once more, his gaze again becoming distant, leaving Lilith empty and alone.

Lilith sighed. She wished she'd had the patience to reach her quiet brother. He was so rarely given to strong emotion. Except, of course, in response to Sammael. Only their impetuous brother could make Seder lose his temper.

Seder's eyes blazed with fury. "How dare you do such a thing! Why do you insist on sowing chaos when you know it ultimately leads to the destruction of those we instruct?"

Sammael sneered. "I thought you were interested in teaching. Why should you care what I teach those creatures? I've given them the ability to utterly destroy their enemies. I'm proud of their achievements."

Lilith shook her head. "Sammael! You've given that world the keys to their destruction. Have you no regard for their threads of destiny?"

Sammael scoffed and hitched his thumb back toward Seder. "You're sounding like him. These creatures are made to kill. Why not nudge them into serving their base instincts? Yes, I want to see them fulfill their destinies—but who's to say this isn't their destiny? And not just the destiny of this world." He smiled. *"Imagine it. World upon world filled with the chaos of dissent, the toppling of civilizations, wars among species... even wars between worlds! How exciting that would be!"*

Seder gathered power into himself. "Brother, I'll not have it. I will not allow this to happen again."

Sammael laughed. "You can't stop chaos, brother."

They had both been right, her brothers, each in his own way. But in the end, it wasn't her brothers who influenced her to change. The spark that changed Lilith's destiny was another being entirely.

An elf named Nicnevin.

Lilith had existed in the spirit realm for millennia, looking for a reason to exist. Her followers on the worlds she could touch were her only treasures, but though the spiritual contact was significant, she wanted more.

It arrived unexpectedly. She felt it, but did not understand it, when the roots of the spirit world shook. Something new had happened.

Lilith stretched her senses across the spirit realm. She easily found the bright beacons of power that were her brothers, and near them was another light—a mere faint spark. Lilith joined them—her two brothers and the frail creature cowering between them.

Seder and Sammael were arguing, as usual.

"This is your doing, brother of mine!" Sammael said, lifting the cringing blonde creature by the arm. "You have brought this thing here to serve some advantage, I know it."

"I have done nothing. Clearly you are behind this, Sammael."

As her brothers argued, Lilith gently separated the creature from her brother's grasp and held it in her arms. The poor thing, a female, was struggling to breathe. What was she? And why was she here?

Lilith reached into the fragile creature's mind and sifted through her memories.

The creature's name was Nicnevin. She thought of herself as an elf—a beautiful race that Lilith yearned to know. And then Lilith saw a memory that made her gasp in astonishment.

This elf had had not been brought here by either of Lilith's brothers. Nicnevin had brought herself here on her own!

A weak thought was projected into Lilith's mind. "Am losing myself here... please... let... me... leave..."

Lilith released the elf and took a step backward. "You are free if you will it."

With a gasp of breath, the elf nodded, shimmered with power, and disappeared.

Lilith scanned the spirit world. Once again, it was only her and her brothers. But though the weight of her loneliness was a shroud... it had become just a bit lighter.

She had witnessed something she hadn't thought possible. And it gave her hope. Hope, and a yearning to change. All thanks to the most insignificant of creatures.

. . .

Lilith thought back to that day, thousands of years ago, when she decided to forgo her life on the spirit plane. She had no regrets then, and no regrets now. She'd committed herself to join those who truly loved her in the physical universe. True, her powers in the material plane were but a shadow of those she possessed in the spirit realm, but that had been a sacrifice worth making. In this world, anything she wanted was possible—as long as she had her followers.

And she had many. Though her brothers tried to influence her world, her physical presence here allowed her to override them with ease, and over time, she developed a strong gathering of devotees. The elves were the first of her minions, but eventually, they were joined by members of all the intelligent species.

Females only, however. They proved to be the strength of the races, as Lilith had known they would be. Females saw and felt the wisdom of Lilith's ways. They understood the folly of a male-dominated society. And with her influence, they came to know the truth. Lilith's truth.

THE THREE TITANS OF POWER

Five hundred and seventy-one years ago

Lilith had her mind's eye stretched across the plains of the Aboveworld when her senses were rocked by a presence she hadn't felt directly in millennia.

Sammael.

It seemed he had used the same method to escape the spirit world that she'd used thousands of years ago. But why here? Of the thousands upon thousands of possible locations he could've chosen, why come to *my* world?

She clenched her fists in frustration. She refused to seek him out, and hoped he would not come to find her either. Perhaps they could coexist, each with a portion of this world to rule as their own.

But she was wrong. Within only a few years of Sammael's arrival—a blink of an eye to one such as Lilith—he managed to attract a host of followers. She heard the screams of violence as the land prepared for war, and she feared for her own minions. She demanded that they retreat to the deepest recesses of the Underworld, leaving Sammael to his wars and destruction.

She knew it would not be enough. Eventually Sammael's gaze would turn to those she cared for.

It was time to make a plan.

Lilith caressed the cheek of the pale elf with pitch-black hair, soaking in the warmth of this creature's sparkling green eyes.

"Anarane. I have a sacred duty for you."

The elf had a dreamy look on her face. "Anything for you, my Lady."

Lilith pulled an egg-sized diamond from her robes. It glowed with a sparkling blue-white light that pierced the gloom of the torch-lit cavern. "My dearest, how long has it taken you to charge this crystal?"

As Anarane gazed at the diamond, her pale complexion took on a greenish hue, and she looked nauseated. Without removing her eyes from the glowing crystal, she declared, "My lady, it has taken me the fullness of three years." She looked at her feet. "In my life, I've never been as tired as I was while charging that thing." She looked up at Lilith, tears glistening on her eyelashes. "Please, mistress. Don't tell me I have to do it again. I don't think I can bear it."

Lilith smiled and beckoned for her minion to follow.

With the diamond in hand, they approached an arch hewn into the dense stone of a cavern wall. It was fifty feet wide and twenty feet tall, with hundreds of round sockets marking its border, but it led nowhere. Beneath its span was only the smooth stone of the wall.

Lilith placed the glowing diamond into one of the sockets, then turned to Anarane. She bent and kissed the elf's forehead, sending a surge of power rushing into her. The elf staggered. Her eyes squeezed shut. Sparks of energy coruscated over her body.

And then she stood still, and her eyes flicked open once more. They were now purple, flashing with hints of the power that lay behind them. A smile crept across her face.

Lilith pointed to the diamond in the arch. "My greatest follower, you will need to seek more of these crystals. Many more. I foresee a time when they will be needed, and I will depend on your special skills to infuse them all with power. You are now my high priestess, and I've activated abilities within you that you didn't know you had. Among these is the power to absorb the life essence of others. That energy, combined with your own, will enable you to infuse the gems that will one day fill this wall.

"Go into the Aboveworld. Recruit assistance as needed, and find more of these crystals. I sense deposits of them in the land north of here. Do not return until you and I agree that you've gathered enough for our people's needs."

As Anarane turned to exit, Lilith added a warning. "Be wary of the escalating violence above. Travel cautiously."

Anarane nodded, and with a flutter of her robes, left the cavern in silence.

Five hundred and sixty-six years ago

Lilith felt Seder's hand reach down from the spirit world, and a giant surge of energy shone like a beacon in the Aboveworld. For a moment, she thought Seder had joined them in this material world, to directly confront Sammael.

But then she extended her senses, and detected a vast amount of energy emanating from a life somewhere in the world above. The energy was unstable, but there was no doubt about it. Huge surges of Seder and Sammael's powers were being deployed by one of the puny creatures of this world.

How could this be?

A mighty explosion erupted, with a terrible ripping that tore right through the world. Lilith crumpled in pain as she felt the tremendous loss of life in the Aboveworld. Left in its wake was a new pulsing object of power: an impenetrable barrier, splitting Trimoria, glowing with Seder's influence.

And Lilith couldn't sense a thing beyond it.

Seventy-five years ago

Lilith fell to her knees as the world tilted on its edge. She felt impossibly weak, and for the first time in her existence, she knew she'd been a fool. In a desperate moment of unthinking hubris, she had taken the one diamond Anarane had charged… and she'd tried to reach out to another world.

Now she clawed at the rock wall for support. The world was tilting, shifting, rocking, sending waves of nausea through her.

I knew that wouldn't work. I'll never second-guess my instincts again.

The diamond still rested in her fist, but it was drained, broken. Moments ago it had glowed with massive energy. Now it was cold, dark. Useless.

Lilith threw down the ruined artifact and closed her eyes. She still sensed her brother's malignancy spreading in the world.

I must somehow find safety for those I care for.

A metallic creaking echoed through the cavern, followed by the sound of breaking glass and a human cough. Lilith turned in the direction of the sound.

All that energy I expended, and instead of creating a gateway to another world, I dragged some pathetic object from that world to join me.

Forty-one years ago

Malphas carried a large metal cage that gave off a strange hum. He wasn't sure what Sammael had done to the metal; all he knew was that the whining creature trapped within it was the first elusive blink dogs ever to have been captured.

He entered Sammael's throne room carrying his burden, and his lord waved him closer.

Malphas set the cage in front of Sammael's throne and knelt beside it. The blink dog barked and whined, its yellow eyes wide with fright.

"An amazing trick, isn't it, Malphas?" said Sammael. "These creatures are instinctively capable of blinking out of existence and appearing elsewhere—yet when you surround them with damantite, infused with just a little of my own power, of course, they are powerless to escape."

"My lord, may I ask why you asked me to capture one?"

"No you may not. But… you may watch."

Sammael stepped down from his throne, opened the cage, and pulled the blink dog out by the scruff of its furry neck. He then forced the quivering animal onto its side and placed a glowing hand on the animal's belly.

Vibrations emanated from the demon lord, and Malphas barely controlled the resulting spasms in his stomach. The blink dog lacked the same restraint; it coughed up its last meal as it squirmed under Sammael's ministrations.

Sammael stood, and the vibrations ceased. He then waved his hand toward one of the throne room's distant walls, where an exit suddenly appeared.

The blink dog wasted no time leaping to his feet and sprinting toward it. And as he passed through the exit, the wall flexed, and a shockwave blasted across the room. Malphas was sent flying backward.

Sammael filled the room with his grating laugh. "*Da qualche fessura sia entrato il fumo di Satana nel tempio di Dio...*"

Malphas looked up at him in confusion. "My lord? I don't understand."

Sammael smiled as he resumed his seat on his throne. "From some fissure, the smoke of Satan has entered the temple of God... I'll show them some smoke."

"My lord, do you want me to retrieve the blink dog?"

Sammael shook his head. "No. With the dog's own help, I've sent her to a place where she'll do the most good."

Today

Malphas was on his way to the throne room to report on the status of the troops when an explosion rattled the tunnels of the Underworld.

Maybe one of the hatchlings was an exploder.

Malphas raced ahead, sprinted into Sammael's throne room, and ran right into a visitor he'd never seen here before. An elven woman. To his surprise, she sent him flying backward with a thunderous backhand, leaving Malphas's ears ringing.

He gathered himself and stood straight, showing his full

height. She was a mere seven feet tall. Yet it was obvious that she possessed great power.

From his throne, Sammael sent him a silent command. *"Show respect, for you are the first to meet my sister, Lilith."*

A shiver of fear raced through Malphas, and he kneeled before her, lowering his eyes in a sign of respect.

Lilith reached out and brushed her fingers across his scale-covered cheek. She leaned close and whispered, "I could make you mine if I wanted to."

Warring emotions raced through Malphas's head. He felt her controlling his mind... and only when he grudgingly turned to Sammael, whose eyes blazed with power, did that control evaporate.

Lilith laughed and walked over to her brother. To Malphas's surprise, Sammael had changed into his more human-like form, and had adjusted his height so that he was only slightly taller than his sister.

"Lileet, ma shlom ech?"

Lilith waved dismissively. "I've shed the old language, Sammael. You should embrace the new world and all that it offers." She nodded toward Malphas. "I see you've begun to embrace the creatures that roam this world. Maybe you've learned that destruction isn't the way of things."

Sammael arched one eyebrow. "Destruction isn't the way of things? Coming from you, who just blew through the stone barrier we erected for our breeding grounds?"

Lilith shrugged. "I needed a more direct route. I'm sure you've felt the changes in our brother's barrier. Is that your doing?"

"I'm working on it, yes. Seder is clever, and he's always been able to see things in ways I've never understood, but he isn't infallible. The barrier will be down soon, and I'll be able to finish what I started."

"Sammael, what is your goal? You realize there is no need for war. I'm sure your minions can exist without destroying others. If not, change them. Even in our diminished capacities, we can do such things."

Sammael's eyes blazed and his lip curled. "Not *this* argument again. What do you want? Are you here to join your minions with mine? I'd welcome that, my sister."

Lilith's eyes blazed purple. "What are you trying to accomplish, Sammael?"

"What has always been," Sammael hissed. "Chaos. Destruction. Bring down all others so they see me as the only power in all the worlds. Why else exist? Are you joining me or not? If not, stay out of my way."

Lilith stepped back with a look of regret and began gathering up energy. She shimmered with power, then erupted in an explosion of light—along with a shock wave that knocked Malphas from his feet.

Blinking, Malphas stared at the spot where Lilith had stood. Standing there now was a perfect likeness of her, carved of pure white stone.

Sammael growled, raised a balled fist, and shattered the statue. He turned to Malphas and snarled.

"Tell me about the army."

Anarane sat reading in the recesses of the temple that she herself had erected in honor of Lilith centuries ago. Sconces on the walls emitted a lavender glow, and the temple's stone reflected and spread a warm purple light throughout every room. It was dim, but Anarane would allow no ordinary torches. She'd noticed long ago that flames released soot that spoiled the pristine white surfaces of her retreat, so she'd forbidden their use within the temple's walls. Fortunately her eyes had long ago grown accustomed to reading with only the dim purple light.

She would never forget the moment when she realized she was stuck on the wrong side of the barrier—and the subsequent intense grief she felt at being separated from her mistress. But she knew, even then, that it could not be forever, and that she'd need a quiet, private place in which to fulfill her mistress's orders. So with the help of her recruits and slaves, she'd arranged for the construction of this temple deep within the long-abandoned tunnels of the Ta'ah. And she'd been following her mistress's last command ever since.

As she flipped a page in the tome she was reading, she detected motion in the cavern outside her temple. With the briefest push of her will, she sent the front door swinging open. Then she rose to meet her visitor.

A fifteen-foot-tall ogre was striding up the temple stairs, dragging a pair of human slaves by their chained collars. She met them at the top of the stairs, where she ran her fingers across the humans' cheeks, tasting of their life essence. A thrill raced through her as their eyes lost focus and they collapsed on the floor.

Delicious.

She pulled a glowing diamond from her robe; it was nearly full. Exercising her powers as Lilith's high priestess, she placed a hand on the first slave's chest. It was like taking a deep breath—she felt the slave's life power pour into her in one long inhalation, and she exhaled the energy into the diamond. Then she repeated the process with the second slave.

Only then did she turn to the ogre. "Report."

The ogre pointed at the two unconscious slaves. "Slaves try run. Three run. One dead. Two I bring." He handed her a small leather pouch. "Find another shiny rock."

"Good." She curled her finger at the ogre. "Follow me."

Anarane led the ogre into the temple, and pointed to a large granite slab in the floor, with a metal loop attached.

"Lift that for me."

The ogre happily gripped at the metal ring and pulled. The slab slowly inched upward, revealing stairs leading down.

"Heavy rock no resist Stonecrusher," the ogre boasted. "Me great mover."

Anarane nodded. *They are such simple and misunderstood creatures.*

"That's right, Stonecrusher, you are a great mover. But remember, don't make the mistake of killing the slaves." She opened the pouch he had handed her and removed the diamond inside. "If you do, I'll put your life inside one of these."

The ogre shook his large head and snarled. "No be bad. I watch hoomans and dorfs. No kill dem. If dey bad, bring to you. And bring shiny rocks. Right?"

Anarane nodded. "That's right, Stonecrusher. Now take the slaves to the megapede pits. Come back after."

When the ogre departed, Anarane stepped down the stairs into the hidden storeroom below. She sent a thread of power into the air, creating a ball of light that pierced the darkness. Though she could have found what she sought even in the dark. At the far end of the room stood a large damantite chest with no adornments, no handles, no latches, and no lock.

She still remembered the look the dwarven smith had given her when she'd had it constructed centuries ago. *"By Seder's white beard,"* he'd said, *"der be no way to lock it or unlock it if'n you don't show a keyhole."* He thought she was crazy.

She held her hand over the chest and sent some of her energy into the hidden inner locking mechanism. With a click, the trunk sprang open, and a flood of blue-white light poured into the room.

With a smile and a silent prayer, she placed her full diamond inside the chest, where it would remain, along with the hundreds of glowing gems already inside, until her mistress needed it.

"Sloane," said Mother, "I have no problem with Zenethar taking on the Thariginian name. In fact, it's something I think we should all be proud of."

Sloane's father nodded in agreement.

"But there is no way I can allow you and Aaron to get married without more notice—whether the First Protector requested it or not. You're the only princess the people have. Maybe in six months I can make the arrangements, and—"

Sloane screeched in frustration. "Absolutely not, Mother! Who knows what could happen to us in six months?" She fixed her father with a glare. "You could do this right *now*."

Her father's mouth hung open, but her mother shrieked in horror at the idea. "How can you even suggest such a thing? It isn't proper. A princess needs a big wedding. And a big wedding requires *time*. Throll, please explain this to your daughter."

Father opened his mouth to speak, then closed it. His eyes

darted from his daughter to his wife and back again. And then a sly grin grew on his face. "There is a way you could *both* get what you want. We could… do this twice."

Sloane's heart beat faster at this thread of hope, but Father's response was clearly not what Mother was expecting.

"What?" she yelled, her eyes flashing with fury.

Father shrank back. "I just mean… we could do something small and informal now, and when we reclaim our castle across the barrier, we can have a huge ceremony for the public. Then everyone's happy," he added, without conviction.

Sloane rushed her father and wrapped him in a giant hug. "Oh, thank you, Father. Thank you thank you thank you." Then, before her mother could object, Sloane broke her embrace and wrapped Mother in her arms. "Thank you, Mother. I promise, when the time comes, I'll be the best bride you could hope for. Very surprised, too. And so innocent!"

Mother stiffened, then relaxed and returned the embrace. Still, Sloane was sure she was glaring at Father as she muttered, "Fine. But I'm not making any of the arrangements."

Aaron couldn't believe Sloane had succeeded in convincing her parents to allow the wedding right away. In fact, he'd been so confident in her failure, he hadn't even considered how he'd tell his own parents. Fortunately, they were receptive to the idea of a two-part wedding. Their only complaint was that Ryan wouldn't be present for "the real wedding," as Mom was calling it, as he and Arabelle had gone to Eluanethra in search of information on Nicnevin.

"I can't believe we're doing this without your brother," she clucked as she buffed his armor. "Of all the times to go running off after some elf queen."

The two of them stood with Dad in the heart of the castle, the pulsing purple light above them, awaiting Sloane and her parents. The six of them—Aaron and Sloane, and their parents—would form the entirety of this ceremony. Not even Zenethar and Rebecca were invited, as they might spill the secret.

The next wedding would, of course, be substantially larger.

Dad chuckled. "Your son and his elf queens. The first one he kills, the next one he dances with. Hard to predict what he'll do with this one."

Mom frowned. "He'll be fine as long as he's got Arabelle with him. I trust her. She's got a good head on her shoulders."

Aaron laughed. "Aha! So you don't trust Ryan!"

"That's not what I meant. I just—"

She was cut off by Throll, who walked into the room with a bellow. "I hear there's a wedding about to take place."

Sloane and her mother followed right after. Gwen's eyes were red and puffy from crying, and Mom immediately went to her, giving her a hug that started the tears flowing yet again. But Aaron had eyes only for Sloane. She wore a simple, form-fitting white dress, and she had never looked more beautiful. When she met his gaze, blushing, he thought his heart was going to pound through his chest.

Am I ready for this?

Throll began immediately. He motioned for Aaron and

Sloane to stand next to each other, facing him, and the others lined up behind them. Both mothers dabbed at their eyes, while Dad smiled through his thick beard.

"Since this will be an informal ceremony," Throll said, "I won't bother with the ribbon binding and all that."

Sloane glared at her father and shook her head slightly.

His shoulders slumped. "Okay… I stand corrected. I guess I *will* bother with the ribbon-binding." He looked to the two mothers. "Do either of you…"

They both held out white silk ribbons.

Throll chuckled. "Of course you do."

He took one of the offered white ribbons and addressed the young couple. "Now face each other."

Aaron's heart thudded in his ears as he looked into Sloane's eyes. The Sloane he knew was the strongest, most willful, most confident girl he'd ever met. Yet at this moment, he saw in her a vulnerability and nervousness that betrayed her innermost feelings. Her chin quivered, and her eyes shone brightly with unshed tears.

Aaron breathed deeply.

I'll never give her a reason to doubt me.

"Sloane Lancaster, do you vow to be matched from this day forward to Aaron Riverton, to have and to hold, for better or for worse, in sickness and in health? To love and cherish him, to keep no secrets from him, to bear him no ill will? Under the Creator's witness, do you vow this?"

Tears dripped down Sloane's cheeks, and her voice cracked as she said, "I d-do."

Aaron felt his nervousness disappear, and he gave Sloane a

warm smile, trying to reassure her.

"Aaron Riverton, do you vow to be matched from this day forward to Sloane Lancaster, to have and to hold, for better or for worse, in sickness and in health? To love and cherish her, to keep no secrets from her, to bear her no ill will? Under the Creator's witness, do you vow this?"

"I do."

Sloane exhaled and smiled.

Throll ceremoniously lifted the silk ribbon in the air. Aaron and Sloane turned to face Throll, and held their arms out to him. The king looped the silk ribbon around their arms, loosely binding them together.

"With this ribbon, I bind you. Let this ribbon symbolize the binding of two lives as one. Just as two trees can be grafted together, I now bind you both—"

Gwen let out a loud sob. Mom hugged her, and they both motioned for Throll to continue.

The king gave the young couple a reassuring smile. "May the roots of your shared life and the strength of your love bring you happiness and prosperity. Let nothing in this world tear this binding asunder. I call upon the blessings of the Creator to sanctify this pairing, and to show his pleasure by giving them a long and productive life together."

The purple light in the ceiling flared white for just an instant.

"As the Protector-General and King of Trimoria, I pronounce you husband and wife. Aaron, you may kiss the bride."

Aaron gently wrapped his free arm around his new bride, and they shared a gentle kiss that warmed him from head to toe.

Throll cleared his throat. "This would normally be when I

introduce you to the crowd, but since everyone present has known you for quite a while, might I instead ask a favor of the newly married couple?"

Aaron and Sloane looked up at him.

Throll blinked away tears. "Would you be willing to share a meal with your parents before you truly depart as husband and wife?"

Sloane threw her arms around her father's midsection. "Of course, Father. I'll always have time for you."

Jared arrived at the newly installed fountain to discover a line of students from the academy already waiting. The student in front kneeled and washed his hands and face in the water, and in response, the orb atop the statue of the First Protector glowed briefly. Jared took up position in the back of the line and waited his turn.

The young girl in front of him turned. "Oh, headmaster! Please, you can go in front of me."

He shook his head. "No need, Elaine. I can wait my turn like everyone else."

She blushed prettily. "Oh, you remember my name!"

Jared smiled. "I try to know all the students' names, though it's getting harder these days with all the new arrivals. Tell me again, what form of magic are you attuned to?"

"Master Eglerion said I'll likely be a war wizard when my training is complete."

"A war wizard… like me." Jared grinned. "Try to do this."

He held up his hand and sent arcs of lightning between his fingers.

Elaine raised her hand, palm up, and concentrated hard. At first, nothing happened. Then a glow appeared in the center of her palm. And then an uncontrolled blast of energy shot outward.

Thankfully, Jared had placed an invisible shield around her hand. He'd learned that precaution the hard way.

Elaine gasped. "I'm sorry! I didn't mean to do that."

"No harm done. Control is one of the most difficult things to learn. But that's why you're at the RAM. You'll be taught what you need to know."

She beamed with pride—but then her smile faltered. "My father says… he says I'm a freak."

Jared clenched his teeth. *The fool man.*

"My dear, you are no such thing, and I would not give another thought to it. There will always be a place of importance for someone of good character who works hard at honing their knowledge and skills. Your abilities should never be a source of shame. Be proud of who and what you are."

The girl still looked uncertain. "Father says a girl shouldn't go to school at all, and definitely shouldn't learn reading and writing. That it spoils her for other things."

"Your father may say that, but that doesn't make it true. Your being a girl has nothing to do with it. Did you know that, centuries ago, some of the most powerful wizards were women?"

She shook her head. "I didn't know that."

"Trust in yourself, Elaine. Work hard, and listen to your instructors. I've no doubt you'll fulfill the great potential I see within you."

She blushed and looked down at her feet. "Thank you, headmaster."

As Jared strolled through the training ground, his mind was preoccupied with finding Castien. Unfortunately, whenever he sought someone with his mind's eye, he gave off a glow that he still hadn't learned to control—and the soldiers on the grounds, trained though they were, tended to stop their sparring and stare at him as he passed.

His power told him that Castien was in the captain's barracks, which also doubled as a school of tactics for the officers. Aaron was one of the best students there, which was important to Trimoria, given his destiny as a general, but Sloane was nearly his equal. They made a good pair.

The door opened as he approached, and Eglerion's wrinkled elven face appeared. "Lord Riverton." Clearly, Jared's arrival had been expected.

"Eglerion, how do you do that? I know you're the elven lore master and know more about magic than I could ever hope to, but you aren't a wizard, and yet you always seem to know right when I'm about to show up."

Eglerion waved a hand dismissively. "Just because I can't use the powers, doesn't mean I can't *hear* them being used. And you… well, the energy crackles all about you. I can't help but hear it. You could learn a thing or two from Ryan about hiding your presence. He's much better at it."

"I know, I know. Subtlety is not my strong suit."

Castien appeared beside Eglerion. "Ah, Lord Riverton, you're here. Unfortunately, I haven't been able to find Sloane. Do you know where she is?"

Jared nodded. "I'm afraid she's busy. That's why I asked Eglerion to join us today. He's fluent in the old language if there are any communication issues."

"Busy?" Castien looked skeptical. "I can't see Sloane passing on this opportunity. What could be more important than the dragons?"

Jared shifted uncomfortably. "I'm afraid it's a private matter. She's not to be disturbed."

"Does this private matter involve young Aaron as well? I haven't seen him in the last two days."

Eglerion squinted thoughtfully at Jared, then chuckled. "Ah."

Castien looked slowly between Jared and the lore master, and an uncharacteristic smile grew on his face. "Are you saying they…?"

Jared couldn't keep from smiling back. "Keep it to yourself."

Castien beamed and clasped Jared's shoulder. "I'm happy for them. And for you. Now. Let's go ride some dragons."

The three men arrived at the scene to find that Ruby had already been fitted with her new, custom-made saddle, and the saddler and his apprentice were pulling a larger saddle from their wagon. Pyre stood some distance away, watching warily, smoke twirling lazily up from his nostrils.

Ruby grumbled at her brother. "*Al tedag. Ze no-ach.*"

Without Sloane around, Jared looked to Eglerion for a translation.

"She told him not to worry," the lore master said. "The saddle is comfortable."

Jared chuckled and walked over to Pyre. "How are you today, my friend?"

The dragon grumbled in the common tongue. "I don't like this."

Jared scratched under Pyre's chin. "Do you still like *this*?"

Pyre closed his eyes and leaned in. His tail swished, and his throat rumbled in the dragon's equivalent of a purr.

"I know you're uneasy about the idea of taking on a rider. But we've discussed this. It's for your own safety. When last we tested your breath, you had a range of about sixty to eighty feet. Right?"

Pyre grumbled an "Uh-huh" and tilted his chin for more scratching.

"Well, dwarven crossbows have double that range, and the elves can triple that range with their longbows. Which means you may encounter circumstances in which you need a rider with a similarly ranged weapon. I'd prefer to save your breath weapon for attacks against flying demons, and for strafing swarms of unranged ground fighters. You understand that, right?"

"I understand. I just don't—" Pyre raised his head and turned to see the saddle lying on him. "You tricked me."

Ruby walked over. "Boys are so easily distracted."

Jared called across the field. "Castien, bring over the two volunteers!"

Castien jogged over to them with an elf and a dwarf in tow.

"I only have one *volunteer*," he said, tilting his head toward the elf. Then he smiled at the dwarf. "But I also have Oda Rockfist."

Oda sputtered as he approached. "What have ye gotten me into? Der be no way I can ride that thing!"

Pyre turned his head toward the dwarf. "Thing?"

"Oh, don't be so sensitive," Oda said. "You've known me since you were fresh from your egg. It's dat *saddle* I've a problem with. How can I hang on and aim my crossbow at the same time?"

Jared shrugged. "The same way you do it on your mountain pony—stirrups. I had the saddler make them extremely adjustable, so the saddle can be used by anyone from your size to folks as tall as our king." He kicked the wooden steps into place so Oda could climb up without being lifted. "Unless there's another problem? You aren't... you aren't telling me you're afraid, are you?"

Oda growled, stomped up the stairs, and plopped down on Pyre's saddle. The elf bowman, who had already mounted Ruby, chuckled.

Jared stepped back and addressed the two dragons. "Okay, you two. For this run, we just want to test the comfort of the saddles during ordinary flying. No diving, no tricks, no fire-breathing. Just fly gently around the practice field for a bit and then come back."

Pyre leaped into the air without warning. Oda gripped the pommel with both hands and let out a squeal of fright as his mount gained altitude. Ruby's lift-off was much smoother, and the elf handled the trip far more calmly—though his expression suggested that he, too, was more uneasy than he pretended.

"I feel sorry for Oda," Castien said. "I have a feeling Pyre is going to make this difficult."

Sure enough, Pyre suddenly banked steeply, pulled into a loop, then executed a barrel roll. He might have complained about having a rider, but now he was making the most of it. Jared flashed back to twenty years earlier, when he was a fighter pilot. Remembering how sick some candidates were from spatial disorientation in the simulators, he hoped the dwarf didn't vomit on the dragon's back. That wouldn't go well for either of them.

Ruby, meanwhile, was following instructions. She was at a much higher altitude, but she was merely gliding casually across the sky.

After a couple more circuits of the field, Pyre came down first. Perhaps he'd decided to take mercy on poor Oda, for his landing was smooth as silk.

"*Zeh hiye kef!*" he declared.

Eglerion chuckled. "Pyre says that was fun."

Oda still held tightly to the pommel, his eyes squeezed shut. "Is it over?"

Castien laughed. "Are you telling me you had your eyes closed the entire time?"

Oda cracked his eyelids open, as if to confirm he was safely on the ground, then dropped from the dragon's back. "Bah!" he said, with false bravado. "I just knew my lookin' around wasn't required for dis test." He turned to Jared. "So, did you learn what ye needed to know?

"Actually, we learned a bit more than that," Jared said, frowning at Pyre. "Not only do we know the saddle worked, we also learned that a dwarf can fly upside down."

"I did *what*?" Oda cried, turning on Pyre, who responded with a grating laugh.

Ruby came down next. She landed gently, but the instant she was down, the elf rider literally fell out of his saddle, landed on all fours, and dry-heaved on the grass.

Ruby looked innocently at Jared. "I was very gentle."

"Ha!" said Oda. "Just shows you dat elves have weak constitutions. I didn't get sick one bit."

Pyre turned to Ruby and snickered. "He kept his eyes closed the whole time."

Jared walked over to Ruby and whispered in her ear. When she nodded, he made a few adjustments to her saddle, then hopped aboard.

"Lord Riverton!" Castien yelled. "What are you doing?"

Jared waved and grinned as Ruby spread her wings. "What does it look like I'm doing! It's been years since I've flown."

Ruby leapt into the air, and Jared held on tight.

SEEKING AN ANCIENT QUEEN

Ryan nearly fell off his horse as he and Arabelle arrived in the elf stronghold of Eluanethra. As the groomsmen led their horses to the stable, she forced Ryan to sit on a wooden bench and relax.

He smiled wanly. "I'm sorry, Belle. I just can't seem to get it together lately. I'm getting plenty of sleep, yet I always feel exhausted."

"Just sit still."

She frowned at the dark circles beneath his bloodshot eyes, drank deeply from her flask, then knelt in front of him and infused him with all the healing energy she could manage.

Ryan kissed her forehead. "Thank you. I feel fine now." He smiled and stood, as if to assure her that he was all right, but she knew better. He hadn't felt "fine" is a long time. Every night he struggled with his demons, and every night she did what she could to soothe him—but it wasn't enough.

"Welcome back to Eluanethra," said a familiar voice.

Arabelle turned to see Xinthian approaching. "Greetings, Xinthian. It is good to see you again."

Xinthian turned to Ryan. "I understand you seek information on Nicnevin. On behalf of the council of elders, I would like to understand why."

"To be honest," said Ryan, "I'm not entirely clear on the 'why' myself. All I know is that I'm to seek Nicnevin's guidance —at the request of the First Protector."

Xinthian's eyes widened. "Zenethar Thariginian? How come you by this request?"

Ryan shrugged. "We spoke with him. Well, Sloane did. He said that I needed to find Nicnevin, 'past the end of the world,' and learn from her. Arabelle is to accompany me."

Xinthian blinked with obvious surprise. "Incredible..." he whispered to himself. Then he nodded curtly. "It looks like some research is in order. Fortunately for you, we currently have a scholar hard at work in the library. A friend of yours, in fact."

"A scholar?" Arabelle asked. "Who?"

Xinthian smiled. "Wat Crazybeard."

They found Wat in the library, sitting at a table stacked high with books. Two years earlier, Wat had won a contest among RAM students, and the prize had been full unrestricted access to the Eluanethran library. In the intervening years, he'd made the most of the opportunity.

Xinthian put his hand on Wat's shoulder. "Wat, my friend. We are in need of your help."

"Of course, elder," Wat replied.

"Our young couple here needs to do some research. They're looking for information on one of our ancestral queens: Nicnevin."

One of Wat's bushy eyebrows arched upward, and he smiled. "I know just where to begin."

"Good. I leave you to it. I must go and speak with our queen about this… development."

As Xinthian departed, Wat retrieved a large leather-bound book and set it on the table where he had been working. Ryan and Arabelle pulled up chairs, and they all sat together.

Arabelle gasped. "I've seen this book before! My father has a copy. This tells a story of a crazy dwarf, doesn't it?"

Wat grinned. "I suppose that's one way of describing it." He opened the tome. "This was actually one of the first books Eglerion showed me after I won my prize. See how there are two columns of print? One tells the story in the common language, and the other in the old language. It was immensely useful to me in learning the old language."

He nudged the book toward Ryan and Arabelle. "Anyway, since this is in the common language, you two can go ahead and start reading this on your own. I'm going to go gather some more things from the restricted section."

He hopped off his chair and walked off, and Ryan turned to the book and read aloud.

. . .

I am but a humble servant of the elven people. These words you read are not my own, but the words of a depraved dwarf author who spent time with someone he believed to be Nicnevin, our queen from many thousands of years ago. Despite its title, the story of Nicnevin is not for this book, but suffice it to say that according to the legend, Nicnevin challenged the gods and was forever cast down to live at the end of the world.

Many have searched for this mythical "end of the world," but none have found it, nor has any document or creature possessed even a hint of its whereabouts.

Until now.

Two weeks ago, this book's author stumbled into Eluanethra, naked and alone. How this dwarf managed to wander into the stronghold of our people without our scouts noticing is still a mystery. In his hands he clutched this book, which he had apparently written with his own blood. He shouted crazed warnings about the doom of all of Trimoria and the end of the world. He raved of demons yet to come, and of a savior amongst the humans which we must join. And he demanded that he be presented to the Archmage of Seder.

Since we knew of no such person, most among our people thought the dwarf crazy.

Xinthian is not so certain. He asked that I take the dwarf seriously and talk with him. Unfortunately the dwarf is fevered, and nothing we've been able to do has helped him. I fear that he will perish soon unless something changes.

With the assistance of my apprentice, Eglerion Mithtanion, I have translated the dwarf's blood script into modern Trimorian and included it on these pages. And on the off chance that it is meaningful, I have also placed notes within this book from the fevered ravings of the lunatic. If any of what he says comes to pass, I fear for the survival of our race.

—Bryan Greenwalker

"Wow," Ryan said. "Eglerion was still only an apprentice. This book must be hundreds of years old."

He turned the page and continued.

There will be a time when the demons arise and spread through the lands like a plague. Only the avatar of Seder can hope to meet with the leader of this host and survive....

———

Wearing white silk gloves, Wat placed a few sheets of parchment on the table. "Please be careful with these. I'd estimate these are two thousand years old—maybe more. And even then, these are only transcriptions of the original scrolls, which are now so ancient that they're too delicate to handle."

Ryan pushed his chair back a foot, fearing to even breathe on the documents.

"Given their age, naturally they're written in the old language, so allow me to translate."

Wat read aloud, translating from the old language with almost no hesitation:

Today, most of our people have forgotten that the greatest of our queens, Nicnevin, the one who brought us awareness of Seder, still haunts the end of the world. It has been thousands of years since any of us have seen her, but she is still the most powerful to have ever walked among us. Before her departure, she relinquished a portion of her great powers to her daughter, and that power has passed to every queen of our people thereafter. Once she named her chosen heir, it was her wish to exile herself for reasons unknown to even the eldest amongst us.

When a great power arrived in Trimoria, some amongst us were fooled into following that new power—who called herself Lilith. The women seemed to be most susceptible to her sway, and at first we believed it to be Nicnevin causing mischief.

Some of us sought guidance from the end of the world, and the only response we received was the shrill screams and cackling of a woman gone mad.

"So there really is a place called the End of the World," Ryan murmured.

Arabelle took his hand and gave it a kiss. "Apparently so."

Wat carefully moved the parchment away and slid another one closer.

. . .

Queen Reiluanni insisted on visiting the end of the world despite our advice against it. She said that it wasn't proper for one of our people to live in exile forever. Any reason for such an exile has been lost in the millennia and we should strive to rehabilitate our ancient queen if possible.

The council of elders advised against it, but unbeknownst to others, Reiluanni departed in the middle of the night two weeks ago. We feared the worst when her daughter, the heir apparent, suddenly came into her wizardly powers. It is known by many that the queen only relinquishes her power at the time of death.

We were in mourning when to everyone's surprise, Reiluanni returned to Eluanethra. Her mind had been broken, and even the conclave of wizards could not explain what had been done to her.

She clutched in her fist a hand-drawn picture of a woman none in Eluanethra recognized. Some speculate that it might be a drawing of our own ancestral queen, Nicnevin. I hope one day to understand why such a sacrifice was required of our Reiluanni. After all, what good is a drawing?

Wat moved the page aside, revealing an ancient drawing. "I believe this is the illustration being referred to."

The drawing depicted an elven woman in tattered and worn clothing, standing majestically in a clearing in the woods. Her haunting stare suggested annoyance at having been disturbed.

It's almost like I'm invading her privacy just by looking at her picture, Ryan thought.

Arabelle closed her eyes and hummed quietly. "That is Nicnevin."

"How do you know?" Ryan asked.

Arabelle opened her eyes. "I told you that Seder gifted me with his presence. That wasn't his only gift." She closed her eyes again, and after a moment she lifted her arm and pointed to the northeast. "She lies in that direction."

She opened her eyes again. "If I have a visual of what I'm looking for, I can usually sense the direction and distance someone is from me."

"That's amazing!" Wat exclaimed.

Ryan snaked his arm around her waist and gave her a gentle squeeze. "So, how far away is she?"

"I would estimate a day's march if it were across open fields. But as we're in the middle of a forest, and I don't know the terrain, it could be much longer."

Ryan clasped Wat's shoulder. "Thank you for your help, Wat. I can't tell you how useful this has been."

Wat lifted a hand, and sparks of energy crackled at his finger-tips. "Do you need assistance in your search?"

"No, my friend. I've been advised that it will be best if it is just myself and my healer."

"Healer?" Arabelle elbowed him. "Is that all that I am to you?"

"Hey!" said Wat, moving between the couple and the fragile parchments. "Take it outside if you're going to fight. Eglerion will kill me if anything happens to his treasures."

Late that evening, Ryan and Arabelle walked arm in arm toward the house that had been set aside for them. The sun had long since set, but the lichen that grew along the path glowed green to light their way.

Arabelle stopped suddenly. "We have company."

Labri stepped out of the woods in front of them, followed by an elf carrying a bundle in his arms.

"Your wife has very sharp eyes, Ryan Riverton," Labri said. She turned to Arabelle and raised an open hand with splayed fingers. "Arabelle Riverton, though you and I have seen each other many times, we've not formally been introduced. I am Labriuteleanan Sirfalas, queen of the elven people, wizard, and final authority in the city of Eluanethra. I welcome you and your husband to my domain, and I have a belated wedding gift for you."

Arabelle smiled and raised her open hand with fingers splayed. "Thank you for the kind greetings. I am Arabelle Riverton, princess of the Imazighen, healer, and named minion of Seder."

Ryan's eyes widened. *Minion of Seder?*

Labri stepped forward and embraced her. "Welcome, sister in Seder's glow," she whispered. Then she stepped back and wiped tears from her eyes.

Ryan saw that Arabelle also had tears dampening her cheeks. "What… what just happened?" he asked, confused.

The two women both laughed, then Labri grabbed Ryan and gave him a quick embrace. "You just witnessed our formal declaration of friendship between two people."

Ryan's brow furrowed. "I thought you were friends already."

"Of course we're friends," said Arabelle. "She meant *people*, as in the elven people and the Imazighen. I hadn't formally met with Labri since she officially became queen of her people. Haven't your parents taught you how these things work?"

Ryan shrugged. "In truth, I'm not sure *they* know about this custom either."

"Well, then you can teach them," Labri said. "Now come," she added, waving for them to follow, "let's go to your cabin. I want to show Arabelle her gift."

Labri unwrapped the bundle and held out a camisole that looked to be made from a fine doe hide. "Arabelle, I had this made for you."

Ryan wondered what the big deal was. *It's just a shirt.*

But Arabelle's eyes widened as she held the shirt and rubbed it between her fingers. "There's something woven into the fabric. I can feel it."

"Try it on," Labri said.

Arabelle glanced at Labri's male elf escort, and Labri laughed.

"Jasper, can you please stand outside? Humans are modest creatures."

When Jasper had exited, Arabelle removed her shirt and put on the new one. "It's lovely. I can't believe how well it fits."

Ryan frowned. "It looks like fine leather, but my senses are detecting… metal?"

Labri smiled. "Your senses are not betraying you. Our finest metalsmiths worked with our best weavers to create this." She turned to Arabelle. "I know that your fighting style does not allow for traditional armor. This shirt is the perfect solution, as it will prevent most bladed weapons from penetrating. However, if you're hit with a blunt weapon like a mace, you will certainly feel it."

"Thank you," Arabelle said, beaming. "This really is precisely what I need. It's a wonderful gift."

"Nothing for me?" Ryan asked Labri playfully.

The elf queen rolled her eyes. "You use magical shielding, wizard. Besides, this gift is for both of you. You *do* want your wife protected, do you not?"

Ryan took one look at Arabelle's challenging gaze and knew there was only one correct answer to that question.

"Yes," he said firmly. "It's truly a wonderful gift. For both of us."

Two days had passed since they'd left Eluanethra, and Ryan was glad they'd packed a lot of food for their trip. Arabelle had needed it, because she expended so much energy healing him from whatever assaulted him in his sleep; and Ryan had needed nourishment as well, as he'd needed to stretch his powers to their limits to unravel the many magical traps and illusions that blocked their progress.

His wife truly was a creature of the forest. She moved silently, always balancing silently on the balls of her feet, her instincts were tuned to all things within the woods, and she easily sniffed out weak portions of the path that were set as traps. When they first began their journey, she even treated her skin with the sap of some pungent leaves of the forest. "There's no need for me to advertise myself," she explained.

So when she suddenly hissed a warning at him—"Go invisible"—he didn't hesitate. He altered the properties of his magical shield to make light wrap around his body as if he wasn't even there.

Arabelle turned invisible as well, but in her own way— through stillness and camouflage. Were it not for her magical signature, Ryan wouldn't have known where she'd gone.

I'd swear she blends into the shadows better than any elf.

A moment later, a huge bear stepped into the path ahead of them. It turned its head in Ryan's direction, sniffed, and growled.

He can smell me.

The bear paused as if confused, then snarled and advanced.

Arabelle leapt from her position, dove across the bear's field of view, and disappeared into the foliage. At the same instant, a cloud of smoke surrounded the bear's head. The bear froze in place, whined, and collapsed onto its side.

Arabelle reappeared to check on the unconscious bear, whose chest rose and fell.

"Belle," said Ryan, becoming visible again, "what did you just do?"

She smiled and held up three straws. "I blew a few strawfuls of powdered *Tishkakh* leaves in his face. It causes forgetfulness and sleep. The bear will be fine."

Ryan continued to stare. "And you just… happened to carry around straws full of this stuff? Just in case you run into a bear?"

Arabelle gave him a devious smile. "A bear, a thief… maybe a misbehaving husband. It works on all sorts of things."

She turned and continued down the path, and Ryan couldn't help but smile.

That's one dangerous girl I've married.

Once again Arabelle paused on the path, but this time it wasn't because of a bear.

"We're close," she whispered. "Nicnevin lies just ahead. She's almost within reach."

Ryan extended his senses and detected no magical traps. "The way is clear—magically, anyway," he whispered back.

But Arabelle shook her head. "Strengthen your shields. There's an obstacle here. It may not be magical, but I have a feeling there's something…"

She scanned the path thoroughly as she crept forward.

Ryan followed Arabelle as carefully as he could, but somehow he seemed to scratch against every branch and thorn that she had so deftly avoided. He picked up his pace to keep up, and suddenly found himself tripping over a vine.

"Look out!" Arabelle cried as she somersaulted forward.

Ryan felt several small impacts on his shield, and a dozen deadly-looking thorns fell to the ground. They were covered with foul-smelling sap that was no doubt poisonous.

His heart beat faster as he looked ahead to Arabelle. She was unharmed.

"Looks like you found the trap," she whispered.

"Yeah. That's one way to do it."

She beckoned him forward. "Come on. We're nearly there."

But before Ryan could take another step, the trees all around him filled with a fast-moving mist. His shield was up, but the mist poured right through it like it wasn't there. A fuzzy, distant voice cried, "Duck and run past it," but it was too late. The ground rose to meet him and the world around him dimmed.

SEDER'S PALADIN

Ohaobbok stared at the mountain pass with some misgiving. He knew very well the dangers that lay in wait even for someone like him, yet here he was with the Rock-fist clan, readying for a journey deep into the territories of the ogres. This would be his first return to his homeland since his mother threw him from the top of a cliff as a punishment for befriending the local dwarves. That seemed like a lifetime ago, though in truth, it had been only five years.

His mother had disliked him even before then, because he was different. It irritated her to no end that he didn't eat meat. *All* ogres ate meat. Except Ohaobbok. For as long as he could remember, the very thought of eating meat made him sick. As a child, he lived on berries, bark, and other root vegetables; and he suffered the beatings he'd receive when he turned down a haunch of deer or a piece of dwarf.

But this unique attribute for an ogre was part of what had

caused that first dwarven clan to trust him. For it seemed a dwarven prophecy had foretold of his coming. He still remembered the moment when Mattias Hammerthrower first related the words of that prophecy.

You will know that the time of the First Protector's return is upon you when you are greeted by a saintly ogre that eats no meat. This ogre will serve as guardian in the abyss, when we face the ultimate evil.

Guardian in the abyss. That was Ohaobbok's fate. It had been revealed in the visions.

"Ohaobbok! Food be ready!"

Ohaobbok looked down to see a dwarf with a long brown beard jumping up and down in front of him, trying to get his attention.

"Sorry, Barnaby. I was just reliving the past."

"Oh? And what do ye remember?"

"I remember wishing I could leave my ogre family. Did you know that I watched the dwarves for a long time? I had a hiding spot from which I could look down on one of your clans. That was how I came to learn your race was prone to merriment instead of violence. I'm glad that circumstances turned out the way they did."

"Oy, we Rockfists enjoy our parties. That we do!" Barnaby jabbed the ogre's thigh with his elbow. "But if'n you don't recall, I'll remind you dat my family isn't known as our people's ogre-slaying crew for being peaceful-like." He grinned slyly. "You be different, o'course."

They walked back into the camp, and one of the other Rockfists handed Ohaobbok the gigantic mug they'd created just for him, filled to the brim with a foamy dark ale. The ogre took a healthy sip, feeling the warmth of kinship.

The clan's cook then waddled over with a huge kettle of stew, which he set down in front of the ogre. "Siddown an' eat, you freak o' nature." He sniffed at the kettle with a look of disdain. "I not be knowin' how you keep up yer strength with only dem vegetables."

Another dwarf shouted over. "Hey, don't be calling that big bag of muscles names. He's one of us."

The cook snarled. "Don'tcha be telling me what to do, you over-muscled half-wit. Ohaobbok be knowin' I says dat stuff cuz I likes him. If'n I weren't likin' him, I'd be shovin' those vegetables up his arse."

The dwarves around the campfire roared with laughter, and Ohaobbok chuckled too as he sat down to eat his stew. These Rockfists might be tiny, but they were his family.

Another dwarf let out a loud burp. "Hey, Ohaobbok, you never explained why you're out patrollin' wit' us." He pointed with his mug at Ohaobbok, sloshing some ale on the ground—to the grumbling of his fellow clansmen. "Are ya really gonna hunt yer own kind?"

Before Ohaobbok could answer, Barnaby cut in. "Oy, let the ogre eat! He just sat down. Asides, I got the letter from me brudder Oda right here explainin' it all. You all remember me brudder be servin' proudly as a captain in the king's army?"

Groans went up around the camp. "We know, Barnaby. You only be tellin' us two times a day."

"Well now I be tellin' you agin!" Barnaby pulled a rolled-up parchment from under his chainmail vest. "Oy, here it is." He read aloud.

"Barnaby,

I'd be there m'self to tell you, but I'm showing the humans how to fight proper and can't be spared.

The Archmage himself asked me to enlist the help of our clan to further investigate the remnants of the First Protector's home and fountain. The Archmage said that he previously sent Wat, one of his most powerful wizards, to investigate, but Wat didn't get full cooperation—"

"Bah!" someone cried. "He be the clanless dwarf!"

Several others nodded their heads in agreement, but Barnaby glared at the speaker and kept reading.

"You tell my rock-for-brains clanmates that when the Archmage sends an emissary, no matter who he be, he need be honored. I was shamed when Lord Riverton told me about my clan's lack of assistance. It be an insult to Lord Riverton and the Archmage when one of his emissaries be treated as such. We can't be allowing such a stain to blemish our honor, and we must redeem ourselves."

. . .

At these words, the looks on the dwarves' faces changed. They were a jovial and carefree bunch, but it was quite a jolt to have one of their own question their honor.

"I believe that our dwarf-friend Ohaobbok will be sent in good time to continue where the prior emissary left off. Know that I'll come bash each and every one of you with my mace if'n I have reason to apologize to Lord Riverton again."

"And see here," said Barnaby, holding up the parchment, "Oda signed it… and added his captain's mark."

Another groan rose from the assembled dwarves.

Barnaby turned the parchment over and showed the outer wax seal. "And this here be the crown of our king." Barnaby patted at Ohaobbok's knee. "Now, dwarf-friend, if ye've filled your belly a bit, p'raps you'd like to tell us more about what we be plannin'. I be feelin' certain ye'll get da full attention of da clan."

The bearded faces all turned to Ohaobbok with a look of respect that made him a touch nervous.

He drained the remainder of his ale, then cleared his throat. "Basically, we just want to take a closer look at what you folks discovered. The Archmage is interested in knowing more about the First Protector's home itself, of course, but also the fountain. He wants me to verify whether the fountain is a magical fountain like the ones in the city squares of Trimoria.

"In addition, Wat mentioned there was a well-worn path

leading to the fountain from up in the mountains. That suggests somebody has been visiting it on a regular basis. We'd like to find out who."

"Do you tink der be another wizard in dat forest?" asked a black-haired dwarf.

Barnaby shook his head. "No way he'd survive alone. He'd have been gobbled up by ogres. Even if he be strong enough to fight 'em off, we'd have seen evidence of da wizardy battles."

Another dwarf nodded. "That place has certainly seen no battles. Heck, there's a bunch o' flowers growin' all over that area, all garden-like. There not only be no wizardy battles, there be no ogre battles neither. I guarantee it."

"And that too is of interest," Ohaobbok said, "seeing as the fountain is in the middle of the hunting grounds for several ogre clans."

Barnaby clapped his hands and stood. "All right, brudders, it be time to set watch. Deneb, Gathrun, and Dathane, you're on first. Rest of you boys, get some sleep. You'll be woken when yer needed."

As the dwarves shuffled off, Barnaby looked up at Ohaobbok. "Dwarf-friend, you be havin' the last watch wid me. Hurry up and finish that stew, then rest as ye can. We're countin' on ya to be ready fer action if'n we run into any trouble."

The next morning, the dwarves and Ohaobbok climbed several thousand feet into a thick forest that smelt of pine. For most of their travel, they followed trails trampled through the undergrowth by wildlife, but now they used the foliage as cover as Barnaby pointed ahead.

"See da path in dem flowers?" he whispered in the ogre's ear.

Ohaobbok nodded. A short distance ahead the tree line ended, and in a clearing at the base of a towering stone cliff were two beds of wildflowers with a small path between them.

"Just down dat path be da fountain," Barnaby said. "So I tink dat mean it now be your turn to lead. What now?"

Before Ohaobbok could answer, the booming call of an ogre thundered through the forest, and everyone froze.

"Dat sounded like a hunting ogre," Barnaby whispered. "Though I tink not too close."

But Ohaobbok knew better. He not only recognized what sort of call that was, he knew precisely what ogre had made it. The memory of that voice sent shivers up and down his spine.

Mother.

"No," he said. "That call was a warning to any trespassers to depart."

"A warning?" said another dwarf. "I'd not be tinkin' dem ogres be so civilized." He glanced up at Ohaobbok and added, "I be meanin', th-that not be sayin' that ogres can't be civilized if they be trained…"

"Oh shut up, Gypsum." Barnaby smacked the back of the younger dwarf's head. "Your tongue's run ahead of your brain again."

But Ohaobbok was lost in his thoughts, and was barely even listening to them. "It's not like my mother to warn people away," he mumbled.

"Did you say yer *mother*?" said Barnaby.

Heavy footsteps sounded nearby, and all the dwarves went silent, crouching in the undergrowth. Ohaobbok squinted through the leaves, trying to silence the booming of his racing heart.

Could Mother have smelled me? Is she coming to investigate? Will I be forced to fight her to save my companions?

He quietly flexed his limbs, readying himself for a battle.

But as the footsteps came closer, and a figure at last appeared on the path before them, it was not his mother.

It was a female ogre, about twelve feet tall—but she looked oddly… human. Her tangled mass of hair was chopped off roughly at the middle of her back, and she was dressed in furs from the hides of goats, though she wore no shoes. And when she passed close enough for Ohaobbok to see her face, he drew in a silent breath.

She was beautiful.

Fortunately, she had not detected the ogre and the two dozen dwarves hiding in the trees. She apparently believed she was alone as she followed the path, coming down from above and heading toward the fountain in the shadows of the cliff.

Barnaby nudged Ohaobbok and handed him a tube with a glass on either end. When Ohaobbok looked back at his friend in confusion, Barnaby indicated through gestures that Ohaobbok was to look through it. So the ogre put it up to his eye.

To his surprise, the things he saw through the tube appeared to be much closer than they actually were.

I didn't know dwarves had such magic. I must bring this to the Archmage's attention.

Using the device, he could easily see the fountain in the distance. It was just like the other fountains, featuring a statue holding an orb. He continued to watch as the female approached its waters, removed her furs—Ohaobbok blushed—and she stepped into the fountain.

The orb glowed furiously.

Ohaobbok almost dropped the magic tube in his shock.

She's a wizard!

"Now we know who be comin' to the fountain," Barnaby whispered.

Ohaobbok continued to watch. After the female bathed and dressed, she held her hands over the flowers, and Ohaobbok felt a prickly sensation that confirmed what the orb had told him. He'd spent enough time among wizards to know what strong magic felt like when it was being used.

He lowered the tube and turned to the dwarves. "I'm going forward to investigate. You stay hidden. If I have trouble, do *not* come after me. It's your mission to ensure the Archmage learns of whatever we see today. Am I understood?"

Barnaby frowned, but nodded reluctantly.

"Remember, no matter what you see, do not make yourself known. It may make things worse. Especially if she acts like most ogres would."

Without waiting for a response, Ohaobbok rose to his full height, pushed through the foliage, and walked into the clearing.

The female didn't notice him right away. Her eyes were closed in concentration as she continued to hold her hands over the flower, applying magic in some way. Ohaobbok didn't want to startle her—that would only make things worse—so when he was about thirty feet away from her, he out his bare hands to show he held no weapons, and softly cleared his throat.

Her eyes snapped open, and she took two steps back and bared her teeth.

Human teeth.

Ohaobbok ran his tongue over his protruding lower incisors, feeling suddenly self-conscious.

She growled at him, sounding just like a cornered ogre. Yet her appearance… was she a human, or was she an ogre?

"Hello," Ohaobbok said. He tried to speak slowly and enunciate clearly. "I mean you no harm."

Her defensive posture relaxed then, and her snarl transformed into an expression of curiosity. She cautiously sniffed the air.

Did she understand me?

For a long moment they both stood like that. Then she started toward him—slowly, tentatively. Ohaobbok had the impression that if he made even the slightest movement, she'd bolt. Or worse, she might use her wizardry on him.

Ohaobbok tried to stay calm as she came within arm's reach. Then she stopped, looked up at him with uncertainty—and swung her fist into his cheek. *Hard.*

Stars erupted in his vision, and he felt a trickle of blood from his lip. Whether she was human or ogre, she certainly possessed an ogre's strength.

Still Ohaobbok didn't move. He was determined to present no threat. He did not come here to fight, and he prayed the dwarves heeded his command to stay out of this.

His hands still held out to his sides, he stubbornly repeated, "I mean you no harm."

She slowly raised one hand out to her side, fingers splayed, mimicking him. Then she reached forward with her other hand

and laid her palm on his face. Immediately he felt a warmth flow into him. The pain in his lip subsided, as did the throbbing in his cheek. When she pulled her hand away, he felt no pain at all.

Ohaobbok was stunned. *A healer?*

The female smiled at him then, and for the first time, she spoke, in a voice that sounded hoarse and unpracticed.

"Greetings, Paladin of Seder. One such as you has been in my dreams for many winters. My name is Nyra, and I knew you would come."

AN ENIGMA WRAPPED IN A MYSTERY

As Ryan opened his eyes, he saw Arabelle hovering over him, her wisps of white healing energy dissipating in the breeze.

She brushed a stray lock of hair away from his eyes. "I told you to duck and run through it."

Ryan sat up and grimaced, his head throbbing with pain. "What was that stuff? My shields were useless against it."

"Spores from that thing." She pointed to the clearing ahead, where a huge plant grew. It looked sort of like a dark-green cabbage, except it would be the biggest cabbage ever, and it featured long green vines lined with dark thorns.

Yet as Ryan rose to his feet, he realized it wasn't a cabbage at all, or even a plant. It was the head of some enormous creature. It had two huge eyes and a toothy maw. It also featured deep gashes that oozed a thick green sap—which explained why Arabelle was now cleaning her daggers with a handful of grass.

"What is it?" he asked.

Arabelle shook her head. "I was going to ask you the same thing."

At that moment, hysterical laughter sounded from ahead, and a dense fog filled the far side of the clearing. A breeze blew into their faces from that direction, bringing with it the fetid breath of something long dead.

"Ugh," said Ryan.

"Ugh is right," said Arabelle, waving a hand before her face. "But we have to deal with it. My senses say she's directly ahead."

They started forward into the clearing. But they had only just passed the giant head when they stopped short. Because there *was* no clearing anymore. In its place was a giant gap in the forest floor.

"What?" said Arabelle. "How is that possible?"

They were standing at the edge of a ravine so deep that shadows obscured its bottom—if it even had one. And it was wide, too—at least a hundred feet across.

Arabelle closed her eyes, then opened them again. "This is an illusion."

Ryan frowned. "I can see magic being used here, but… it could be related to the fog, or something else. Maybe the clearing was the illusion, and this is real."

Arabelle shook her head. "No. I told you, I can sense her distance. The vision gift from Seder has never failed me, and it tells me she's directly ahead. So either she's hovering in midair over this ravine… or there is no ravine."

A flash of blinding white light was followed by a deafening

crack of thunder. The ravine disappeared, as did the fog, and the clearing was present once more.

But this time it was no longer empty.

A woman approached from the far side. She wore no clothes, but her long blond tresses covered most of her body. And she pulsed with a power that Ryan feared would more than match his.

"It's her," Arabelle whispered.

Ryan strengthened his shield and expanded it around Arabelle.

Who knows what this crazy elf will do.

As Nicnevin stopped before them, she faced Ryan and sneered. "Pathetic. You can't even shield your thoughts of disgust against my race. And you think you are worthy of calling yourself a wizard? I think not!"

Ryan's face heated, but Arabelle touched his elbow as if to say, *Stay calm.*

He cleared his throat and measured his words carefully. "I have no hate for elves. Some of my best friends are elves."

Nicnevin's green eyes flared with power, and her shriek shook the clearing, sending a flock of blackbirds erupting from the trees. "*Lies!* You have none that you can call true friends!" She pointed to Arabelle. "She *would* be your friend, but you've not yet accepted who she is. She is superior to you in every way that matters."

Calming, Nicnevin turned to Arabelle and gave a bow of respect. "*You* are Seder's weapon. You are your people's savior." She stepped closer and said in a stage-whisper, "I'm sorry to tell you, you'll need him to achieve your goal.

Sammael has his good moments, but they are usually cloaked in chaos. Of course I don't need to tell you, Seder, that the threads of destiny weave and unweave. However, this is how I see it, for now."

Arabelle exchanged a look with Ryan, who shrugged. The elf queen seemed to be more than a bit confused. Her words made no sense, and she didn't even seem to be fully present. Her eyes darted wildly about, sometimes remaining unfocused for seconds, other times staring intently.

Arabelle spoke gently. "Nicnevin, we were asked to seek you out." She pointed to Ryan. "He was told he stands at a precipice. He suffers from nightmares that cause him damage. We were told you could give him guidance."

Nicnevin sniffed with disgust. "Yes... Sammael and his night-time visits. He knocked on my door many times, but like a proper maiden, *I* never opened that door." She cackled with glee, then pointed a shaking finger at Ryan. "You invited this on yourself, young wizard. I see that you touched something that belonged to him."

Ryan frowned. "Something that belonged to Sammael? I don't think so."

Arabelle's eyes widened in understanding. "Ryan, at the altar —the one Labri's grandmother erected. You threw that blackened orb into the barrier."

Nicnevin stepped uncomfortably close to Ryan. "Yes, it is as Seder says. You've been tainted by an object infused with the essence of Sammael." Then she sniffed at him, moving her nose from his neck, to his arm, to his hand. "Aha!" She lifted his right hand. "Poisoned it is."

Then her eyes went far away again, and she let go of his wrist. Her voice was distant as she continued.

"Now Sammael visits you at night. Soon he will visit you in the day. You'll be his. Unless…"

Ryan waited, but the elf queen didn't continue. She seemed lost in her own thoughts.

"Unless what?" he asked. "Please. Tell me what I can do to stop this."

The queen seemed to awaken from her stupor. She shook her head and took two frightened steps back. "I'll not teach Sammael my tricks. He is simple, but brilliant. Leave!"

Arabelle reached out and gently took Nicnevin's hands. "Please, Nicnevin. Please show him how to avoid Sammael's influence. Do it for me?"

Nicnevin stared in astonishment at their joined hands, as if the very idea of physical contact was foreign to her. Then she looked up at Arabelle and smiled. "For you, Seder, I will do this."

She pulled free of Arabelle's grasp, stepped over to Ryan, and rested her forehead against his, so that they were staring directly into one another's eyes. Then Nicnevin closed her eyes —and Ryan had the unpleasant sensation of fingers crawling *under* his scalp. After a moment, it dawned on him what she was doing.

She's manipulating my powers.

He'd done something like this himself once—before he knew how dangerous it was. By connected one end of a loose thread of magic that he'd detected within Sloane, he'd given her the skill of telepathy. Nicnevin was doing something like that, but far more complex. Whereas Ryan was convinced that he had merely repaired an ability within Sloane that she had been destined to possess, Nicnevin was manipulating areas of his magic that had never been active to begin with.

Then her voice sounded inside his head.

"Yes, I am giving you a power you do not deserve. When I am finished, you'll be able to shield your mind just as you've learned to shield your body. Are you ready?"

Ryan answered aloud. "Yes. I'm ready."

Nicnevin did a few more manipulations, then pulled away and smirked.

"Now use it, for I am about to visit upon your mind a nightmare you will never recover from. You have five seconds."

Ryan pushed aside his fear and uncertainty as he raised a secondary shield. He didn't know how he did it, precisely, and it felt entirely unnatural, like blinking a second set of eyelids.

Nicnevin laughed. "You haven't fallen over screaming for death like all the others… so you have passed the test." She grinned wickedly. "Too bad it does you no good at night. For that…"—she hitched her thumb back toward Arabelle—"you'll need his blessing."

Without further comment, Nicnevin walked to the head of the giant plant-creature and raised one hand high in the air. The dead cabbage head rose from the ground with a deep groaning and ripping, followed by a dirt-encrusted body. When it had fully emerged from the ground, she snapped her fingers, and the creature was instantly incinerated in a ball of fire.

Nicnevin turned to Arabelle with a pout. "It wasn't necessary to kill my creation. He would not have eaten you—only him."

Then she glared at Ryan. "Young wizard, you owe me a new dwarf! Go find one and send him to me!"

"A—a dwarf?"

Nicnevin's green eyes flashed dangerously. "*Go!*"

Arabelle grabbed Ryan by the arm and forced a smile. "Yes, I'm afraid we must depart. Thank you for your help, Nicnevin."

As they fled from the clearing, Nicnevin's voice followed after them, sounding uncharacteristically pleasant. "It was lovely having you visit. Farewell!"

In the six nights after their encounter with the mad queen, Ryan's nightmares became much worse. Arabelle did everything she could, but her healing no longer seemed to have any effect. And the last two nights had been unbearable—for both of them. Ryan tossed about in his sleep and screamed in agony, and Arabelle felt as though her husband was being tortured in front of her.

The days were not much better. Arabelle could tell that her husband held on only through sheer will. She had to support him as they walked. And though she didn't mention it to him, he began to smell unnatural. Like the hot springs in the wastelands that stank of sulfur.

So it was with great relief that on the seventh day of their travels, Castle Riverton came into sight—and Sloane came riding out to meet them, a spare horse in tow.

"Arabelle, we got your message!" She gasped at the sight of Ryan. "Oh! It's even worse than you let on!"

Together they lifted Ryan onto the spare horse, and Arabelle mounted behind him.

"Let's get him to the healers immediately," Sloane said.

"No," said Arabelle said. "The only way to help him is to attain Seder's blessing." She kicked her horse into a gallop. "To the fountain!"

Sloane took the lead, shouting for everyone to get out of the way. Wizards and students were lined up to wash their faces and hands, but they all stepped aside at Sloane's cry.

Arabelle dropped down from her horse, dragged Ryan down after her, and practically carried him into the fountain with her. She plopped right down into the waters, cradling his head in her lap.

The crowd gasped—for the orb atop the statue did not glow with pure white as it always did in the presence of a magic user; instead it swirled with ribbons of red and white.

Arabelle pulled Ryan up so that he could lay back against her, then wrapped her arms protectively around him and infused him with what little energy she had left. "It'll be all right, my love," she whispered. "I'm here with you."

Sloane sat on the edge of the fountain and read the inscription aloud. *"A weekly bath will inoculate the wizard from the sway of evil.* You think that means Seder's blessing?"

"It is only a hope." In Arabelle's arms, Ryan shivered. She looked up at Sloane, trying to keep the panic from her voice—

and failing. "Can you—can you look into his mind and see if...?"

Sloane nodded. "I will look."

She closed her eyes for what felt to Arabelle like an eternity. But as Sloane concentrated, Ryan's shivering subsided, and his body relaxed against hers.

Finally Sloane opened her eyes and let out a long breath. "He's coming back now. In fact..." A blush lit her cheeks. "He's dreaming about you."

Arabelle looked up and nearly cried out with joy as the statue's orb exploded with waves of brilliant white light—any hint of red had vanished.

CROSSING THE BARRIER

Aaron silently approached his new wife from behind as she hollered instructions at her wolves and swamp cats. But just as he was about to grab her around the waist and snatch her from her feet, she growled.

"Aaron, when are you going to learn that I can hear your mind from a mile away?"

He let out a frustrated sigh.

She turned and smiled at him. "Aww, my poor soldier wanted to grab the damsel and cause her some distress." She gave him a quick kiss, then stepped back. "Maybe one day I'll let you do that."

He put one arm around his wife and watched what Sloane had her animal troops doing. She had paired them off, wolf and cat, and had the pairs attacking over-sized training dummies. Their moves were fluid and devastating.

"At first, I saw that the wolves instinctively tried to

hamstring an enemy, while the cats often aimed for the neck," Sloane said. "But you can see they're getting much better at working together, coordinating their attacks. Together, I think they'll be able to take on some of the largest demons."

"What if one of the pair is killed or injured?" Aaron asked. "Will they still be effective if you have to pair them up with different partners?"

Sloane frowned. "It's a concern. Once they formed their pairings—they chose their partners on their own—they've stuck with them. I'm waiting until they've mastered this attack, then I'll work on switching partners. Though it might require a bit of convincing. They're stubborn creatures."

Aaron kissed the top of Sloane's head. "Well, what you've done so far is amazing. Your troops are better than any cavalry."

An explosion sounded in the distance, and Aaron squinted at the horizon, raising his hand to block the sunlight. One of the dragons was rocketing upward, and a huge puff of smoke rose from the land below.

Sloane laughed. "Pyre is having a lot of fun with your father. They both really love setting things on fire."

"Do you mind if I run over there to watch?" Aaron asked.

Sloane held a finger. "I have a better idea." She turned to her troops and yelled. "Continue to practice, and when the light departs, go rest. You're doing very well!"

Then she started running toward the dragons' training grounds. "Race you there!" she shouted over her shoulder.

———

Aaron scanned the skies, looking for his father. The smell of burning wood filled his nostrils as he heard the warning shouts from the soldiers charged with fighting any stray fires that leapt over the practice area's fire barriers.

One of the captains bellowed. "Get yer arses out of the field or you'll be lit up sure as anything!"

One of the nearest soldiers noticed Aaron and Sloane and pointed toward the sky. "Sir, your father's dragon flew into that cloud. One thing is for certain—we'll all see him when he comes back out. The first time I saw Lord Riverton strafe the field, I got so scared I nearly soiled myself."

Aaron watched as Pyre and his father burst through a bank of clouds. The whistling in the air grew louder as the dragon tucked its wings and plummeted. The setting sun shone brightly off the dragon's dark scales as he unfurled his wings, pulled up from his steep dive, and breathed a gout of sulfurous flames across the field of fake soldiers.

Aaron heard his father's laughter as a thick bolt of white-hot energy flew from his fingertips and struck a distant rocky outcropping. As the rock exploded, the dragon pulled up for another run.

Castien and Oda were watching as well, and came to join Aaron and Sloane.

"Your father is like a child up there," said the sword master. "He truly enjoys this practice."

"What about the others?" Aaron asked. "We need more than my father as a dragon rider."

Castien pointed to another part of the sky, where Ruby was

approaching at high speed. "No one rides like your father, but that's Charlie Carbunkle. He does passably well."

Ruby flew overhead with a blast of wind as she too strafed the field with gouts of flame. Charlie sent forth a bolt of energy, but his aim was erratic, and it disappeared over the horizon. Ruby flapped into the sky, quickly gaining altitude.

Sloane arched one eyebrow. "That was passably well?"

Oda laughed. "Compared to where he started, it's amazin'. Give him time."

Castien patted the dwarf's shoulder. "Your friend Wat did really well. In fact, nearly as well as Lord Riverton. He would be even better if he didn't spend so much time in Eluanethra. I will have to talk with Eglerion about that. Our dragon riders need practice."

Oda's thick beard waved up and down as he nodded. "Yup. Dat Crazybeard does dwarfkind proud, he does. Dunno how he does it. War wizard, librarian, *and* dragon rider."

Aaron put his arm around Sloane. "How about you and I grab something to eat?"

Oda smiled. "Oy, I know da place! Follow me." Without waiting for an answer, he started off.

Aaron held his hand out to Sloane. "I guess Oda is joining us."

She frowned. "Didn't we get sick at the last place Oda recommended?"

"That was only you, my dear. Hopefully this place has some options more to your liking."

The tavern Oda led them to was obviously popular—a good sign. Dozens of patrons were gathered along a bar or sitting at the tables.

Sloane squeezed Aaron's hand. "I smell freshly baked bread."

The three of them sat at a table, and a waitress hurried over.

"Oy, lovely lassie." Oda put down two copper coins. "I'd like an ale, if you be so kind."

Aaron shoved the coins back toward Oda and placed a silver coin in the girl's hand. "Ale for the three of us, please."

"And a loaf of your freshest bread," Sloane added.

The waitress rushed away and returned shortly with the ale, bread, and some freshly pickled cucumbers, before describing the specials of the day.

"We have trout with a spicy tomato broth served on a fragrant rice. It's too spicy for me, but lots of the customers seem to like it. I highly recommend the roasted beef tongue served with potatoes and carrots. There's also a roast fowl served with a creamed spinach and baby onions, which is quite good."

Aaron drank deeply from his mug. "Roast tongue."

Oda hummed as he ran his fingers through his beard. "Fowl for me, dearie."

"Can I get the spicy tomato broth on the rice, but instead of the fish, can I have some added carrots?" Sloane asked.

"Yes, Your Highness." The waitress turned to Aaron. "General, that will be one silver and three coppers."

Oda dug some coins out of his belt, but Aaron quickly placed two silvers in the waitress's hand. "Keep the rest."

The waitress smiled and twirled away.

"Bah!" Oda sputtered. "You makin' me feel like a girl and all for not payin' me way."

Sloane rolled her eyes but held her tongue.

As they sipped their ale, a group of dwarves across the room started making a ruckus, banging their empty tankards on their table, apparently trying to encourage one of their members to do something. Finally the reluctant dwarf, whose long red beard hung over heavy armor, stood on his chair, and the dwarves cheered.

The red-bearded dwarf then began to sing.

"Polish the armor, hone the blade
Dance to the music, while it's played
Kiss the ladies, one two three
Look out boys, that one's for me
Enjoy the fun, while we can
For soon it's over, you know the plan
Beyond the barrier, lies our fate
Battling the demons we surely hate
Seeking victory ere the break of day
Hurry, boys, the war won't wait!

The entire tavern cheered, and there were calls for an encore. The entire group of dwarves joined in for a second verse, and some of them even got up and started dancing.

Aaron enjoyed seeing the merriment, but he couldn't resist

frowning. There was too much truth in the dwarf's song. The end really was near.

Sloane, having read his thoughts as always, projected a silent message into his mind. *"So where's my kiss?"*

As the dwarves belted out the passage, "Kiss the ladies, one two three," Aaron gave his smiling wife a lingering kiss. At just that moment, the waitress arrived with their food, and she grinned and gave them both a quick wink.

As Aaron bent over his steaming plate, he deliberately pushed aside thoughts of what awaited them beyond the barrier. The dwarves were right: *Enjoy the fun, while we can.* Now was a time to relax and enjoy; for tomorrow, everything might be different.

Malphas's fist connected with the skull of an unruly demon. The snarling Mazikim was knocked back into his brethren, blood pouring from his caved-in eye socket.

"I told you to be careful and not race ahead!" Malphas barked.

The Mazikim were the troops he used most commonly during raids. Their dark scales and small eight-foot frames served well in the Underworld's tunnels. But occasionally they could become undisciplined. Fortunately, Malphas enjoyed the opportunity to bring them back into line.

They'd just passed through several passages with unusually large quantities of glowing mushrooms. Malphas had learned over the years that it was the Ta'ah who farmed these mushrooms, so he knew the Ta'ah had to be near. He hoped so. It would be nice for the Mazikim to have someone to fight other than themselves.

They crept down another passage and arrived at an intersection. As Malphas sniffed deeply, searching for a hint of prey, the unruly and now half-blinded Mazikim suddenly bolted away to their right.

Malphas growled. *I'm going to rip that one apart.*

He chased after the demon, the others following close behind, but he was forced to slow when a light appeared down the passage ahead. Creeping along more carefully, he stepped out of the tunnel into a cavern lit by a single torch in a sconce.

The foolish demon was here, staring at a granite door in the far wall. An inscription was written above the door, which gave off a hint of magic.

Before Malphas could even bark an order, the demon slammed his fists against the door. A flash of energy burst forth as he made contact, and the demon was incinerated.

Malphas sneered. *Lesson learned.* Though he would have liked to have ripped that fool apart with his own hands, this outcome would do.

He walked across the cavern and studied the door. Yes, it was definitely protected by a magic barrier. Then he looked up at the inscription, translating the letters:

In the wake of demons and strife
There arrived a newfound life
He comes from a place beyond the stars

Yet knows the meaning of the planet Mars

Malphas read the words a second time, yet they made no sense. As he was pondering the riddle, voices sounded from an adjoining tunnel, along with running footsteps.

The Ta'ah.

Malphas turned to his troops and growled. "Your idiot brother has brought the Ta'ah defenders on us. You aren't prepared for a group of them. Retreat to our tunnels."

As Malphas raced into the tunnel through which they'd come, he felt a bolt of energy in the cavern behind him, and heard one of the Mazikim screech in pain.

Hopefully that's another lesson learned. Maybe next time they'll know to listen when I give a word of caution.

Ryan smiled as Arabelle snuggled next to him under the covers. The headache that had been plaguing him for months was finally gone, and he felt like a new person.

It had been three days since he'd awoken from his months-long nightmare. He didn't even remember the last part of their journey home. He remembered Nicnevin, but after that, all he had was hazy snatches of stumbling through the woods, Arabelle at his side.

And to think, so much of his problem could have been avoided if he'd used the fountain regularly—like he was supposed to do. He felt like an idiot. From now on, he was determined to not only make his regular visits to the fountain, but to give thanks to Seder for his protective blessings every time.

It was still very early in the morning, but he decided to chance a message on his ring, and just hope he didn't disturb anyone who was still sleeping.

Ryan. Dad? Are you awake?

Dad. Yes, I'm eating breakfast with your mother.

Mom. Good morning honey.

Good morning. Dad, you said you wanted to talk. Is this morning all right?

I'll be in my study in thirty minutes. Come as soon as you're ready. Bring your staff.

All right, I'll talk with Belle and be there in a bit.

Arabelle's grumbled from under the covers. "My ring is vibrating."

He flipped the covers off her head. "Sorry I woke you."

Arabelle squinted against the light and buried her head under her pillow. "What's your father got planned for you?"

"I'm not sure, but I want to get it over with. I have my own plan for later today. It involves you, Aaron, and Sloane."

Arabelle popped her head back out. "What's on your mind?"

"Oh, nothing much." He smiled. "I was just thinking about trying to cross the barrier today."

Arabelle's mouth fell open. "You really think we can do it?"

Ryan nodded confidently. "Remember how I had that vision years ago about us crossing the barrier and landing in Castle Thariginian? Well, I had that vision again last night."

"Did the vision tell you how to do it?"

"Well… not exactly. But why would I get the vision now, if we couldn't figure it out?"

Arabelle bit her lower lip. "Ryan, that's great, but…" Her brow furrowed. "You know, I'd feel better about this if you were more worried. It's not just some adventure. Who knows what we'll encounter there?"

"Believe me, I know that. But we've got to do it at some point. Why not now?"

"I suppose. But if we're doing this, we're need to be prepared."

She leaped out of bed, opened her supply chest, and started pulling things out. Several bags, a mortar and pestle, a bunch of straws. She took everything to the table in the corner and started grinding up some leaves from one of the bags.

"Making some sneaky elven stuff?" Ryan asked.

She winked. "Just readying my tools. Now go see your father. Do what you need to do. When I'm done here, I'll let Sloane and Aaron know what's going on."

Ryan found his father in his study, which was a mess, as usual. Several chalkboards were propped up around the room, filled with scrawled equations that made utterly no sense to Ryan. Dad had been an engineer before they came to Trimoria, and he approached magic as just another science that needed exploration.

His Dad was at his main worktable, using tweezers to put

tiny crystals into sockets on a small plate of damantite. Ryan waited patiently while his father worked.

When Dad placed the final crystal, he waved Ryan over. "Come. Hand me that lens."

He pointed to a convex glass that looked sort of like a magnifying glass. Ryan picked it up and brought it over.

"Now watch. This is going to be cool."

Dad held the lens over the plate of crystal-infused damantite, then raised his other hand over the lens, and released a flow of energy. As usual, the energy that came from Dad's hand was thick and unfocused, but when it passed through the lens, it became a thin needle of power. He precisely moved the needle across the plate, moving it from one of the tiny crystals to the next, sealing each in place.

When he was done, he flipped the plate over, revealing a bunch of copper lines scrawled across the back. "Okay, check this out. These lines are copper traces. They connect the gem sockets to one another. I've created a transdermal connection."

"A what?"

His father flipped the plate back over and pointed at the sealed crystals. "The milky one on the right is quartz, the bottom is ruby, the left is an emerald, and at the top is a diamond." He tied some leather straps to the ends of the plate. "Now hold out your arm."

Ryan had no idea what was going on, but he obediently held out his arm.

Dad put a thin cloth over Ryan's wrist, laid the damantite plate on top, and secured it with the leather straps. It was like an oversized watch that didn't tell time.

Dad grinned. "Here's the best part."

He pulled the cloth out from under the watch. Instantly, the quartz and ruby sockets glowed brightly, while the emerald gave just the faintest sign of light.

"Whoa. That is cool," Ryan said. "But what's it doing?"

His father sat back. "It's measuring your magical energy."

"Care to explain?"

Dad laughed. "Sure. It's taken a great deal of experimentation, but I've finally been able to create a magical circuit. The copper leads underneath the plate tap into the magic coursing through your body. The quartz is the most sensitive to magical energy, so it will glow with maximum brightness even if it senses a small amount of energy. I've calibrated the ruby to be ten times less sensitive, so it will be at max brightness when you possess ten times the amount of energy required to max out the quartz. The emerald is adjusted to have full glow at roughly one hundred times more than the ruby—so a thousand times more than the quartz—and the diamond will light up fully when you possess a thousand rubies' worth of energy. Which is a million more than the quartz."

"So is this like a gas gauge in a car?"

"Exactly right. Let's treat the quartz as one unit of energy—which is next to nothing, but it's there to prove that the device is working. Right now, you're just barely tickling the emerald, so that's one thousand units of energy. Which our prior experiments showed is your normal level when you're not tired."

"What's your normal level?"

Jared shrugged. "I made the emerald glow a bit more than

yours. But now I want to try something else. Pick up your staff and tap its energy. I want to see if this detects that energy."

Ryan picked up his damantite staff and tapped into the power he'd stored in the diamond on its end. A surge of power raced through him.

"Look!" said Dad. "You maxed out the emerald, and I swear I saw the diamond flicker for a second."

Ryan played with the device for a bit, grabbing and releasing his staff, and watching the gauge's measurements change.

"It's amazing that you were able to make this, Dad. So no offense, but… what do we need it for? We can already feel when we're low on power."

"Sure, you can feel it," Dad said, "but it's a very imprecise measurement—and unreliable. How many times have we had a student pass out in class when they insisted they could continue in their lessons? We can't afford to have wizards passing out in the battlefield because they pushed too hard without replenishing their reserves. I'm going to make more of these, so we can at least equip all the war wizards."

Ryan nodded. "That makes sense."

"You can keep that one," Dad said. "Remember, if you get down to the ruby, you're pretty low. If you get to the quartz, you're about to pass out."

"Thanks, Dad. You know, it's been years since I've worn a watch. It brings back the old days."

His father chuckled. "I don't think they had magic sensors back home. Now have a seat. I'm not done with you quite yet."

"Dad… I'm not really up for any experiments today."

"Don't worry, it's not an experiment. The castle just wanted me to explain something to you."

"Did you say the *castle*?"

"Actually it was your sister who started it."

Now Ryan was definitely intrigued. He sat down. "I'm listening."

Dad took another chair. "Okay, where to begin. It seems that ever since Rebecca played a part in the ceremony to wake the castle, she's been talking with it. I did some research, and it seems like we should have expected this. The person who acted as the Dedicate for Castle Thariginian was said to do the same thing.

"Anyway, yesterday Rebecca came to me with a message. She said the castle wants me to explain quantum entanglement to you."

"Ooookay," said Ryan. "Because that's a totally normal thing for a four-year-old to do."

Dad laughed. "I felt the same way. Trust me, it was even weirder hearing her say the words." He removed one of his rings and twirled it on the table. "You remember when we made these?"

Ryan nodded. "Of course."

"And what did we learn?"

Ryan sighed. His dad was going into professorial mode. But he knew from experience that there was nothing to do but to go along with it.

"We learned that if you infused energy into a solid metal bar, and then split that bar into pieces, whatever we did to one of those pieces happened to *all* of them, no matter how far apart they are. It's like they're always directly connected, even though they're separated by miles."

"Exactly. A quantum physicist would say that those two pieces are 'entangled.'" Dad stroked his beard. "And that mirrors the concept of quantum entanglement. Quantum theory describes how a photon can be split, and its parts entangled. Meaning that no matter how far apart the pieces are, if one changes, the other will change as well. And remember, this is back on Earth. No magic there, just science. But it works out exactly the same."

"Okay. I understand that. But why would the castle want me to know this?"

"I wondered the same thing—and I came up with a hypothesis. We know that, through its heart, our castle is connected to another plane of existence. Castle Thariginian must have the same type of connection. And if the power coming into the heart for both castles stems from the same source…"

"Then the two castles might be entangled?"

"They might be. But it was just a hypothesis—and hypotheses need to be tested. So I went to the heart of the castle, placed a stone in the center of the room, and then stood outside. With your sister's help, I asked the castle to run a test—"

Ryan didn't need to hear the details. "The rock disappeared, didn't it?"

"The rock disappeared."

"It went to Castle Thariginian."

"Maybe. I then had Rebecca ask the castle to repeat the exercise. We left the room for a moment, and when we went back in, the rock had returned."

Ryan smiled. "It's just like my vision about appearing in Castle Thariginian."

Dad nodded. "That was my thought too. It's pure speculation at this point, but think about it. The castle wants me to explain to you what quantum entanglement is; the results of my experiment; your vision." He leaned forward. "We might have a way across the barrier."

Ryan also leaned forward. "Would you be surprised to learn that last night, I had another vision? And in this one I'm sitting in the heart of our castle, then finding myself, along with Belle, Aaron, and Sloane, within a new castle? In fact, even before I talked to you this morning, I was already planning to try to cross the barrier today—like… like the vision had told me I needed to. I just didn't know how to go about it. But now… now maybe I do."

Jared's eyes widened. He sat back and raked his fingers through the knots in his beard. "Be cautious, son. I trust in your judgment, but don't take any unneeded risks."

"I swear, we'll take as little time as possible and be right back."

Jared stood and wrapped him in a bear hug. "Don't tell your mother anything. She won't take this well. I'll tell her afterward. And make sure you take extra healing draughts. And that you're well-rested before you go."

Ryan laughed. "Okay, Dad. I know."

"Then know one more thing." His dad smiled. "I love you."

In the heart of the castle, Ryan, Arabelle, Aaron, and Sloane sat cross-legged on the floor, forming a circle. They linked hands and closed their eyes.

"Just keep your mind clear," Ryan said, "and lend whatever powers you have to the circle."

"I have no magic powers," Sloane said.

"Just keep your mind clear then."

Ryan opened his eyes and concentrated on the flashing ball of magic near the ceiling—the castle's heartbeat. He saw their own magic energy flowing through their ring, pulsing and synchronizing with the magic above.

Then the color of the ring's magic deepened to match the heartbeat's purple. Filaments of violet light snaked from the ball above and connected to all of them. Suddenly, a brilliant flash of light filled the room, and Ryan's ears popped.

The room was different.

It was still an empty room surrounded by four stone walls, yet it was obviously not the same one. And the ball of energy pulsing above was green, not purple.

"Guys… we did it. You can open your eyes now."

The others opened their eyes, and Sloane, who was facing the door, gasped.

Ryan turned to the door, and saw an inscription on it.

Welcome, my friends. I've been awaiting your arrival.

CASTLE THARIGINIAN

"Are we really in the other castle?" Aaron said.

Arabelle walked to the door and studied it. "It isn't trapped." She looked over her shoulder. "Are we ready to see what's on the other side?"

Ryan strengthened his shields, walked to the door, and motioned Arabelle aside. "Let me open it. If there is a nasty surprise, my shields should hopefully stop the worst of it."

Aaron brought up his own shield and drew his sword, while Arabelle stood near Sloane, twirling a dagger in each hand.

Ryan lifted the latch and pulled at the door. It swung open noiselessly, bringing in hot air smelling of sulfur. Ryan poked his head out into a hallway. At one end were stairs leading down; at the other end was an open terrace.

Ryan walked to the terrace, with the others following. Apparently the heart of Castle Thariginian was much higher in the structure than the one in Castle Riverton, because they found themselves near the top of the building, with an amazing view of the lands to the north. Sadly, those lands were scarred—and ended at the barrier of mist, no more than a mile away.

"Praise Seder, we did it!" Arabelle gasped. "We've crossed the barrier."

"I can hardly believe it," Sloane murmured.

Arabelle suddenly spun around and crouched in a defensive posture, her black daggers glowing faintly in her hands. Only then did Ryan hear the approaching footsteps.

A tall, thin elf wielding a thick wooden staff emerged from the shadows. For a moment he merely stared in disbelief at the four newcomers. Then tears welled up in his eyes, and he began to shake. He fell to his knees, his staff clattering on the stone tiles, covered his face with his hands, and wept.

"Seder," he whispered. "After so long a time, I'd lost faith in your visions…"

The elf's name was Bryan Greenwalker—the very same Bryan Greenwalker who had, according to Ryan and Arabelle, written an ancient history of Nicnevin. As they all sat cross-legged on the terrace under the bright midday sun, Sloane was amazed at how animated the elf was—so unlike the largely unemotional elves she'd encountered before.

I suppose the desperation for company might do that to even the most stoic of them.

The elf pointed across the terrace at the vast plain of desolation. "As you probably know, it was over five centuries ago when all of that happened. We were beset by the demons, and the Archmage foolishly left the safety of these castle grounds."

"You mean the First Protector?" Aaron asked.

"First Protector?"

Arabelle chimed in. "Zenethar Thariginian became a hero to those of us north of the barrier. We called him the First Protector."

Bryan frowned. "Ah. Had I been to the north, I suppose I might view him in that light as well. But here in the south…" He paused, as if weighing his words. "I understand that the Archmage did what he felt was necessary. But those of us in the south were left much worse off due to his decision."

Sloane felt the elf's resentment, and understood it. The First Protector had essentially sacrificed him—treated him as though he were expendable.

"How have you survived here, on this side of the barrier?" Ryan asked.

"That's a long story. After the battle, and the creation of the barrier, I was captured by the Avud. In the common tongue, Avud means 'the lost ones.' They are elves from my people's ancient past who chose to leave Seder's path and instead follow the chaotic beliefs of a being who calls herself Lilith." As he spoke, he lifted a lock of blond hair, revealing an angry red scar that ran from his forehead into his hairline. "I'd been knocked out in battle, and at first I thought they had rescued me. I quickly learned that was not the case. The Avud are… not like my people."

Aaron leaned forward. "Then I must learn more about them. I need to know what I'm facing."

Bryan shook his head. "I don't think you'll need to fight them. They aren't like that; they're not interested in conquest. In fact, they avoid violence unless..." The elf's brown skin paled. "Unless they're provoked."

Sloane caught the flash of a memory, and dove after it. It came to her as clearly as if she were re-living the moment herself...

My manacled wrists were scraped raw from trying to escape. My head still throbbed from the club that had struck me on the battlefield. The damned Avud couldn't care less for my injuries, and I wasn't the only one they'd grabbed. All along the wall of the torch-lit cavern were other captives—those who'd been trapped between the entrance to the Underworld and the mist barrier that had appeared out of nowhere.

I leaned against the chains that held my arms to the walls and watched as more of the dark-haired Avud women entered the cavern, dragging a tied-up dwarf. He strained against his bonds and screamed incoherently.

The leader of the group faced the chained prisoners and yelled over the din. "You men will be given a very pleasant choice in the coming days."

She smiled then, and I saw the horrid glistening of her fangs. I detected a crackling magic emanating from her, too, and a shiver ran down my spine. How could such a corrupted creature use magic? Was this the queen of their twisted new race?

She pointed at the dwarf, who frothed at the mouth as if he were rabid. "Witness my daughter's birth. The dwarf refused me, and my lady Lilith requires us to spread our numbers." Still facing the prisoners, she hissed, "Refuse me, or any of my sisters, and this will happen to you!"

The dwarf's midsection bulged, spewing blood, and the dwarf released an ear-splitting scream, then fell still. I heard the tearing of flesh—and the squall of an infant.

The Avud leader knelt beside the dwarf, reached into the split in his gut, and pulled forth a wriggling baby girl—a young, bloodied version of the women who held us captive. My stomach roiled at the possibility of such a thing erupting from my chest, and several of the chained prisoners retched.

Then one of the women stepped toward me. She licked her lips, flipped her long dark hair over her shoulder, and smiled. I broke out in a cold sweat. But as she came closer, I breathed a quiet sigh of relief. For it was not me she was walking toward, but the prisoner next to me.

I knew then that I had only one hope. I had to avoid their attention long enough to escape.

Sloane shivered as she absorbed the memory. Her eyes strayed to Bryan's heavily scarred wrists. She must have missed part of Bryan's story, because Ryan was now talking about something else.

"And when you were back in the safety of the castle, how did you survive?"

Bryan pulled a clump of green moss from a stone tile and held it up. "With this. The castle provides all the sustenance I need. And all I get. I dare not leave the grounds." He pointed at the ancient battlefield surrounding the castle. "Strange things lie in wait out there. Demons, mostly. But others, too, both good and evil."

"Good?" Arabelle asked. "Are there good races surviving on this side of the barrier? I'd have thought they were all killed."

Bryan shrugged. "I can't speak confidently, but I believe the Ta'ah remain hidden deep within the underground tunnels to the south. In the time after I escaped the Avud, when I was wandering those tunnels, I spied hints of them, and felt their magic."

"You can sense magic?" Ryan asked.

The elf's eyes flashed, and his back stiffened. "Of course. I was Queen Ellisandrea's most trusted advisor, and lore master of my people. I've trained in the art of magic for nearly a millennia, young wizard."

"Lore master," said Aaron respectfully, "would I be correct in guessing that you would like to be reunited with your people?"

Sloane felt overwhelming waves of sadness, guilt, and hope coming from the stunned elf. But outwardly, Bryan merely nodded silently.

Ryan stood and held out a hand. "Come, then. Let's not stay here any longer. I believe I know someone who would love to see you again."

Bryan's hand firmly clasped Ryan's wrist, and as Ryan pulled him to his feet, the elf spoke with a hoarse voice. "Bless you. Bless all of you."

Ryan's ears popped as they reappeared in the heart of Castle Riverton. The familiar ball of purple energy pulsed overhead.

"I cannot believe it!" Bryan exclaimed. "You've dedicated another castle. Brilliant!" He frowned. "This is how you managed it, isn't it? My visions showed your arrival in the heart of the castle, but I couldn't puzzle out how it was done."

Ryan smiled. "You really are a lore master, to have figured it out already. There is so much that's transpired on our own side of the barrier over the last five centuries. There'll be a lot for you to learn. Perhaps you would like to meet our own lore master."

"Yes, please," said Bryan. "I would be most pleased."

Ryan raised an eyebrow at Sloane, who nodded. "I already projected a message to him. He's on his way to the main hall."

"Who is this lore master of yours?" Bryan asked.

"Someone who, I'm certain, will be delighted to see you." Ryan wrapped his arm around Bryan's shoulder, and they started through the corridors. "Come. You'll see soon enough."

As Sloane had promised, they found Eglerion waiting in the main hall. Bryan froze in shock at the sight of his former apprentice.

Eglerion gave a formal bow. "I have missed seeing your face, Master."

Bryan's eyes couldn't have been wider, and tears streamed down his face. "It cannot be!" He touched the cloth of Eglerion's robe as if to prove he wasn't a hallucination. "Young Eglerion? Is it really you?"

Eglerion held up a splayed hand. "Yes, Master, it is I."

"Eglerion! I had never thought—" He stopped himself. "And Xinthian?"

"He's in Eluanethra."

"You must tell him that I've found the Avud. They truly have left Seder's flock. Trust them, and our people may become lost with them."

Eglerion's expression turned somber. "You'll tell him yourself, Master. We'll go to Eluanethra. This isn't something we can leave to a courier."

AN ANCIENT GRAVE

Ohaobbok held out a skewer of meat for Nyra. She snatched it from his hand and scurried away from him and the others. Despite his assurances that the dwarves wouldn't harm her, she refused to interact with anyone but him.

Barnaby nudged him with his elbow. "She be a skittish lass."

Ohaobbok nodded. "We must make accommodations for her, my friend. We don't yet know her story."

Barnaby patted his friend's knee and stood. "Well, it's late, and I'll get some rest. I trust that we have nothing to fear from our visitor?"

Ohaobbok studied the giant woman, who was attacking her skewer without taking her nervous eyes off him and the dwarves. "I'll make sure no harm comes from her."

He drained his tankard and walked toward Nyra. She didn't flee, but she watched him very carefully.

As he sat near her—but not too near—his ring vibrated with an incoming message.

Arabelle. Ohaobbok, we are within a day's ride from you.

Ohaobbok nodded in response, and to his surprise, Nyra nodded as well.

He tapped out a return message.

Ohaobbok. Nyra is with me. I'm an hour's walk from the cave of the First Protector.

Ryan. Don't worry, Arabelle can find you easily. Nyra's story has piqued her interest. We'll meet this new healer tomorrow.

Nyra pointed at Ohaobbok's hand. "Itch?"

Ohaobbok laughed. "No. I was receiving a message from some friends. The ones I mentioned before. One is a healer like you. The other is a great wizard."

Nyra pointed her chin at the dwarves. "Friends like that?"

"No, they are human. More like you, but smaller."

Nyra looked down at her feet. Her pale complexion reddened. "I must sleep."

Ohaobbok swept the sticks and rocks away. "We can sleep right here." He gestured to the dwarves. "You don't need to worry about them. They won't harm you if you don't harm them."

Nyra shook her head and held out her hand. "No. Come. I will show you where I sleep."

He stared at her outstretched hand, then cautiously took it. With a firm tug, she pulled him away from the dwarven camp.

As he followed her along mountain trails, getting farther and farther from the camp, Ohaobbok wondered if he was making a terrible mistake. Yet he knew that if he was to convince her to trust him, he needed to trust her as well.

After thirty minutes of fast-paced hiking, Nyra finally came to a stop. "My bed."

She gestured to a shadowy recess dug beneath a rocky overhang. Within the recess, layers of live vegetation grew on a thick green moss.

It's like a mattress, Ohaobbok thought.

Nyra lay down on the bed and patted the spot next to her. "There is room."

Ohaobbok paused to listen to the sounds of the forest. He knew there were ogres out there, hunting for their evening meal, and he could see how exposed Nyra was in this spot.

"How is it the ogres don't attack you here?" he asked.

She smiled brightly. "I hide well."

A look of concentration crossed her face, and she and the bed of vegetation disappeared from sight.

"Nyra?"

"I'm here." She reappeared and reached out to Ohaobbok. "Come, Paladin of Seder. I'll keep you safe."

He took her hand, and she pulled him down to her bed of moss. The greenery cupped him in a comfortable, pine-scented embrace. *It's even* more *comfortable than a mattress.*

Nyra lay on her side and wrapped her arm around him, pulling him closer. He sensed her using magic, and the surrounding forest shimmered and dimmed.

"Rest," she murmured. "We are safe."

Ohaobbok closed his eyes, feeling the warmth of Nyra's body against his back.

"As soon as the disobedient Mazikim touched the barrier, there was an explosion of power that destroyed him and alerted the Ta'ah to our presence," Malphas explained.

Sammael's clawed fingers tapped on his throne. "Repeat to me the inscription."

Malphas began to relax. He'd prepared himself for a harsher reaction than this after he'd lost half of the troop of Mazikim. He recited the inscription once more:

"In the wake of demons and strife
There arrived a newfound life
He comes from a place beyond the stars
Yet knows the meaning of the planet Mars

Sammael looked down at Malphas, and a chilling smile crossed his face. "This message feels... familiar. It can only mean one thing. Seder."

Malphas clenched his fists. "What would you have me do, my lord? Assault the cavern? Attack the Ta'ah?"

"No, Malphas." Sammael stood. "This is beyond you. You aren't prepared for what I'll gift Seder's followers with."

Aa crackling ball of energy formed around Sammael's hands, and before Malphas could scramble away, the demon lord slapped his hands together. The shock wave sent Malphas tumbling to his knees.

As Malphas regained his feet, he saw a rope-like fountain of energy emanating from his lord's clenched fists and burrowing into the stone floor of the cavern. Sammael was snarling with the effort of controlling such immense power. And then the stone shuddered beneath their feet

"Aha!" Sammael cried. "Come and do my bidding, titan of the rock!"

Titan of the rock?

Sammael released his energy and sat back on his throne, but the vibrations in the floor only grew stronger. Fine cracks appeared in the stone, and stalactites dropped from the ceiling eighty feet above. A fissure appeared twenty feet in front of Sammael's throne, and widened into a crevasse.

With the scraping of scales, a creature emerged, the likes of which Malphas had never seen. It was like a fifty-foot-long armored snake with eyes of blazing fire.

The creature hissed at Sammael, who laughed.

"You may retrieve the thoughts of my general," he said, pointing at Malphas. "He has witnessed the location. I want you to seek this doorway, and when you find it, either retrieve what is hidden there or prevent others from gaining access to it."

The snake turned and faced Malphas. Its hiss shook the cavern, and Malphas felt something grip his mind with intense force. He could do nothing to stop the creature from clawing through his memories; in fact he barely had the will to stand.

Visions of the failed expedition with the Mazikim flashed in front of his eyes. He saw once again the magic barrier, the explosion caused by the one-eyed fool, and the flight from the territory of the Ta'ah.

Then, mercifully, the creature released him and slithered away.

Malphas fell again to his knees. For the first time in centuries, he felt weak.

I'm not as strong as I need to be.

Ryan sat cross-legged with Arabelle, Ohaobbok, and the giant woman named Nyra, absorbing the story she had just, haltingly, told them all. She'd explained that she was born in these mountains, and that her mother was an ogre who had visions and magic powers. She'd never known her father, but suspected he was human. Nyra was shunned by the other ogres, who knew her as "the witch's cub."

"Mother was hard for me to understand," she continued. "She was a good mother… but she was also quite bad."

"Very similar to my own mother, I think," Ohaobbok said. "Violent and unpredictable… and yet she tried to care for me in her own way."

Nyra smiled. "Yes. That is Mother."

"Did you have any brothers or sisters?" Arabelle asked.

Nyra looked sad. "He was called Kirag. He was tiny. Taller than you, but much smaller than me. Mother liked to hurt him. I haven't seen him in many winters. Mother broke him, I think."

Arabelle's eyes were wide as she breathed the word, "Kirag…"

Nyra stood. "I am done talking. Come, Ohaobbok. I will show you this."

"Show me what?"

She pulled at his hand impatiently. "Come. It's your destiny. We must visit the paladin's grave."

Ryan stood as well. "We would like to come also. Is that all right?"

Nyra ignored the question, but kept pulling at Ohaobbok's arm. With a shrug, he rose and let her drag him along, but not before beckoning the others to follow.

Minor demons screeched in fear as Malphas plowed through them, knocking their gangly bodies aside. *It must still be there,* he thought as he raced for the Aboveworld. One of the demon guards at the exit from the Underworld challenged him on his departure, but without slowing, Malphas plunged his fist into the twelve-foot-tall demon's chest, pulled out his still-beating black heart, and took an enormous bite.

He then raced to a secluded cave near the great mist barrier, one he hadn't been to in several seasons. He swallowed the last morsel of heart and felt some of the demon's strength infuse in his own muscles.

Eating my brethren is insufficient for what I hope to achieve. My hope lies in that which I've kept hidden. Will it have a greater effect?

Malphas was larger and stronger than any in the demon horde, yet his recent experience with the titan had shown him how insignificant he really was.

He needed more power.

He found the cave in which he'd buried his treasure. Fourteen paces in, he frantically dug into the hard-packed ground. His claws became cracked and bloody, but still he dug. And a dozen feet down, he found what he sought. A headless demon skeleton, and a dirt-encrusted black orb.

Ignoring the skeleton, he lifted the orb to eye level. A great power emanated from within, making it vibrate, and shaking away the dirt. Shimmering streaks of energy swirled on its surface. And as Malphas held it, a surge of power traveled up his arm, sparks floated in his vision, and he felt a tickling sensation scratched at the base of his neck. When he tightened his grip, the crackling energy increased, feeling like thousands of pinpricks against his hand.

Malphas shoved the orb into his mouth and swallowed it.

Fire coursed through his veins, sheets of energy flooded from his every pore, and he screamed.

He tried to stand, but instead fell into the pit he'd dug. His last vision was of his clawed hands sparking with arcs of energy as the ceiling collapsed on top of him, sealing him in a bed of dirt and rubble.

As Ryan hiked after his companions, he was struck with a vision of the moment he'd uncovered the Seed. The feeling of evil pulsing from the dark orb sickened him, and the vision ended with him throwing the crystal into the barrier. \

His stomach twisted in a knot as he raced up the mountain path.

I hope that evil thing doesn't come back to haunt me.

He breathed heavily as he struggled up the overgrown mountain trail. Up ahead, his wife scrambled easily after the two behemoths leading their expedition. She smiled back at him and encouraged him to pick up the pace.

"It has long been feared by those who know of it," panted Nyra.

Ohaobbok climbed the steep incline after her. "Why would a grave be feared?"

"You will see, my hu—Ohaobbok." Nyra cleared her throat. "This is an ancient burial site. It is feared by many of our people."

"By ogres?"

"Yes."

Ryan's legs were burning when Nyra at last stopped at a large, mostly level area. Even the ogres were winded from the fast-paced climb, and Ryan was sucking air in the higher altitude. He also had a painful cramp in his side.

Arabelle reached her hand out to him, and as he grasped it, he felt the energy of her healing. The cramp disappeared, and her warmth relaxed his sore muscles.

"We are here," Nyra said. "On these grounds, my ancient ancestors are buried."

She walked to the mouth of a huge cave, partially obscured by masses of vegetation. Then she paused and gestured for Ohaobbok to enter first.

"It's time. This is your destiny."

Ohaobbok looked at Nyra uncertainly. He sniffed at the cave, shrugged, and stepped forward.

But as he crossed the threshold of the cave, Ryan sensed the awakening of an ancient magic. A shimmering apparition materialized before him, and Ohaobbok took several steps back.

A translucent armored warrior stood before them. He was a good thirteen feet tall and wore plate armor from head to foot. Emblazoned on his chest was the image of a splayed hand.

Ohaobbok unsheathed his sword. "What is this?"

The glowing knight pointed at Ohaobbok's sword. "Sheathe thy sword, for 'tis not the day you will die. Forsooth, I have already died for thee."

Nyra knelt, her head bowed. The shimmering apparition bowed in return.

"I thank thee, daughter of the races. Your role was destined to be, and now thy position in the prophecies is set. I wish thee success, for you will be needed in the end."

The knight turned to Ryan and bowed again. "Our lord hath allowed me to foresee thine arrival, Champion of Seder. 'Tis my wish for your greatest success, for my people depend on thee."

The giant then faced Arabelle and bowed a third time. "I know thee as well, but not thy role. Thou art Seder's weapon. Dangerous. Yet thy mission is unknown to me."

Finally he faced them all. "I am honored to be greeted by such an august set of heroes." His helm evaporated, revealing his overly large head and overgrown lower incisors.

"You're an ogre!" Ohaobbok exclaimed.

The knight's laughter echoed around them. His gauntlets evaporated, and he studied his hands. "Why… you are correct, my friend. Forsooth I am an ogre."

He smiled and held up a hand to forestall any questions.

"Listen well, for I have little time. 'Twas more than seven hundred years ago when I was struck down, the last of mine order. I was, and still am, a paladin of Seder. I have watched my people perform many ill deeds. They have allowed themselves to cede to their base instincts, and have discarded the teachings of Seder."

The knight drew his sword and showed Ohaobbok the runes etched along its blade. "Know thee what is inscribed upon my sword?"

Ohaobbok shook his head.

"It reads strength, honor, wisdom, and life. Those are the values a paladin holds dear. His strength, used in defense of the weak. A paladin's honor prevents him from embracing deceit. With wisdom, he spurns rash action, and ill intent would ne'er guide his actions. And finally, life. A paladin of Seder would ne'er take a life unless 'twas in defense of himself or another."

The knight pointed at Ohaobbok. "Life is listed last, but not because 'tis least important. A true paladin of Seder wouldst forsake the destruction of life even if it meant his own hunger."

Ryan smiled. "Ohaobbok is a strict vegetarian. I've never seen him eat flesh in any form."

The knight nodded and placed the flat of his blade on his fellow ogre's shoulder. "Ohaobbok. I can detect thy intent even when you remain silent. Thou art who you are, and in that, I name thee heir."

A powerful surge of energy bloomed from deep within the knight, and threads of power wrapped themselves around Ohaobbok.

"I bequeath to thee the last vestiges of my powers, and in Seder's name I wish thee well. Go forth and fulfill thy destinies."

Brilliant white energy erupted from the knight, and hundreds of apparitions flew from the cave, filling the air. All of them ogres. All of them armored knights with the splayed hand emblazoned on their chests. They, too, lent their remaining power to Ohaobbok, explosions of energy fountaining forth and slamming into Ohaobbok.

For a moment, the brightness was too much, and Ryan had to squeeze his eyes shut. Then the light dimmed, and he heard Arabelle gasp.

He opened his eyes.

The knight was gone. As were the apparitions. But Ohaobbok remained, and he now wore a brilliant white suit of plate armor. The energy of Seder was infused in the metal, making it glow like a beacon of hope. And on his chest plate was the red symbol of the splayed hand.

Ohaobbok drew his sword, and it, too, had changed. The handle was red, the blade a brilliant white, shining with Seder's power. And the same runes were etched on the blade as had been written on the dead knight's sword.

Nyra wrapped her arms around him. "My dearest," she said, "you've been blessed beyond imagining. It's your destiny to bring our people back to the ways of Seder."

SCOUTING ENEMY TERRITORY

A curl of smoke rose from one of Ruby's nostrils, and the air in front of her shimmered. The practice fields were nearby, so the sounds of horses neighing and the clash of swords were a constant chaos, yet as the dragon concentrated, Jared noticed the background noises seemed to fade. And the prickling sensation at the base of his neck told him that strong magic was being used.

After a moment, the noises returned, and Ruby blew out two jets of sulfurous smoke in frustration.

"Dad, can you explain it to me again?"

Pyre flapped over to join them. "I want to hear this too."

Jared repeated his theory of teleportation, and Ruby and Pyre both listened intently.

"You both understand that Castle Thariginian and Castle Riverton are linked by their connection to the spirit world, and that with the use of sufficient power, objects can be moved through that connection. Right?"

The two dragons nodded their great heads.

"What I'm saying in addition is that, with enough localized power, I think this connection can be made between *any* two points—not just the hearts of the castles. In fact I've accomplished this myself, but only to transport a pebble from one side of a table to the other. I'm unable to transport anything larger—or farther. That's where you come in. You two have natural magical powers; it's part of what's allowed you to grow at such a fantastic rate. I think you might have a better chance at succeeding than I do."

Ruby sniffed with frustration. "Yes, but I've already tried to do it. Nothing happens."

"I'm convinced you can. But maybe… let's try something a little different. This time, don't try to send anything. Just open a portal to…" Jared looked around, and pointed at some trees about a mile away. "To those trees. And to better our chances, I want you to work together on this."

"Where should we put the portal?" Pyre asked. He seemed confident they would succeed.

Jared scorched a line in the ground. "How about right here? Are you ready?"

"I'm ready," said Ruby.

"This will be easy," said Pyre.

"Just remember to work *with* your sister, Pyre," Jared said, stepping back.

The two dragons assumed a look of concentration. Pyre

focused on the line in the dirt, while Ruby stared at the distant trees.

This time, the effects were almost immediate. Directly above the scorched line, a shimmering image began to waver. The image it displayed looked remarkably similar to the distant trees —but viewed from close up.

"Keep doing what you're doing!" Jared shouted with excitement.

He looked around and found a hand cart that had been used for hauling supplies. He rolled it toward the shimmering image, released it with a heave, and sent it rolling…

… right through the gateway.

It kept on rolling until it hit a tree trunk on the other side of the portal—a full mile away.

The shimmering gateway collapsed, and Pyre roared. "It worked!"

Jared smiled. "Kids, I think we can use this in many ways."

"All right, Charlie," said Aaron. "You understand what to do?"

Charlie was only twelve, but he'd already proven to be a strong war wizard. "Yes." He pointed to the dragons with a shaking hand. They were all gathered in the courtyard of Castle Riverton. "The dragons will open a portal to Castle Thariginian, and you and I will go across the barrier into the castle."

Sloane sensed Charlie's anxiety. "Don't worry, Charlie. We already know that the passage between the castles works. And Aaron has a ring of communication that will allow him to communicate with me from there. We've tested that part already."

Aaron put a hand on Charlie's shoulder. "She's right. We've done it before—though through a different route. And I need you, Charlie. It takes a strong wizard to activate the castle heart to get us back home—and that's why I chose you."

Charlie's lower lip quivered. "But what if I can't activate it? What if it only works if you went there from *this* castle? Maybe it won't work if you went there through a dragon portal."

"We don't think that's the case," Aaron said.

"And more importantly," Sloane added, "there are other ways to get you back. We can open another dragon portal, or send someone through the castle portal to help you come back. Okay?"

Charlie bit at his lower lip and nodded.

Aaron slapped him on the back. "I have every confidence in you. And just think about it—you'll be one of the first people in *centuries* to set your eyes on the First Protector's castle!"

Charlie brightened a bit, and straightened his back. "I'm ready."

Aaron looked to Sloane. "We both are."

Sloane nodded to the dragons, and sent them images of Castle Thariginian. They squinted their yellow eyes at a line drawn in the middle of the courtyard.

A shimmering portal formed precisely where they stared, revealing another castle courtyard… this one belonging to Castle Thariginian.

Aaron clasped Charlie's shoulder, and together they stepped through into another castle.

The cave collapse had left Malphas entombed in rock and darkness, but this meant nothing to him. All he cared about was one thing.

He'd never been so powerful.

Not only had his body absorbed the power of the orb, his mental capacity had expanded as well, and he understood things like never before. Until this moment, he'd had no idea what he possessed. He'd stolen the orb because he thought it was an artifact of power.

Now he knew that it was so much more.

The orb was known to many as the Seed. It was a lodestone of power especially tuned to Sammael, and in fact it was the very object that his lord had used to corrupt those across the barrier. With its power...

I can do anything.

Despite being buried under tons of dirt and rock, Malphas clawed his way upward and outward. Fiery sparks flew from his claws, and in moments he was free, staring across the desolate land of the Aboveworld.

With a mere flex of his arms, his scales popped back into place. He saw that one of his legs had been shattered and shredded in the cave-in, and yet he stood on it without pain. Another flex, this time of his mangled limb, and the bones and flesh knotted themselves back together.

With every move and stretch, Malphas felt new strength flow through him. Many of his scales popped off him, replaced by stronger, more flexible armor. He sensed that even his internal structures were realigning themselves.

I'm a creature to be feared.

"May I please be excused?" Rebecca asked. "I'm full."

Her mother looked up. "Are you sure you don't want anything else to eat?"

Rebecca shook her head. "No, Mommy, I'm fuller than Maggie!" She showed her parents her favorite doll and poked at its overstuffed belly for emphasis.

Her parents chuckled and waved her away from the dinner table.

Rebecca hopped off her chair and raced to the playroom. Daddy's deep voice chased after her. "Remember, tonight all of us are going to the fountain. Afterward, I'll tell you a story."

Cloud was curled up in the corner of the playroom, as usual. The silver swamp cat was now quite a bit bigger than Rebecca, but Rebecca knew she had nothing to fear from her friend. She scratched at his whiskery face and gave him a kiss on the nose. "Where's your brother, Cloud?"

She heard the voice of the castle whisper in her mind.

"There are three swamp cats wandering within me. You are making odd faces at one of them. His sibling is currently being fed scraps from young Zenethar's dinner plate. The largest of the cats is now departing the kitchens, where one of the cooks has fed him. He is likely seeking a warm place to rest."

"Castle," Rebecca said, "can you tell me what Aaron is doing?"

"He and twenty-three other soldiers are gathered in the courtyard. The dragons are summoning a gateway."

Rebecca stuck her lower lip out in a pout. Nobody ever told her when interesting things were going on. They thought she was still a kid. She'd never be allowed to join her brothers on their adventures.

Suddenly she felt dizzy, and a vision formed in her mind. She saw the castle everyone talked about. Castle Thariginian. Then the vision raced to the south and west, revealing several large caves. Dozens of misshapen creatures were clambering out of them and loping toward the castle. Some looked like spiky dogs; others like giant lumbering ogres with sharp horns protruding from every joint. Rebecca shivered at the sight.

Zenethar came into the playroom with Shadow following behind. "Hi, Rebecca. Sorry I'm late. Mother caught me feeding Shadow my food and made me eat a second helping."

Rebecca dismissed the vision and raced to the toy chest. "I've got the perfect game we can play. I invented it last night."

FINDING AN OLD FRIEND

As Ryan ate his bowl of mutton and root-vegetable stew, he kept an eye on Nyra. She was clearly nervous among the dwarves, her back straight as an arrow, her eyes constantly darting about. They'd given her every assurance that she was safe, but he supposed a lifetime's worth of prejudice would take some time to overcome.

The cook staggered as he came over to her, carrying a huge metal skewer loaded down with select cuts of roasted mutton. She rewarded him with a smile, and easily took the heavy skewer from him with one hand.

"Thank you, good dwarf."

The dwarf wiped the sweat from his brow and bowed deeply. "My lady, I'm Hammerthorn Rockfist." He flushed red underneath his brown beard. "But my friends be callin' me Hambone."

Nyra bent lower so she could see the cook face to face. "Thank you for the meat, Hambone."

Arabelle leaned over to Ryan and whispered, "I think our cook is enamored with Nyra."

The dwarf bowed again, his beard scraping along the ground. As he turned and walked back to his cooking fires, he had a huge grin on his face.

"I think you're right," Ryan said. "He's normally quite a grumpy little guy. Don't think I've ever seen him act like that before."

A voice called out from behind them. "Oy, Archmage! I've got yer delivery fer da army."

Ryan turned to see a dusty dwarf and a team of mountain ponies pulling a series of covered wagons. He stood, walked to the nearest wagon, and looked inside. "All damantite ore?"

"Dat be what yer paps asked for, isn't it?"

Arabelle came over, ran her hands over the lead wagon's wheels, examined the axles, and nodded with satisfaction. "Wagon looks sound."

The dwarf sputtered with indignation. "Whatchya tink, I gunna produce for him a shoddy wagon?"

Ryan patted the dwarf's shoulder. "My wife grew up living with wagons, so she can't resist paying careful attention to such things. She's just being cautious."

Arabelle gave the dwarf a sweet smile as she twirled a glowing damantite dagger in each hand. "I like to ensure my husband's safety."

Ohaobbok and Nyra walked over. "Are we almost ready to depart?" Ohaobbok asked.

Ryan patted his friend's armored elbow. "Yes, Belle and I need to head back right away." He turned to Nyra. "Have you met the maker of the fountain that you've been bathing at?"

Nyra's eyes widened. "He lives?"

"In a way." He turned to Ohaobbok. "Before you two return to the castle, it seems right that she gets an opportunity to pay her respects to the First Protector. And both of you make sure you visit the local fountain one last time before you depart. I don't want any of us taking any chances."

Nyra grabbed Ohaobbok's arm and nodded.

Barnaby walked up, grunting with effort as he tossed two leather packs onto the wagon. "Gotchya da supplies ye asked fer. Not knowin' why ya'd need three weeks of provisions for a trip dat's only a handful of days, but you got it." He patted at a medium-sized keg. "If'n you don't mind, I'm packin' a keg o' the good stuff for my brudder Oda."

Ryan laughed. "If I know Oda, he'll be very appreciative."

As they bounced along in the lead wagon, Arabelle closed her eyes and rested her head against her husband's shoulder. "Let me know when we're there."

He kissed her head. "I will."

She let herself drift off, and it was not long before she once again had the same vision that had been haunting her nights.

Arabelle stands with Ryan on an island in a swamp. The half-moon hovers high above in the night sky, insects swarm over the stagnant water, and flashes of light reflect from the eyes of predators within the trees.

She turns to see her love raise his hand and release a blue-white orb of sparkling energy into the air. It rivals the brightest of full moons, and chases the shadows away.

A pack of twenty swamp cats approaches. The lead cat, a giant among his brethren, bares his teeth and roars, his tail twitching nervously.

When Arabelle woke, she wondered yet again what her vision meant. What was Seder trying to tell her?

Whatever it was, she could no longer ignore it.

Arabelle and Ryan had waded through miles of swamp, always following her vision, but the swamp cats they were tracking shunned human interaction.

And then a warning growl sounded.

Arabelle immediately pulled her cloak around her and disappeared into the darkness of the swamp. Ryan summoned a light and hissed, "I'll try not to hurt them, but if things go bad, I can't promise anything."

It was just as her vision had predicted. They stood deep within the great swamp in the northern reaches of Trimoria, and above Ryan's head shimmered a brilliant orb of light as a pack of swamp cats approached.

The lead cat bared his teeth and opened his mouth in a roar.

Ryan walked forward with the mystical light hovering high over him. He held his arm out and sent a thread of shimmering light into the cat's head. The cat slashed at Ryan with his giant paw, but his claws raked against an invisible barrier.

"There's something odd about this cat," Ryan said.

Arabelle gripped her daggers, uncertain what she should do.

Ryan's rope of white energy continued to pulse between him and the giant cat, but then he released it and backed away. The cat swayed and fell to the ground, its body shaking with spasms.

The other animals closed in menacingly.

Then white energy pulsed from the shrinking body of the cat, and in seconds, the cat disappeared. In its place, a disheveled dwarf staggered to his feet, blinking rapidly as if he had trouble focusing.

Arabelle gasped.

"Grisham!"

AMBUSH!

Aaron stepped into the portal, and the world flashed white. A bout of dizziness hit him, and he crouched, ready for anything.

Before him was the ancient battleground. Rotting hulks of broken battle engines lay in the knee-high, sun-scorched grass. A scent in the air told him that nearby was a fumarole, a vent in the land that spewed noxious gases that could overcome those who were caught unaware.

This was his second trip through the dragons' portal. The first one, with Charlie, was just a test of the portal itself. This trip was about exploration—and as such involved a lot more travelers.

With a pop, Oda appeared behind him, grimacing through his disorientation. More pops followed, as two dozen popping soldiers arrived.

These men were some of Trimoria's best, as indicated by the crossed sword and lightning bolt on their collars. This was the symbol of the elite corps, soldiers who had undergone the direct tutelage of Castien, the sword master of the armies. Their armor and weaponry were formed from damantite and infused with magical power that made them glow.

Two of the soldiers glowed themselves. These were the war wizards, marked as such by the dual lightning bolts on their collars. One was Wat, the determined dwarf who had shown himself to be not only among the most powerful war wizards, but also the most learned. The other was a self-taught wizard named Graystone. Prior to his arrival at Castle Riverton six months ago, he'd been living as hermit in the elven woods—the only place he could find to avoid Azazel's purge. Both wizards held long damantite staffs.

Aaron gestured toward the castle behind him. "Men, welcome to Castle Thariginian. You're the first of our armies to set eyes on it in half a millennium." He nodded to Oda, who stepped forward.

"Boys, it be time we scout da area. Our mission be to find out what scurries about here and return whatever information we can."

"What if we find some baddies?" someone asked.

Oda tapped his mace against his shield. "We're not to be seekin' trouble, but if trouble be findin' us, we give it right back. Ya hear me?"

"Aye, sir!"

Together, they crept south toward the mountains. Unfortunately, they were moving through grasslands, which provided little cover. It made Aaron uneasy. If there were "baddies" about, he and his men were sitting ducks.

Suddenly his foot sank into the ground, and he fell forward. Oda grabbed his belt and pulled him back to solid ground.

"Watch yerself, General. Otherwise you're gonna end up boiled like a shrimp."

Aaron had nearly fallen into the bubbling and steaming mud surrounding a sulfurous hot spring. "Thanks, Oda. I owe you one."

"I'll take ye up on dat, don'tcha worry." Oda laughed. "Just keep yer eye out where ya be—"

He was cut off by a shriek from above. A flapping demon dove from the sky, claws extended, toothed beak open.

An arrow flew into its gullet, and the demon struck the ground with a tremendous thud. The nearby soldiers patted the shoulder of the archer who'd shot it down.

Then Aaron turned toward the castle, and his heart sank. Between his men and the castle, nearly a hundred figures had risen from the grasses. They were vaguely wolf-like, but stood taller than humans.

"Enemies!" he cried. "Men, stay in formation! Archers and wizards, use the distance to our advantage."

"Fire when in range," Oda yelled.

The thrum of bowstrings sounded, and arrows streaked across the field and slammed into the charging enemy. Before the first arrows had even hit their targets, the bowmen had sent a second barrage, and they followed it with a third.

Many of the enemy fell, but the rest were not dissuaded from their charge. And Aaron was not eager to take them on in hand-to-hand combat, for spikes protruded from their every joint.

Oda was clearly thinking the same thing. "Don't fight dem

beasts up close or yer gonna get skewered!" he yelled. "Keep dem at da end of yer weapons, and avoid dem spikes!"

Two thick ropes of brilliant white energy erupted from Wat and Graystone, splashing across the densest part of the oncoming assault. At least a dozen demons burst into flame under the assault.

"Above!" Aaron yelled.

Three flying demons were streaking in, claws extended and tearing at anything within reach. Aaron raised his shield just in time, and sparks flew from it as he absorbed the impact. A soldier beside him was not so lucky; a claw ripped across his forehead before he could react.

The archers sent arrows into the air, bringing down the flying creatures, but the war wizards continued to throw their massive bolts of sparkling death at the incoming wolf-men. The power of the attacks created a wall of heat that flung burning demons in all directions. For the first time, the assault faltered.

Aaron seized the opportunity. He smashed the pommel of his sword against his shield and roared a bestial cry. "Charge!" he shouted as he raced forward.

The opposing sides came together with a roar. One of Aaron's soldiers took a massive blow to the chest that would have crushed a man without magic-infused armor. As it was, the soldier shrugged off the assault and plunged his sword into the attacking demon's neck. Greenish ichor spewed from the wound, and the monstrosity fell backward.

In seconds all the soldiers were deeply engaged in melee, making the arrows and bolts of energy ineffective, except to pick off stragglers.

It's now my fight.

A misshapen demon came loping toward him, a club in each of its four hands. It snarled as it jumped at him, its clubs whistling through the air.

Aaron raised his shield, dove under the swinging arms, and slashed up into the demon's chest. He leaped to the side and saw the look of surprise on the demon's face as his entrails spilled from his gut.

Nearby, Oda yelled, "I'm Oda, da one dwarf army! Die by my mace, ye spawn of da Abyss!" The dwarf smashed the leg out from under a demon, and as the beast collapsed, Oda caved in its skull with a devastating blow.

Aaron heard the crunch of armor and a man cry out in pain. He turned toward the sound to see a thirteen-foot-tall demon bellowing a challenge. Two of Aaron's soldiers were already dead at his feet.

Aaron met the creature's bellow with one of his own, and raced to engage. "Come at me you, insignificant worm!" he yelled across the din.

The demon's lip curled into a smile, and his red eyes glowed as if a fire raged within his skull. As Aaron closed, the demon raised a mace that was longer than Aaron was tall, and swung it with surprising speed and dexterity. Aaron dove to the side, and the weapon smashed into the ground, barely missing. As Aaron rolled past, he slashed at the side of the behemoth's leg. but his sword failed to penetrate the monster's scale-covered knee.

"For Cammoria!" shouted one of the Trimorian soldiers, coming at the demon from the other side.

But the demon spun about and casually kicked the soldier.

The man's leg buckled with a sickening crunch, and he screamed in pain.

Aaron launched himself forward, grabbed the soldier, and with the strength of a giant, tossed the man out of range of further attacks.

He barely managed to duck behind his shield before being struck by a stream of sticky green fluid that burst from the demon's mouth. And a good thing, too, for the grass sizzled and burned wherever the acid touched.

Aaron again dove forward, slashed again at the same spot on the behemoth's knee. This time his blade sliced through, and he felt the popping of tendons. The demon fell sideways, his leg folding underneath him.

Aaron didn't slow. He jumped through the demon's flailing arms and swung his glowing blade with all his preternatural strength. When the damantite blade connected with the demon's neck, the black scales shattered with a brilliant shower of sparks.

A wet gurgling sound came from the demon as he grabbed at the wound on his neck. And then a sizzling bolt of white-hot energy smashed into the demon's head. It exploded, sending gobbets of flesh and bone in all directions.

Aaron felt the battle changing around him. The thrumming of bowstrings picked up again. The demons were scrambling to escape. Graystone and Wat joined with the archers, sending blasts of energy at the retreating enemies.

Aaron's sword craved blood, and he spun about, looking for an opponent, any opponent. But there were none to be found. All had fled.

He turned and found the soldier that he'd flung aside. The

man was attempting to stand on one leg, but his face was a mask of pain. His other leg was twisted horribly.

"Stop, soldier. Sit back down!" Aaron ran over to him, pulling a flask from his waistband.

The soldier collapsed, screaming as he twisted his leg even further.

Aaron looked into the frightened man's eyes. "Soldier, I'm going to have to set your leg before we heal you. Do you understand?"

The soldier pulled a dagger from his belt. "Whalen, sir. My name is Whalen, and yes, I understand." He bit down on the blade's handle and nodded bravely.

Aaron grasped the man's ankle with one hand and put his other hand on the knee.

Am I really doing this?

"All right. One… two…."

Aaron quickly pulled and twisted the leg. He felt the bones crunch, and he heard them too, even over Whalen's muffled scream. But the leg was straight. His mother's healing draught would take care of the rest.

He was surprised Whalen hadn't passed out. The man was indeed a survivor. He gratefully took the flask and drained it. Aaron gave him a second flask, and he drained that one too.

"Well?" Aaron asked.

Whalen moved the leg. "Sir, it's much better. I can't believe it."

Aaron stood and helped the man to his feet. Whalen tentatively tested his injured leg, then with a laugh, he jumped up and landed hard. He looked up at Aaron with a smile. "I thought for sure that leg was beyond repair. I'll never forget what you've done."

Aaron clapped his hand on the man's shoulder. "Just be careful with the bigger demons. Now get yourself ready; we'll be returning home soon."

Aaron scanned the battlefield and saw Oda kneeling over another soldier, his head bent in mourning.

"Romley," said the dwarf, "you were brave to da end, and died a hero. I promise you I'll be bringin' ya home fer a proper burial. I swear it."

Aaron crouched next to Oda. "He's the first, but he won't be the last, my friend."

"Oy, dat certainly be da truth. We lucky to nae have lost more today. Dis healin' magic is a true wonder." He pointed to a soldier who was being given a healing flask. "I'd have sworn good ole Simson over der was a goner. And Girol over dere"—he pointed to another, who was being helped to his feet—"I'd have sworn his back be broke."

"Indeed. We owe a great debt to the healers, and must thank them when we return." He stood and cupped his hands to his mouth. "Everyone, gather up! Let's get into Castle Thariginian and head home."

We've certainly learned more than we expected to about the creatures we'll be fighting.

Oda stood up beside him. "Well, what ye be waitin' for! The general's spoken. You boys done good, now is not the time to celebrate, nor is it the place to lick yer wounds. Fer all we know, the entire demon army is comin', so let's *move!*"

A LONG-DELAYED MISSION

Arabelle rode with Grisham in the back of the lead wagon. Despite the days that had passed since she'd found her old friend, he still looked troubled.

"Grisham, don't worry. We'll be there soon."

The sullen-looking dwarf shrugged. His wild black beard hung down over the oversized clothes he'd borrowed from Ryan. "I don't see how they can help. Were it not for your husband's somehow calling me out of my swamp cat form, I'd never have remembered who I was." He nodded toward the family of cats that followed the wagon toward Eluanethra. "I'll not leave my family, Arabelle. I won't. I'm not right for the two-legs world."

Ryan spoke from up front. "I'd never suggest such a thing, Grisham. But there are those in Eluanethra who will better understand your ability. Even I've read about it before, though it's said to be very rare."

"And you believe that this understanding will help? Because if you ask me to choose, I'd rather go back to the swamps and dismiss knowledge of who I am."

Ryan looked down at the ring on his finger. "I just received confirmation from Labri—"

"She's the queen of the elves," Arabelle noted.

"Both Eglerion and his master believe they can help you keep your identity when you transition. In fact, the lore master's mentor claims to have aided someone in your exact situation."

Arabelle gently touched her friend's shoulder, and he jumped back, startled. "Grisham. When you and I met, you were a young, only twelve years old or so. Do you remember what you told me? You told me that you had a mission to accomplish, but had resigned yourself to failure."

Grisham frowned, and a faraway look came over him. "I remember knowing that my mission didn't matter anymore."

"No, Grisham! I won't believe that our having met, and Seder having sent me repeated visions of your rescue, is for naught."

Suddenly Grisham's mouth fell open and his breathing increased. His eyes turned white, and he fell back.

"What's going on? Is he all right?" Ryan asked.

Arabelle pooled some of her healing power and reached out to the dwarf. "I think he's having a vision." Just as she was about to touch him and see if something physically ailed him, the dwarf's eyes flew open.

"I remember!"

Bryan tilted Grisham's head up and looked in his eyes. "Do not fear, young dwarf. This is an extremely rare and useful gift. And although it can be very easy to lose yourself in an adopted identity, with some simple guidance, that is just as easily avoided."

"I have no guidance, sir. I was orphaned before anyone I knew could teach me."

Ryan looked over at the dozen swamp cats that were curled about the fireplace. They seemed not to care that Grisham now looked like a "two-legs." They were comfortable, non-threatening, as long as he was in their presence.

"Lore master," he said, "he claims to be of the Ta'ah."

Bryan frowned. "A Ta'ah? Now how is that possible on this side of the barrier?"

Grisham pulled his fingers nervously through his beard. "Sir, I wasn't born on this side of the barrier. I don't know the details of how it worked, but my father and I were sent here by our elders. I'd never even been in the Aboveworld until the day we walked through the portal with the flashing crystals."

Bryan nodded slowly. "Fascinating. I'd heard of such things, but have never witnessed the like." He turned to Ryan and Eglerion. "With a dozen fully charged diamonds forming a ring, it is possible to create a portal between any two known places. I know the theory, but our people have never had the benefit of an Archmage. Nor did we have the diamonds required."

"An Archmage?" Grisham asked. "Won't any wizard do?"

Bryan shook his head. "No, young Ta'ah. Only an Archmage can transfer energy into an object." He pointed to the glowing diamond on the end of Ryan's staff. "See how the diamond glows with our Archmage's infused energy? Those flashing lights you passed through were diamonds, I suspect—diamonds that held power sufficient to warp, stretch, and then tear a passage through the fabric of our world. This mission of yours… it must have been quite important."

Grisham's face grew somber. "Yes, it was very important. My people have histories that speak of Zenethar Thariginian in the time before the coming of the demons and the raising of the great barrier. And our people knew that the line of the king still lived, because his castle remained standing. So when Father and I crossed over, our mission was to find that heir—and help him reunify the people on both sides of the barrier."

"Grisham," said Ryan, "you need to meet King Throll and tell him this."

"Do you think he'd see me? I'm just an orphan."

Ryan laughed. "Just an orphan? No. You're an emissary from a race of dwarves our people haven't seen in many centuries. That makes you very important."

Arabelle put her arm around Grisham's shoulder. "Come. Let's get you dressed in something befitting an ambassador."

Grisham looked down at his borrowed clothes. "I *would* prefer clothes that fit."

Arabelle laughed. "We'll see what we can do."

As they all rose, Ryan noticed that Bryan was wiping sweat from his brow, and his normally tanned face looked pale. "Are you all right, lore master?"

Bryan smiled. "I'm fine. It's the food. It seems centuries of castle moss have made my stomach a bit sensitive to anything else."

Throll motioned for Grisham to rise and take a seat. "Tell me, Ambassador Grisham, what set your feet on such a tragic path. The Ta'ah must have foreseen a great need for such a sacrifice."

Grisham shifted nervously. He stood in Castle Riverton's audience hall, facing not only the king, but the entire royal family. The Rivertons were there as well, along with several of the king's senior captains. Arabelle knew it had to be intimidating. She was glad that his swamp cat family had stayed by his side—and that they weren't causing any trouble.

As if reading her mind, Ryan whispered in her ear. "He'll be fine, Belle. His people expected him to do this without someone mothering him."

Grisham cleared his throat and let out a breath. "Sire, my people have long been isolated from their cousins who live in the Aboveworld mountains of Trimoria. I should probably speak of my people and fill in some history.

"It has been nearly a millennium since Seder began sending visions to warn my people. He showed us a great calamity that would befall us all if we didn't help prevent it. At the time, my people still sought the diamonds that our Archmages treasured beyond all else. We dug very deeply into the ground, following the promise of ever larger crystals, when we encountered the chamber…"

Grisham breathed deeply and glanced at Arabelle, who gave him a comforting smile.

"We fear that this was the beginning of the terror unleashed in this world."

"The Abyss?" Ryan asked.

Grisham nodded. "The records show that our miners had fully expanded the lowest portion of the thirty-third level of the diamond mines, and we'd just dug another fifty feet down into the bedrock to open the thirty-fourth level. That was when we discovered a subterranean chamber whose air smelled of sulfur. It was huge, unlike the tight quarters provided by the tunnels above. From ceiling to floor was over one hundred feet, and the records indicate that the walls were so far away as to not even be visible."

Sloane gasped. "I see… two glowing crystals. And you're afraid of them. What are they?"

Aaron smiled. "You must excuse my wife. She can read minds, and sometimes she gets overly excited."

A smile crossed Grisham's bearded face. "Yes, I can see the pink aura that extends beyond her reddened cheeks."

Ryan leaned toward Arabelle and whispered, "Your friend has the ability to see auras around people? I wonder if that is common among the Ta'ah."

"Yes, princess," said Grisham, "my ancestors encountered two crystals. I never saw them myself, but Father shared with me the mental image."

The young dwarf then squinted in concentration, and a scene materialized in Arabelle's mind. It must have been affecting the others in the room as well, for she heard several sharp intakes of breath. At first she saw only mists, smelling horribly of rotten eggs. But then the mists parted, revealing two glowing orbs sitting atop mounds of much smaller crystals. The crystals in the pile had no glow, but the two on top pulsed with unbelievable energy.

Then the vision dissipated, and the audience chamber appeared around them all once more.

"The one on the left!" Ryan exclaimed. "I recognized it! That's the Seed."

Grisham nodded. "The Archmage is correct. We immediately noticed the orb's flaw, and after consulting with the elders, we created a chamber to forever seal it away on the thirty-fourth level."

"It didn't work," Ryan grumbled.

"What's the other crystal? A twin?" Aaron asked.

Grisham shook his head. "The second crystal lacks the flaw of the first. And shortly after discovering this chamber, some of my people received a prophecy from Seder. It spoke of the second crystal and charged us with its safekeeping." Grisham turned toward Ryan. "It also spoke of a time when the power of this crystal was to be used."

"What, specifically, was this prophecy?" Throll asked.

Grisham recited the lines.

"The time will come when the object I give to you must be wielded by my champion. You will know that the time has come when all else is lost, the people aboveground are no more, and life has spontaneously come into the smallest of the crystals.

"When the Dedicate crystals begin to glow, you will know that the threads of destiny have been knotted. Only then will the crystal that represents the power of the people of Trimoria be ready for use.

"On that day, seek the king of the humans. For in his company will you find the blue-eyed Archmage who has arrived from the stars. Only he will be able to wield this weapon against that which means to destroy all life."

Throll settled back in his chair, glanced at Ryan and chuckled. "Now isn't that interesting."

Grisham nodded. "Sire, I was tasked with ascertaining whether the champion of Seder does exist. And I can tell from the nimbus of power surrounding your Archmage—as well as the blue eyes—that he is in fact the one in the prophecy. I ask for permission to escort him to my people so that he can extract from the vaults that which only he can wield."

"Absolutely not!" Aaron exclaimed. "It is entirely too dangerous for someone to simply run around on the other side of the barrier." He pointed to the black ribbon of mourning he wore on his wrist. "I traveled there with a powerful troop of soldiers and wizards, and even so, we suffered a fatality within moments of our arrival."

Throll scratched at his neatly shorn beard, then looked at Grisham and shook his head. "Grisham, I tend to agree with our general. I think it would be too dangerous for you. You are in no condition to fight if we run into trouble."

Arabelle spoke up. "Your Highness, I suggest this is a task for a very small group practiced in stealth."

"Nonsense," Aaron said. "This calls for those who can fight—"

With a flick of her wrists, Arabelle sent two glowing damantite daggers into the arm of his chair. Aaron's eyes widened.

"Don't tell me I can't fight." She turned toward the king once more. "King Throll, I believe that Ryan and I could cross the barrier and find our way there. I'm more than sufficiently practiced with stealth, and he can cloak himself within his magic shield."

Throll turned toward Castien. The elf silently nodded affirmation.

"But how will you know the way?" Grisham asked. "You've never been there."

"Grisham," said Arabelle, "you remember how I could sense Ryan's direction even before I had ever met him? I could do the same with one of your Ta'ah elders. If you can send me an image of one of them, I can use my ability to find my way directly to them."

Grisham concentrated, and Arabelle received an image of a white-bearded dwarf with a scar across his forehead. She then applied her own special sight, and sought out the dwarf she was seeing.

She pointed toward the south, and slightly downward. "Yes. He is there. I can seek him without a problem."

Throll glanced at Jared and raised an eyebrow. "Thoughts, Lord Riverton?"

Jared grasped his wife's hand. "My son and his wife are beyond the need for our permission."

Ryan smiled and turned to Arabelle. "Shall I pack, or will you?"

Arabelle rolled her eyes. "I'll pack. You'd never remember anything other than food."

Throll walked over to them and rested a hand on each of their shoulders. "I know it's unnecessary for me to say it, but please be careful. Much rests on your safe return."

Aaron grumbled, "Like the entire future of Trimoria."

LOST UNDERGROUND

It was just after midnight, and Ryan and Arabelle were in the enormous cave that housed Ruby and Pyre. The two dragons were focused, crackling with magical energy, and the air was just starting to shimmer between them.

They had decided to use a dragon portal rather than the castle portal for their journey, seeing as their destination was so far from Castle Thariginian. Taking the castle portal would mean at least a day's travel through dangerous territory just to get to the mountain ranges where the Ta'ah lived, whereas by using an image Sloane had extracted from Grisham, they should be able to get to the mountains directly.

Pyre grumbled. "It's not right. The place Sloane told us to find doesn't exist."

Ruby exhaled two jets of smoke from her nostrils. "No, it exists, but there has been a rockslide. It isn't suitable for us to send you there."

"Is it possible for you to find us a place to arrive nearby?" Arabelle asked. "I'm not clear on how this works."

Pyre and Ruby closed their eyes. A few moments passed in silence, but for the swishing of the dragons' scaly tails on the cave floor.

"Found it!" Pyre yelled, opening his eyes.

Ruby growled. "Then share the image, you big idiot."

Pyre narrowed his eyes at her. "Idiot? I found it before you did."

"Where is this location?" Ryan asked Pyre.

"Sloane's image was of a cave," Pyre said. "We will make a portal on top of the rocks that closed it off. To get inside, you may have to move some rock, but that's nothing an Archmage such as yourself can't handle."

Ryan squeezed Arabelle's hand. "You ready?"

She nodded. "Ready."

The dragons closed their eyes, and moments later, a portal appeared. Ryan raised his shield and twisted it to make himself invisible.

"Belle, stand close to me so I can make you invisible too."

She frowned. "I'm quite capable of blending into the shadows, thank you."

Ryan rolled his eyes. "All right, let's step through on three. One, two, *three*."

Ryan stepped into the shimmering image, and his foot came down on shifting rock. He was on top of a rock slide in a lifeless wasteland. There was no sign of life nor sign of greenery for miles.

Arabelle appeared beside him, and padded silently toward a

crack in the mountain before them. The cave hadn't been entirely blocked off; that was good. He followed her into the mountain, and the darkness swallowed them.

Just inside the entrance, Arabelle pulled a vial from her pocket. She tilted her head back, put a drop of liquid in each of her eyes, then waved him toward her. "Your turn."

"What is it?"

"She called it a tincture of the new moon. It will improve your night vision."

"She who?"

"I was taught how to make this by an old herb woman who knew my mother. Don't worry, I've used it plenty of times."

"Hard not to worry when the whites of your eyes have turned black," Ryan muttered.

"They'll eventually go back to normal. And in the meantime, it makes me harder to see—which is a good thing."

Ryan shook his head. "I don't need it. My eyes are already adjusting. Look—there's a faintly glowing lichen on the walls. And if we run out of light, I can uncover the diamond on my staff."

"No, you can't, because you'll put a target on us. We're better off remaining in the dark."

"Fine," Ryan said, "I won't uncover the diamond. But I'd rather keep my eyes the way they are."

Arabelle sighed and put the bottle in a hidden pocket. "I guess I'm leading the way then. Let's go."

For the next several hours they climbed around and over obstacles, through narrow passages and innumerable cave-ins. Ryan's muscles were burning from exertion, but Arabelle scrambled along nimbly, not even slowing, except when she stopped to wait for him to catch up.

Ryan quickly gave up on trying to maintain a shield around her, as she was always too far ahead, scouting their path, sometimes raising a closed fist for caution. Instead he dedicated all of his concentration to keeping up with her without injuring himself.

It was during one of those moments when Arabelle had put some distance between them that Ryan felt the ground shake and heard the cracking of stone. And then the rock he stood on fell away—and Ryan fell with it.

As he tumbled straight down, streams of dirt and rock tumbling around him, he looked up to see Arabelle reaching out a hand as she threw herself half over the edge. Then he slammed hard against the ground and everything went dark.

Ryan's head throbbed with pain. In fact, so did his entire body. He opened his eyes to find himself half-buried in rubble—but alive.

Ignoring the pain, he cleared away enough of the rubble to crawl out from underneath it. For a moment, he could barely feel his legs, and panic raced through him, but then he realized his lower body was merely numb with cold. He'd landed in wet mud, which had likely cushioned his fall.

He rubbed vigorously at his legs, trying to get the blood circulating, and looked around.

The lichen was brighter here, illuminating another tunnel. At least he wasn't trapped in a pit. But when he looked up at the shaft through which he'd fallen, he saw only rock. Apparently a huge boulder had come down after him and had gotten wedged in the shaft, blocking the way up.

He shuddered at the thought of what would have happened to him if that boulder *hadn't* gotten caught up above.

He reached to his ring to tell Arabelle he was all right, only to discover that both of his rings were broken at their seams—and the fingers on his right hand were throbbing and horribly swollen.

Damn it! Over the years, the only thing they'd discovered that would make one of the communication rings stop working was if the welded seam of the ring cracked. *Belle is probably freaking out, trying to get to me.*

Carefully biting on the side of each ring, Ryan pulled them off his fingers. Instantly the blood rushed into those two fingers with a wave of pain. Ryan patted at his belt, looking for a flask of healing potion, but they had broken during the fall. He would just have to suffer through the pain.

Luckily, he found his staff, sticking out of the rubble. He grabbed it with his left hand and used it to stand. It felt like every muscle in his body was screaming with pain.

I shouldn't complain. It's a freaking miracle I didn't break anything.

Then a sudden pain hit him in the stomach, as if someone had kicked him, and he bent over in agony, barely remaining upright.

He knotted with cramps and held back waves of nausea. The pain lasted for a full minute before fading.

What the heck was that?

Ryan straightened. He had no healing powers, so there was nothing he could do about his pains but try to find Arabelle—and hope he didn't run into something else first. With effort, and a sharp pain in his temples, he recreated his invisibility shield and started hobbling down the tunnel.

Unlike the tunnels above, the one Ryan limped through now was straight and true, without any intersections or branches, and without any cave-ins either. He had hoped to find a path leading upward, but there was only one way to go, unless he wanted to retrace his steps and go back in the other direction—which he didn't.

So he continued on, and after about twenty minutes, the tunnel opened onto a chamber. Ryan wasn't sure how large it was, but it was huge enough that the bioluminescent lichen didn't reach the far wall.

Ryan sank to his knees, exhausted. The air here was humid and musty, with a metallic taste. The smell reminded him of the mud he'd landed in. Or maybe it was just the mud he was smelling. He was still covered in it, and it was making him itch like crazy.

What I'd give to for an underground lake to wash myself in.

A crash sounded from somewhere up ahead in the cavern, and Ryan instinctively strengthened his shields.

That sounded like armor falling to the ground.

He stood silently, listening, for what felt like minutes, but all he heard was the occasional drip. He now wished he'd allowed Arabelle to treat his eyes with her strange concoction. The light from the moss didn't extend far, and at the edge of its influence, the inky blackness was complete.

He considered uncovering his diamond, despite his promise to Arabelle. But she was right—creating his own light would paint a bull's-eye on him for any enemies who might be present.

He smiled. *Unless that light is nowhere near me…*

He chose a location about fifty feet ahead of him and thirty feet off the ground, and concentrated his magic. Moments later, a small bluish-white ball of light had materialized, casting its glow across the cavern. He made it brighten gradually, until he could make out what lay ahead.

And when he saw it, his jaw literally dropped. The giant object lying in the center of the cavern was absolutely the last thing he would ever have expected to find in Trimoria.

For ahead in the underground cavern, lit by the glow of a magic sphere, lay an old twin-engine airplane.

Ryan's hand shook as he touched the metal of the fuselage.

How the heck did you get here?

He paused as he felt a prickling sensation all over, and a wave of dizziness washed over him. When the moment passed, he continued along the plane, studying it. It didn't seem to have much in the way of structural damage. If not for all the rust, it might even be in flying condition.

When he reached the front, he peered into the cockpit.

A skeleton stared back at him.

If only your bones could tell your tale.

Ryan spied a logbook resting in the empty chair next to the dead pilot. He reached for it, but as he did, his fingers brushed against the pilot's yoke, and a vision exploded in his mind.

A vaguely familiar-looking female pilot speaks into the microphone. "Itasca, we must be on you, but cannot see you. Gas is running low. Have been unable to reach you by radio. We are flying at one thousand feet."

She turns to her co-pilot, a worried-looking man who flips through charts on his lap. "Fred, I'm not sure I trust my instrument readings."

Fred shows her a chart with a line drawn on it, leading from their position to Howland Island. "Don't worry, with Fred Noonan as navigator, we'll be fine." He winks.

The pilot adjusts the ailerons and banks the plane to see the ground below. "I just wish I could see the ground to confirm. If it weren't for this damned mist!"

Fred shakes his head and points again at the chart. "There's nothing to see except ocean. Just stay on this bearing. Any moment now, my dear, and we'll cross over the island."

. . .

Ryan yanked back his hand and shook his head. Another wave of dizziness came over him, and this time he fell backward, landing on his rear.

Clenched in his hand was the logbook he'd been reaching for. Since at the moment he didn't feel much like standing, he took a moment to flip through the yellowed pages. The contents were written by hand, and appeared to document a trip that had started in Miami on the first of June and continued on to locations in South America, Africa, India, and parts of Asia. The last flight logged departed from New Guinea on the second of July.

But hints of trouble were logged on the last written page.

KHAQQ Navigation Log

July 2, 1937

Itasca is gone. Engine sputtered and died. Somehow, didn't crash. Mist everywhere, can't see anything. Noonan is unconscious. We should be dead. I need to find help.

Amelia

Ryan's mind reeled. *Amelia.*

Long before he had come to Trimoria, he had heard about a woman named Amelia—a famous daredevil pilot who was lost at sea in the early 1900s.

"Now we know what happened to Amelia Earhart," he muttered aloud.

A cramping nausea washed over him without warning, and he convulsed with pain. He lost all control of his muscles, and even his shimmering globe of light blinked off. The prickling feeling on his skin transformed into an intense burning sensation, and he felt himself passing out.

And just as consciousness left him, he felt someone grabbing at his arm.

A RESCUE MISSION

Arabelle crept along, trying to find a way down to the lower level where her husband had fallen. She'd tried sending him a message on the personal rings, but he hadn't responded, and she was afraid of what that meant. At least she knew he was still alive; her location sense wouldn't work if he wasn't. And he was moving; her location sense told her that too. But knowing he was alive, even knowing precisely where he was, didn't help her if she couldn't find a route to get there. And she'd now been wandering the twisting tunnels of the Underworld for hours.

She'd been reluctant to use the family communication ring, because she knew she would alarm everyone, but the time had come. She had to do it.

She tapped out a message.

Arabelle. Ryan and I got separated in the tunnels. He's not responding to my ring.

A response came through almost immediately.

Aubrey. Do you still sense him?

Yes. I know he's alive and moving. I don't understand why he's not messaging me.

She explained what had happened, and reassured Ryan's mother that she'd find Ryan no matter what else happened.

Nothing will keep me from him.

Jared was at work in his study when Grisham walked in.

"Sir, you asked for me?"

"Yes, Grisham. I won't coat these bitter words with honey. My son and his wife are lost in the Underworld tunnels. There was a cave-in, and my son disappeared down some god-forsaken hole in the ground. Arabelle is fine, but she's can't find a way to get down to him. Do you think you—"

"Absolutely!" Grisham announced. "I'm sure I can find them."

Jared smiled. "What makes you so confident? You were just a child when you lived there."

Grisham tapped the side of his large nose and grinned. "I can recognize smells better than anyone you know. Better yet, I'm also a swamp cat who knows scents and tracking. If they've left a scented trail, then I can follow it."

Jared put his hand on the dwarf's shoulder. "My friend, if you can find my son and daughter-in-law and return them to us, I'll be deeply indebted to you." He looked out the window and saw the dragons in the distance. "As to finding their trail, that's not a problem. We can place you within feet of where they entered your underground world."

Grisham enjoyed the exhilarating feeling of racing across the fields on all fours, followed by his mate and cubs. Yet today, the experience was different. He was no longer Midnight, the leader of a pack of swamp cats; he was Grisham, a shape-changing Ta'ah who was the head of a rather unusual family of half-breeds.

Long before reaching the dragons' cave, Grisham detected their musky scent, as did his mate. "Are you sure the no-tails spoke truly?" she asked. "Do the lizard lords not eat cat?"

Grisham turned to the beautiful black-furred face he'd loved for five years. "I trust the humans. Besides, many times we've witnessed the dragons hunting in our territory, and never have they attacked a swamp cat."

At the entrance to the cave, he willed himself to saunter in confidently. He even let out a proud roar to announce his presence.

His roar was met with the scraping of claws against stone and the vibrations of heavy footfalls. His family hissed in fear and shrank back, their hackles rising.

And then one of the dragons appeared. The one known as Ruby.

A grinding voice erupted from deep within her chest. "Changeling, you have arrived as promised. That is good. We must now await my brother. He is late—as always."

A thud outside of the cavern announced the arrival of Pyre. His blood-soaked snout poked into the opening. "I heard that, sister. Can I help it if I was hungry?"

Ruby growled in exasperation and turned back to the cats. "You understand that once my brother and I pierce the barrier and you cross over, we have no way to retrieve you. You will be stuck."

Grisham yowled his understanding.

Ruby turned to her brother. "Then let us begin."

<hr>

Arabelle banged her fist against the stone wall.

Another dead end!

She retraced her path, scanning the walls for any side passages she may have missed. But her patience was wearing thin. Worse, her location sense told her that Ryan hadn't moved in many hours.

Maybe that meant he lay down to sleep.

And maybe that meant he was injured.

Or worse.

The tunnel was deathly silent, and Arabelle paid close attention to every sound. She knew that her only tools were her senses, and so when a drop of water plinked in the distance, she froze.

Long moments passed without another sound. Her senses stretched to their limit. And then it came again.

Plink.

She moved in the direction of the sound. Somehow, it had

come from the wall to her right. She moved along it, carefully eyeing the greenish-white moss. And then, with a smile, she clawed the moss aside.

Behind the moss was a narrow passage.

She ripped more of the vegetation aside, and barely held back a laugh when she saw that the hidden tunnel was sloping down.

Hang on, Ryan. I'll be right there.

In a dark stone cavern, a milky-white elf with dark hair read the message written in glowing glyphs above a stone door. But he had a hard time concentrating on the glyphs—for coiled directly in front of the door was a tremendous snake.

He had been told to retrieve the message; no one had bothered to mention the snake.

He moved silently closer, his heart thudding in his chest, so he could make out the thin letters.

One of the snake's fiery eyes opened.

All thought of the message evaporated, and the elf scrambled back. But it was too late.

With the crunching of bones, darkness fell.

Wat had to admit, Eluanethra's library had some excellent reference material on demons. He was paging through the latest tome —one found for him by Bryan Greenwalker himself, despite the elder lore master's obvious illness, when he heard raised voices behind the closed door to the restricted section.

He didn't have to wonder who was arguing; Eglerion and Bryan had both retreated there to further their own research. And though it was surprising to hear Eglerion raise his voice to anyone, it wasn't at all surprising to hear Bryan do the same. The elder master was uncharacteristically emotional for an elf. Eglerion had said that his master had suffered greatly by having been isolated from his people for centuries.

So Wat ignored the muffled voices and re-immersed himself in his book—until a scream sounded.

Wat launched himself from his chair, raced into the restricted room—and stopped short.

Eglerion's lifeless body fell from Bryan Greenwalker's arms, a dagger buried deeply in the younger lore master's chest.

Wat bit back his shock and gathered his power. "Murderer," he snarled. "I'll not let you escape what is your due."

Bryan's eyes darted about rapidly, froth collected at his lips, and he tilted his head back and howled at the ceiling. His stomach began to bulge grotesquely, and he fell to his knees.

The bulge grew, and was accompanied by the sound of tearing flesh, and then… the squall of an infant. And as blood pooled on the floor beneath the elder lore master, something crawled from beneath his robes.

It was indeed an infant, but of no species Wat knew. It blinked its verdant green eyes, bared needle-like fangs, and screeched menacingly at Wat.

With a snarl of disgust, Wat flung a bolt of energy at the monstrosity, filling the air with the smells of burnt hair and flesh.

He had just raised his arm to gather more power, intending to utterly incinerate the remnants of the tiny beast, when a hand landed on his shoulder, and Wat spun about to find Xinthian standing behind him, looking at the scene in horror.

"Eglerion?" he said, then looked down at the dwarf. "Wat, what happened?"

QUEEN OF THE AVUD

A moist cloth dabbed at Ryan's forehead, then a gentle hand dried the dampness with a towel.

"Belle," he whispered without opening his eyes. "I'm so glad you're okay. I think I got really sick when I landed in that muck."

But the voice that responded wasn't Belle's. "You were poisoned, not sick."

Ryan called up his shields and tried to rise into a sitting position, but cracked his head against stone. Thankfully the shield took the majority of the blow. Still, as he fell back down, he couldn't see a thing, except the stars that erupted in his vision.

"You will not come to harm under my care," said the voice. "My lady would never allow it."

Ryan summoned a tiny ball of bluish-white light, illuminating his caretaker—a slender, elf-like creature.

She smiled. "You really *are* a mage."

He looked around. He was lying in a recess dug into the side of a room, covered in only a thin sheet. His clothing was gone. The room was bare but for a single chair, on which the elf sat, a bucket of water, and some towels. Then he saw his right hand; three of the fingers had been splinted.

"Don't you have any healers?" he asked.

The elf shook her head. "None of Lilith's followers have such a gift. Why? Does something else ail you? Did I not remove the mud demons?"

"Mud demons?"

"Yes. Some are very tiny, and you were covered with mud that was teeming with them. They can quickly overcome even the strongest of us without treatment."

"That explains why I felt so sick." Ryan nodded to the elf. "Thank you. I'm deeply in your debt."

The elf blushed and shook her head. "Do not thank me. It was my lady's wish to seek you out. She has great powers of foresight, and knew you would arrive." She looked Ryan in the eyes, unblinking, and Ryan saw that her pupils had expanded. "My lady also determined that I was the least likely to ruin you."

She smiled then, revealing the fangs of a predator, and grasped his uninjured hand.

"My name is Canarane," she continued. "Are you mated to anyone? Forgive my forwardness, but we've had no males amongst us in centuries."

Ryan tried to maintain a look of calm. "It's very nice to meet you, Canarane. I'm sorry, but I'm married."

The elf frowned and leaned in closer. "She must be far away if you are down here with me."

Ryan barely kept his voice steady. "In fact, she is in the

tunnels as well. We got separated. Do you think you could help me find her?"

Canarane stood, her green eyes flashing. Then an eerie smile crossed her lips and those fangs made another appearance. "The tunnels are dangerous. Are you sure she still lives?"

"I'm sure," Ryan lied. "Can you also get me some clothes? I would greatly appreciate it."

"You won't need them. It is warm in my lady's domain within the Underworld."

"Actually, I really do. And did you by chance see a long metal staff? I mustn't lose that."

The elf ducked out of the room and returned with his clothes neatly folded in her arms. carefully placed them next to him. "My lady found your staff interesting. You will have to talk with her about gaining access to it."

"Then I would like to meet her. And I would like your help finding my wife, if you would be so kind."

Another elf walked in, carrying a tray laden with food. But when she looked at Ryan, she froze, her pupils widening just as Canarane's had. Canarane had to pry the tray from the other elf's grip and forcibly escort her from the room.

"Please eat and drink everything," Canarane said as she left. "It will help flush the poisons. I will keep watch on your room and keep out unwanted visitors, and then return when it is time for an audience with my lady."

As soon as Canarane stepped out of the room, Ryan tried to stand—only to be overcome by a wave of dizziness and exhaustion. He quickly lowered himself back onto the bed and looked at the tray Canarane had left behind. It held bread, steamed mushrooms, and two bowls of steaming broth. He popped a mushroom into his mouth. It was mildly spiced and succulent.

From outside his room, he heard what sounded like the hiss of a cat, but he suspected it was one of the strange elves.

I can't trust them.

He prayed that Arabelle was able to find him. He had the feeling these elves would never help; in fact, if they knew where Arabelle was, he suspected they might even try to hurt her.

Anger bubbled within him.

I have to get out of here. I have to find her.

Canarane shook him awake. "The lady says it is time for you to meet. Please hurry."

Ryan was incredibly weary and groggy, and moved sluggishly as he dressed.

Canarane pulled at his arm with a strength that belied her slender limbs. "Come. The lady awaits. You shouldn't delay." She sounded worried. "Please cooperate."

Ryan stood, searching for his staff, only to remember that it was in this "lady's" possession. With his arm outstretched toward the door, he bowed slightly. "Very well. You lead, Miss Canarane."

The elf grabbed at his elbow and escorted him from the room and through a maze of tunnels. They passed several other elves, all female, and every single one of them gave Ryan that same unnerving hungry stare, often accompanied by a fanged smile.

Then their eyes would fall to his chest and their fascination would evaporate.

He looked down at his tunic. Embroidered on the front in gold thread was an image that hadn't been there before. It looked like a tree.

"What is this symbol?" he asked.

"It is the mark of my lady. She has claimed you for herself."

Claimed me?

Ryan's heart skipped a beat. "I don't understand."

"Oh, you will."

Ryan didn't like the sound of that.

Chanting echoed through the hallway, coming from somewhere ahead of them. "We are close," Canarane said. "Those are the prayers of my lady's chosen. They are praying for time with her."

Ryan made a quick prayer of his own.

Seder, please see me through this encounter.

Canarane suddenly hissed and ripped her hand away from his elbow. Blisters rose on her fingertips. And Ryan felt a comforting warmth spread through his body. Did he do that somehow? Or was Seder actually watching over him? Protecting him?

The elf held her injured hand and pointed toward an arch directly ahead. "My lady's chamber is there."

As Ryan advanced, he reinforced his shields, both physical and mental.

The "lady's chamber" was a massive room, hundreds of feet long, with a ceiling at least fifty feet high. The stone walls were polished to a near-mirror-like finish that reflected the purple light of the torches that dotted their length. And the floor was covered with a springy layer of densely packed, faintly bioluminescent moss. At the far end of the room was a large chair—the lady's throne, it would seem—and on the wall behind it was a giant arch made of shining black metal. *Damantite.* But it led nowhere. Just an arch built into a stone wall.

Most notable, however, were the dozens of men prostrating themselves toward the front of the cavern in prayer.

Canarane stepped up beside him, but carefully avoided touching him. She led him down the center of the chamber, past the men, to the empty throne.

"Please do not upset her," she said. "She is all-powerful."

Ryan squeezed more energy into his shields.

A gong sounded, a door opened on the side of the chamber, and the lady stepped in.

She was an elf like the others—pointed ears, dark black hair, delicate build—but something about her indicated that she was also much, much more. Perhaps it was her eyes, which radiated an intense purple light. As she walked toward her throne, Ryan noticed the sway of her hips. She walked with the grace of a dancer and the confidence of a warrior. Her face was perfectly proportioned.

It suddenly dawned on him who she reminded him of.

She looks like a dark-haired Nicnevin!

When the lady reached the throne, she faced Canarane. "Why are you not holding him in case he misbehaves?"

Canarane held up her hand to reveal her new blisters. "My lady, I was—until this happened."

The lady motioned Canarane away and finally faced Ryan directly. A fangless smile crossed her face as she studied him from head to toe. When she stepped closer, he could feel the power emanating from her, and his knees weakened.

This is no normal elf.

She leaned forward and whispered in his ear. "Lower your shields. I mean you no harm."

He actually felt his resolve melting. Perhaps he should drop his shields. But then the lady's lavender eyes darted upward, and she took a step back.

Ryan shook the cobwebs from his head and realized just how close he'd come to giving her unfettered access to his mind.

"Brother," said the lady, still looking upward, "I was but playing with your champion." She let out a lilting laugh. "No need to interfere."

Ryan followed her gaze and saw a white orb of light hovering above and behind him. A voice suddenly echoed in his mind.

Your destination is with the Ta'ah, my chosen champion. Do not allow Lilith to sway you from your cause.

"Seder?"

The lady pouted. "It seems that my brother fancies you, and he forbids my playtime."

"Seder is your *brother*?"

The lady grasped her dress and curtseyed formally. "How rude of me. My name is Lilith, and yes, Seder is best described as my brother. A very *uninteresting* brother, but a brother nevertheless."

She waved at the orb. "You can go now. I pledge to keep him safe and allow him passage toward the destiny you so value."

The orb flickered, and this time the voice spoke aloud, at ear-splitting volume.

"My dearest Lilith, you are missed. I know you are but a shadow of your former self, but I can feel your thoughts. Before I depart, know that the barrier will fail and the one you've been parted from will seek you out."

The orb blinked out of existence, leaving no sign it had ever been there.

For a moment, Lilith stared at the empty spot. Then she turned to Ryan with tears in her eyes and smiled.

"Follow me. I must show you something."

She stepped behind her throne toward the back wall of the chamber. As Ryan followed, he saw his staff leaning against it. Lilith sat cross-legged near the staff and motioned for him to sit as well.

She motioned toward the arch set into the wall. "Do you know what that is?"

"A damantite arch that leads nowhere?"

"No!" Lilith shook her head. "It can lead *anywhere*."

Ryan studied the arch. All along its length were empty holes. No, not holes—sockets. An idea dawned on him.

"It's an unpowered gateway," he said.

Lilith clapped her hands together. "Precisely!"

"But where is it you want to go?" Ryan asked. "I'm sure if you would cooperate with the Ta'ah, they would assist you and your people."

Lilith sighed and shook her head. "I'm afraid I've made several miscalculations when learning to deal with other races in this world. My people are shunned. In fact, they are known as the Avud by some of their former family members."

"Avud?"

"The word means 'lost.' Ha! My people should be known as the *found* instead. They found their destiny with me."

Ryan felt the bile rise in his throat as he glanced back at the mindless men groveling on the other side of the chamber, all waiting for her attention.

"Maybe if you and your minions allowed men to have free will, you wouldn't be shunned."

Lilith shrugged. "I suppose it is possible. But I fear that if men are given freedom, they will become more like Sammael. My other brother. I cannot allow such a thing to happen."

Ryan's mind reeled. *Both Seder and Sammael are her brothers?* And then the full truth finally dawned on him: he was talking with the physical incarnation of a deity.

"You realize that I'm a man?" Ryan said. "I'm completely free, and most people consider me to be honorable and interested in the welfare of others. Would you like my opinion?"

Lilith nodded. "Please."

He leaned in. "You must allow the mortals around you to be themselves. You can punish those who deserve punishment, but you mustn't strip them of their free will. If you do, the resentment it will sow will be profound."

Lilith accepted his comments with an indifferent nod. Then she shot a look at his staff, and it streaked into her hand with a resounding smack.

"This staff has been imbued with an energy that I find quite interesting," she said. "Was it you who did this, or was it naturally occurring?"

"I charged the staff myself."

She ripped the cover off the top, exposing the glowing

diamond. "And this? The glowing crystal has been endowed with a tremendous amount of energy. You again?"

Ryan squirmed under her longing stare. "Yes, I charged the diamond. But this isn't something most mages can do. I seem to be unique in this age."

Lilith's eyes held a faraway look. "No. There is another." She re-covered the diamond and handed him the staff. "You claim to be honorable and interested in the welfare of others. Can I ask of you one favor?"

Ryan's brow furrowed. "What favor?"

Lilith stood, and with only a motion of her hand, she grew from nearly seven feet tall to a perfectly proportioned twenty feet tall in the blink of an eye. Then she ran her hand along the top of the arch.

"Can you imbue this with energy for my people? It must be prepared for the fall of the barrier. We will have need of this creation, and I cannot bear waiting for another such as you to assist."

"What would you do with the arch once it is powered?" Ryan asked.

Lilith frowned as if weighing her words carefully. "My people deserve a new start. I hear the words of my worshippers in other worlds, and to them I will take my people."

Ryan looked at the length of the arch, and shook his head. "I am afraid this is much more than I could handle. Charging this arch would be like… charging hundreds of my staff. I couldn't possibly manage that before the fall of the barrier." He pointed to his staff. "For me to charge just this length of damantite, it takes all of the energy I have contained within me times ten. I must charge it, regenerate my energy reserves, charge it again, and so on. And again, that's just for this one small piece of damantite."

"Energy?" Lilith said. "Is that all you need? What if I provide you with energy? Could you then transfer it into my people's arch?"

Ryan's considered this. *I suppose if she has some charged diamonds I can drain,* maybe *I could do it.*

He nodded. "If you have a way to get me enough energy to do this quickly, I will try to help."

Lilith nodded, and several gongs sounded outside of the chamber. Several elves walked in, then a few more, and within moments, a continuous stream of Lilith's minions poured into the chamber.

Lilith motioned across the expanse of them. "Here is the energy you requested."

Ryan sent invisible ribbons of energy at the arch, making the dense metal glow. Lilith sat cross-legged under the arch and watched his every move.

When beads of perspiration formed on his forehead and he felt his energy levels waning, he nodded to her, and she waved over the first of her minions. The elf glided forward and leaned into him without making physical contact. Ryan felt waves of energy pouring into him, and his outgoing stream sputtered as he felt the shock of unexpected euphoria.

Then the elf groaned and fainted at Ryan's feet.

Lilith waved her finger, and the elf's body slid across the

room to others, who carried her away. Ryan stared after her, his mouth hanging open.

Lilith's laugh echoed through the chamber. "So you are concerned! Don't worry; she has simply exhausted herself. No harm has come to her."

She motioned for him to continue.

Ryan dug into his refreshed reserves and poured more energy into the arch. He was surprised to see that he could already detect hints of a glow emanating from the first ten-foot span of damantite.

Lilith continued to observe, and this time, at the first sign of Ryan's strain, she signaled for the next of her minions to come forward. Again the elf leaned in, pouring whatever innate energy she had into him, and then collapsed.

Lilith brushed her aside with a wave of her powers, and the next elf stood ready, all so Ryan could maintain his incessant stream of power.

I'm going to have a very long day.

Ryan collapsed to the floor; he'd stretched himself beyond anything he'd ever done before. Still, he managed to reinforce his shields as he looked up at Lilith, who hopped up and down in excitement.

Her look was rapturous as she pirouetted beneath the arch, which now glowed with the unimaginable power he'd channeled into it—along with the help of her hundreds of followers. Many of those followers had returned to see the results of his work;

they looked haggard and worn from their draining, but Lilith had spoken true: they were unharmed.

It was then that it dawned on him. *All of these women are wizards. Hundreds of them!*

Lilith danced over to Ryan and crouched in front of him. "Are you sure you cannot stay with us? I know what is in the hearts of men, and I assure you, we could make you happy."

Ryan nodded toward the mindless men who chanted their prayers to Lilith. "Like that?"

Lilith shook her head. "Absolutely not." She pointed from one end of the arch to the other. "I wouldn't have believed any man would have voluntarily served for the greater good, but you've proven that it's possible." She closed her eyes, and the drone of chanting stopped. "I've done it."

Ryan looked toward the back of the chamber. The mindless men who'd prostrated themselves on the floor were now sitting up, blinking as if they'd just awakened from a dream. Lilith's minions swooped in and helped them to their feet.

"*What* have you done?" Ryan asked.

Lilith did a bad job of holding back a smile. "I've given them back their destinies. They are free."

As the chambers cleared, Lilith leaned in and repeated her question. "So... will you stay with us?"

"I cannot stay. My destiny lies elsewhere. And even if that were not the case, I'm already married."

Lilith closed her eyes, and for the first time, Ryan detected the threads of magic coming from her. Long moments passed as he waited uncomfortably in the silent presence of the supernatural creature. Finally he spoke.

"When the barrier goes down, I'm sure there will be others who will be more than interested in *mingling* with your people. Assuming that you choose not to enslave the men again. I can even help with introductions if you like."

Lilith's eyes popped open, and she gave him a lopsided smile.

"Such a service, though appreciated, will be unnecessary. Ryan Riverton, we will not see each other again in this world. However, I will repay your kindness with a kindness."

She snapped her fingers, and a parchment appeared in her hand. She gave it to him.

It was a detailed map of the tunnels.

"One of Seder's minions is in danger," she said. "I've marked her location on the map. You are her objective, but I'm afraid Seder's weapon is about to run into trouble."

Seder's weapon. Arabelle!

"The X on the map signifies our current location," Lilith continued, "and the image of the dagger is Seder's weapon. The weapon needs its champion. Go now, or I will try to convince you to stay with my people again."

Ryan raced from the chamber into the twisting tunnels of the Underworld.

THE WANDERING DWARVES

For hours and hours Arabelle moved through the maze of tunnels, descending ever lower into the darkness. She found new strength within herself when she again detected motion from Ryan's location. And then, finally, she saw evidence of life.

She had just entered some kind of central cavern—dozens of tunnels connected to it—when she spied a lithe dark-haired creature skulking at the far end, a large bag slung over its shoulder.

If I didn't know better, I'd say that was an elf.

The elf stepped into a tunnel that was closest to where Arabelle sensed Ryan. A coincidence? Probably, but regardless, Arabelle was determined to follow. Blending into the shadows, she cut across the cavern after the elf.

But as she followed the elf around a corner into a connecting tunnel, she froze. This tunnel was blocked by a large gate, guarded by a half dozen others of its kind.

The guards were elves as well—but like the first, they weren't the elves Arabelle had come to know. These had nearly white skin and very dark hair, nearly the opposite coloration of the Eluanethran elves. And all of the guards were women.

A sickly-looking elf came up the tunnel from the other side, swaying on her feet. She spoke to one of the guards, and Arabelle caught snatches of her words.

"…replacement… more needed…"

The guard handed her spear to the new elf, and Arabelle saw her leaning heavily on the spear just to remain upright.

The poor thing.

Arabelle controlled her natural instincts to help someone who was suffering. She couldn't risk exposing herself to these unknown creatures. And she certainly couldn't proceed down that tunnel; she would have to take an alternate path.

Following her direction sense, she took another adjoining tunnel that at least went in the right general direction. Covering the floor here were thousands of flexible spiked protrusions, all tilted in the direction she was going. Arabelle paused, wondering if she should backtrack—but just then the floor suddenly tilted. Her feet slipped out from underneath her, and she slid on the slick floor into the darkness ahead.

With his shields wrapping the light around him, Ryan ran through the halls of Lilith's domain, occasionally bumping against a confused passerby. With the slightest exertion, he blasted apart the gate that blocked his way, and as a handful of elves screamed in protest, he raced out of the purple-lit tunnel and into the darkness of the Underworld.

At an intersection of several tunnels, Ryan summoned a pin-sized light that hovered over the map. He turned right and sprinted down a tunnel that led to the dagger symbol. His boots crunched on a slime-covered floor covered with flexible thorn-like projections.

Suddenly, the entire tunnel began vibrating, stretching, undulating. His eyes widened as he saw the thorns rippling. They weren't only on the floor, but on the walls and ceiling.

Am I in—

A shriek of pain sounded somewhere ahead.

Arabelle!

Pulling energy from the power he'd imbued in the diamond, he made his shields crackle with invisible energy as he ran forward.

He entered a chamber, perhaps twenty feet from one end to the other, where the undulating walls were pockmarked with fist-sized holes, some of which had spiked vines that reached into the room. Before him, Arabelle lay on the ground, slashing at the vines, some of which were wrapping around her legs.

Ryan sent a white-hot bolt of energy at the bases of the vines grabbing Arabelle. And as the energy struck its target, the entire chamber shifted.

Arabelle ripped the lifeless vines from her legs and scrambled to her feet. She looked up at Ryan and smiled despite the gashes on her face.

A series of heavy contacts rocked Ryan's shields; a dozen

vines had launched themselves at him. He sent a shock wave of fire in all directions, turning the vines into ashes.

Then he ran to Arabelle's side. "Stay close," he said, expanding his shield around her. "We've got to climb out of this thing."

They backed up the way Ryan had come, but now the thorns had grown rigid, their points sharp and oozing some yellow substance, likely poison or something worse.

"What *is* this place?" Arabelle said.

"I'm not sure, but I think we've found ourselves inside some kind of giant creature."

Ryan sent a wave of shimmering energy splashing across the thorns—but instead of harming them, it merely made them billow with green smoke.

"Ryan! That's what got me! The smoke will make you dizzy."

Remembering the gaseous attack he faced when seeking Nicnevin, Ryan tightened the mesh of his shield, making it small enough that nothing could pass.

"What did you do? I can't hear anything," Arabelle said.

"To block the gas, I needed to block everything coming through the shield. Sound included."

"What about our air supply?"

Ryan groaned. "Yeah. Try not to breathe too much."

Green smoke surrounded the shield, which also continued to be struck by pummeling vines. Ryan raised his staff, building up power for another strike at the thorns, when Arabelle yelled, "Look!"

One wall bulged, and a half dozen knife blades burst through.

Then dozens more blades appeared, and together they shredded the wall, sending ichor spewing everywhere.

A furry head peered into the chamber, silently roared, and disappeared again.

Arabelle pulled at Ryan. "That was a swamp cat!"

More vines blasted against the shield, and Ryan engulfed them in a wave of fire. Then he took Arabelle's hand, sprinted to the hole in the wall and plunged head-first through it.

Arabelle landed heavily on him and they both scrambled to their feet. Sure enough, an entire pack of black swamp cats was waiting for them outside.

Ryan removed the light-wrapping attribute from his shield and loosened its mesh. The unnatural silence was instantly replaced by the stench of the monstrosity's blood and a nervous growl from one of the swamp cats.

The largest of the swamp cats wore a glittering damantite ring on a chain around its neck. It yowled, a white light shimmered around him, and with a popping sound, the black cat was replaced by a bearded—and naked—dwarf.

"Grisham!" Arabelle cried.

"One moment," Grisham said, turning away. The dwarf went to another cat, who had a pack strapped to it, and pulled some clothes from the pack.

As Grisham dressed, Ryan tilted Arabelle's chin toward him and gave her a kiss. "I'm very glad to see you again. I'm also very happy to see our rescuer, even if he is naked."

Grisham stomped his feet into a pair of boots. "What in the world possessed the two of you to visit a cave kraken?"

Ryan shrugged. "I was just following her."

Arabelle rolled her eyes. "*I* was trying to find *him*, and I didn't trust asking those strange dark-haired elves I saw."

"Good choice," said both Grisham and Ryan.

Grisham lifted the chain from his neck and handed it to Ryan. "Your mother asked that I give this to you so you can tell her all is well."

Ryan grinned, recognizing the dragon insignia on the ring.

"Well then," said Grisham, "I suggest we continue on to my home. We aren't far. Only about two hours' walk."

He motioned for everyone to follow as he walked down the tunnel. One of the cats made a guttural vocalization. Grisham responded with a variety of growls and chirps, then turned to the Rivertons.

"I told them not to lick their paws. We can wash them off when we get to Eer Ha'ta'ah."

"Eer Ha'ta'ah?" said Arabelle.

Grisham smiled widely. "In literal translation, it means 'the wanderers' town.' But to me, it means *home*." He waved them forward. "Come on. If we arrive on time, my mother might still have her famous mushroom stew on the fire."

In Eer Ha'ta'ah, they were greeted by four white-robed guards with power emanating from them—wizards. The guards studied the visitors, but seemed to pay particular attention to Ryan. He wondered: could they detect he was a wizard as well? Perhaps, given the staff, it was obvious.

After a short discussion with Grisham, one guard escorted

them to a waiting area while another went to summon the clan elders. As they walked the halls, Ryan felt a warm sensation flowing through him. It wasn't just the temperature, which was comfortable, but a general feeling of order. As if all things were as they should be.

"Please wait here," the guard said at the entrance to the waiting room. "There is mead, tea, water, and mushrooms to snack on."

It wasn't just a waiting room for visitors; it was more like a library. Many of the white-robed Ta'ah were present, sitting at long tables, reading scrolls, and sipping something out of large mugs. Ryan settled in a padded chair, and Arabelle crouched in front of him and removed the splint from his swollen fingers.

When she uncovered the purple and yellow that had spread all across his hand, she grimaced. "Oh, my poor baby. At least it was wrapped well." She looked up at him. "Who did this? I know you can't even wrap a present, much less a broken hand."

"After I got very ill, I collapsed in one of the tunnels. Some of Lilith's people found me and took care of—"

"No!" A gray-haired dwarf yelled as he jumped from his chair, spilling his mead. He ran into the hallway and screamed for assistance.

"What's going on?" Ryan asked.

A matronly dwarf entered the room, following the pointing finger of the dwarf who'd shouted. She walked right up to Ryan.

"Are you the one who was captured by those dark-haired elf demons?"

"Well… I wasn't exactly 'captured.'"

"Lift your shirt. I must examine you."

Ryan lifted his swollen hand and protested. "My wife was about to take care of my broken hand."

"Bah! Who cares about a broken bone or two. You only have days before I can reverse the effects of those demons. Do you want to die in a psychotic rage and have your insides blow out your chest?"

The dwarf lifted Ryan's tunic and placed her ear against his bare stomach. "I don't hear anything. But that doesn't eliminate the possibility of an implantation."

She then placed her cold hands on his abdomen. Waves of white energy shimmered where she touched him, and he felt her warming energy course throughout his body. The bruises on his arms faded, and he felt a crack as a bone in his hand popped into place. His entire body started to glow, and he sweated freely. Three more pops sounded from his fingers, then the dwarf pulled away and faced Arabelle.

"Please remove his boots and socks. While I'm here, I might as well make sure everything is as it should be."

Arabelle did as she was asked, and the dwarf knelt to examine his feet. Ryan noticed that the glow was uneven on his right leg—the one that had bothered him since the cave-in.

The dwarf ran her hand down to his ankle, and Ryan felt an intense heat wherever she touched. Soon the glow evened out, the dwarf withdrew her hands, and the glow disappeared altogether.

She nodded to the dwarf who'd called her. Others had gathered around as well. "He's lucky," she said. "I detected nothing more than a few broken bones and partially torn ligaments." She waved a thick index finger at Ryan. "But you should know better than to allow yourself amongst those demons. Don't you know what they're capable of?"

An older dwarf stepped forward, his hair white, and his beard braided into dozens of white ropes. "Madam Shimmerstone, is he truly all right?"

She bowed respectfully. "He is fully healed now, Elder Firewielder. He had only a few broken bones, remnants of a skin rash, a meniscal tear, a torn—"

The elder held up his hand. "Yes, you are to be commended for a job well done. Thank you, Madam Shimmerstone. You are excused."

The dwarf healer nodded and departed.

Elder Firewielder looked like he was about to speak to Ryan, then stopped short when he noticed Grisham.

"Grisham Farwalker? Is that you?"

Grisham blinked, and a moment passed before he responded. "Yes, it is I, Elder Firewielder." A wan smile crossed his lips. "It has been a long time since anyone spoke my family name."

The elder greeted him with a warm hug and a kiss on each cheek. "My boy, I remember when you and your father departed like it was yesterday." His eyes glistened with tears. "I'm so glad that you have returned. You are the only one who ever has."

Grisham nodded solemnly. "Much has been sacrificed so that we can fulfill our part in the prophecies. Father died soon after our arrival across the barrier."

A tear dripped into the elder's snow-white beard. "I was afraid of that as the years passed. I couldn't know, of course. My son and only grandson departed years before the council sent you and your father. We have not heard from them either."

Several white-robed dwarves entered the chamber, glowing with magical strength. The elder turned to them.

"Ah, good, the entire council. Has Lydia Farwalker been summoned? She could use the good news."

One of the other elders nodded. "Yes, I expect her any moment."

Grisham cleared his throat and put a hand on Ryan's shoulder. "I would like to introduce—"

"Seder's champion," Elder Firewielder said, interrupting. "I recognize the human of the prophecies. Though the prophecies made no mention of this host of furry creatures." He gestured to the swamp cats lounging about. "Nor do I recognize you, young woman," he said to Arabelle.

Grisham cleared his throat again. "This lady is a princess of the Imazighen, married to Seder's champion, and also by marriage a princess of the Thariginian throne."

At the mention of the Thariginian name, several of the elders whispered to each other.

"One more thing," Grisham said. "Nearly eight years ago, my father and I were tasked with bringing news of a treaty between the humans and our people. I met with King Throll Lancaster, blood heir of the Thariginian line. He is the ruler of Trimoria and rules from a council of equals between all of the races. This includes our cousins, the dwarves from the iron mountains, the elves from their forested home of Eluanethra, the humans of the Trimorian plains, and the Imazighen, the true wandering nation of merchants. King Lancaster accepts an offer of alliance, and is willing to meet with our elders as equals."

Elder Firewielder ran his fingers through his beard, then

bowed deeply to Grisham. "For a job excellently done, and surpassing all expectations for one of his youth, I, Flint Firewielder, hereby nominate Grisham Farwalker our people's permanent ambassador to King Throll Lancaster's court."

Several of the white-haired dwarves bellowed, "Agreed!"

Flint Firewielder smacked his palms together. "It is done." He winked at Grisham. "Your father would certainly be at least as proud of you as I am, young Ta'ah."

The elder then turned to Ryan. "Well… we have a lot of things to talk about. But first let's get you comfortable and fed. We can talk while you eat."

As they started toward the exit, a female dwarf burst into the entryway, her eyes darting about, then finally stopping on Grisham.

"Grisham!" she cried.

Grisham ran to her with open arms. "Mama!"

"Told you she'd have stew on the fire!" Grisham said with a laugh.

Grisham's mother ladled another helping into Ryan's bowl. As he chewed on one of the meaty mushrooms, the elder spoke.

"Long before our people settled in the Underworld, the dark-haired elves had found solace in the isolation of the tunnels. The elves on your side of the barrier called them the Avud. The lost ones. We know very little of them other than that their leader has an affinity for the females of any race, and the males are mostly treated like slaves."

Ryan nodded, having seen as much. "What about the fear your healer had about my being among them? She said something about my chest being blown apart."

"Well… over the centuries, some of our people have been caught by those she-demons. They have the ability to overcome the will of others, effectively making mindless slaves of those they capture. Their slaves are unable to… ahem… *perform* sufficiently to help the she-demons reproduce. So instead, the she-demon magically implants an embryo within the midsection of their victim. The slave carries the infant until it bursts from their chest cavity, killing the slave, and adding one more she-demon to the population."

Ryan imagined a scene from a movie he'd seen in another world… another lifetime. "If they're mindless slaves, how did you even learn about such things?"

Lydia Farwalker sat down next to her son. "My cousin Sarnoff Firehammer was captured and escaped. It seems the one who possessed him was killed—hopefully in a gruesome manner—which aided his ability to resist. He described the state they put him in as 'being a puppet with someone else pulling the strings.' He remembered everything that happened around him, he just couldn't do anything more than the rudimentary motions he was commanded to do.

"And then one day, it was like the puppet strings were sliced. He raced from their halls and nearly collapsed when he arrived at Eer Ha'ta'ah. But it was too late for him. The creature inside him was ready to burst."

Grisham took his mother's hand and held it tightly.

Ryan decided it was best to change the subject. He turned

back to the elder. "Why are the Ta'ah living in this dangerous underground world? Why not live with the mountain dwarves?"

"Ahh, that is the root of all things now, isn't it? It's a simple tale. Do you know what the word 'Ta'ah' means in the old language?"

Ryan glanced at Grisham. "Uhh… I know Grisham told me, but I can't remember."

"It means to wander. For ages uncounted, those gifted with magic abilities were thought odd by our cousins. Over the centuries, the clans eventually formed into two separate societies. One with magic skills, the other without. Nearly a thousand years ago, Seder provided visions to the magic-wielding clans, and we departed from the iron mountains."

"Is that when you left for the Underworld?" Ryan asked.

"No, but it wasn't long after we departed that Seder instructed our council to seek an object hidden deep within the ground. We spent many years wandering the great expanse of the lands, seeking this object with our magic. Thus did our brethren know us as the Ta'ah, for we continually uprooted ourselves."

The elder's eyes sparkled with excitement. "This object foretold your arrival." He closed his eyes and recited.

"The time will come when the object I give to you must be wielded by my champion. You will know that the time has come when all else is lost, the people aboveground are no more, and life has spontaneously come into the smallest of the crystals.

"When the Dedicate crystals begin to glow, you will know that the threads of destiny have been knotted. Only then will the crystal that represents the power of the people of Trimoria be ready for use.

"Five hundred years ago, with the raising of the great barrier, the first part of the prophecy came to pass. We knew that none worth speaking of remained alive above our location. Certainly not on this side of the barrier."

He raised his hand and pointed to a golden ring on his finger, a diamond embedded in it. "See the glow of the diamond? This ring has been worn by every council elder since our discovery of Seder's orb. It was only fifteen years ago that this diamond began to glow. We knew it was time."

Ryan picked up his staff and pointed to his own glowing diamond. "Is the orb you're talking about larger than this?"

The elder laughed and shook his head. "How old do you think I am? I've never seen the giant crystal in real life. You must enter the vault and extract it from its place of safekeeping if you want to see it."

Ryan nodded. "When do we start?"

The elder retrieved a parchment from his tunic and handed it to Ryan. "There is a complication. A very dangerous beast has placed itself directly in front of the vault's entrance."

Ryan unrolled the parchment to reveal a bloodstained drawing of an armored snake, with some runic symbols below it. He pointed to the characters, and the elder leaned over the parchment and nodded.

"A creature long thought extinct. It is a demon lord that our records refer to as a titan of the rock."

ENTERING THE VAULT

Nyra sat cross-legged in the First Protector's cave, her eyes closed and her head bowed. Outside the cave, Ohaobbok and some of the dwarves were arguing over her intrusion into the sacred chamber.

"Dwarf-friend, I dinna realize she be goin' in da cave. What if she be hurtin' the First Protector?"

Ohaobbok growled with frustration. "Listen, Deneb. She's not here to harm anyone. Besides, she's been in there a week and no harm has come. Didn't she prove her intentions when she healed your sore back? She feels strongly that she wants to watch over the First Protector. Who are we to deny her?"

"Just cuz she fixed me back, dat don't mean she's not gonna hurt our charge."

Nyra allowed the arguing to fade from her mind as she concentrated on the shimmering man lying before her. From the moment she first entered the cave, she'd sensed feelings of suffering from within his shield. She'd been applying healing energy at regular intervals, and was pleased that the turmoil subsided for at least a few hours each time.

The problem was, the healing was only temporary. And despite her efforts, the First Protector was getting worse.

A crackling sounded within the cave, and Nyra opened her eyes. She didn't see anything out of the ordinary—other than the faces of Ohaobbok and Deneb, who were peeking in, curious.

The crackle came again, followed by a voice that was so loud, Nyra had to cover her ears.

"It is nearly time."

It was then that she noticed the glowing white orb hovering high over the dais.

"Paladin of Seder, you must gather your resources and meet with my champion. Much depends on the threads of your destiny remaining knotted as they are. Go. There is nothing anyone can do for the one I've protected for many of your centuries. His service is nearly complete."

The white orb vanished, leaving a deathly silence behind.

Nyra met Ohaobbok's shocked eyes.

"Nyra," he said, "I must return to Castle Riverton right away."

She reached out to the stone platform and touched it one last time, tears falling from her cheeks. "Goodbye, holy one. You are in my prayers." Then she turned to Ohaobbok. "I'm going with you."

"Stay behind me and keep your shields up," Ryan said to the dozen Ta'ah wizards who insisted on accompanying him. "If what I've been told about this demon is true, you'll need them."

From the strength of the buzzing that sounded as they erected their shields, he could tell that any one of them would have qualified as one of the strongest war wizards in Trimoria's army.

We desperately need this kind of power.

He wished he had Arabelle with him as well, but the elders had decided that since she wasn't a war wizard, it was too unsafe. No amount of arguing from her and Ryan could convince them that she was more capable in a fight than anyone.

In the deep darkness ahead, two flaming orbs appeared, accompanied by a menacing hiss. A few threads of power launched from Ryan's company, and several brilliant white orbs appeared ahead, flooding the giant cavern with light.

The illustrations and descriptions didn't do justice to the beast that lay before them.

The snake was huge—its maw was large enough to swallow a cow without much effort—and its eyes were pure unblinking flame. Its scales scraping against the stone as it slithered in its coil.

And then the snake breathed out a cloud of steam. It sizzled on the rock, and one of the dwarves warned, "Be wary, Archmage. There's acid in that breath."

Great.

Ryan yelled across the cavern. "You have no business here! This is the territory of the Ta'ah. Leave or we will use force."

The snake's body twisted and turned, and Ryan felt it

exerting a mental pressure at his shield. The shield flexed, but held.

"Careful," he yelled over his shoulder. "I feel it trying to invade my thoughts."

"Aye, it's a demon lord," someone replied. "What did you expect?"

Ryan gathered power at his fingertips until they vibrated, waiting for release. With a single thought, Ryan launched a white-hot spear of energy at the snake. It splashed against the beast's armored head, and the creature reared its head up before smashing through the floor of the cavern and disappearing through the hole.

Ryan blinked with surprise and walked forward slowly.

It can't be that easy.

It wasn't. With a loud crack, he found himself flying upward as the creature burst forth through the floor directly beneath him and launched him into the air. He slammed into the roof of the cavern, nearly shattering his shields, then fell back onto the snake before tumbling off and hitting a solid section of floor.

The Ta'ah sent a dozen beams of shimmering fire at the snake, but it seemed not to care. It struck at the nearest of them with its fangs while whipping the rest of its body through their ranks. One of the orbs of light winked out, and the others quivered.

Ryan stood shakily. Channeling the power from his diamond —many weeks' worth of energy—he sent a massive torrent of energy at the head of the demon. The snake must have heard the sizzling stream of power coming, as it turned toward Ryan—and the energy went directly into its open maw.

Its head was instantly engulfed in white fire, and its shrill shriek of pain shook the cavern. For a long moment its body writhed from side to side, slamming the walls, and then it slumped against the floor and lay still, the scent of its scorched flesh filling the air.

The Ta'ah groaned and picked themselves up from the floor. Ryan ran to help a dwarf that had been injured, handing him a healing draught.

"That wasn't pleasant," the dwarf grumbled.

Just as the words left his mouth, the body of the snake shivered, and the armored eyelids flicked open.

"It's still alive!" Ryan yelled as he strengthened his shields and pulled even deeper from his reserves.

As the snake lifted its head, some of its scales flaked off, showing raw skin underneath. It turned to face Ryan, its fiery eyes glaring with a palpable malevolence. In fact, the look in those eyes was familiar. It was the same look Dominic had had when he was possessed by—

Sammael!

Ryan reached again into his staff's power reserves, draining them so deeply that the diamond dimmed. He wrapped himself in energy, prepared to put an end to this battle once and for all.

But before he could deal the critical blow, the fire in the monster's eyes faded, and the creature shuddered, as if it was fighting an unseen battle. It blinked—once, twice—and where the fiery eyes had been, there were now only the cold, black eyes of a snake.

Its forked tongue flicked out, sampling the air, and then it smashed its head through the floor of the cavern and disappeared through the hole.

For a long moment, nobody moved.

Only then did Ryan feel his exhaustion—waves of it that threatened to overwhelmed him. He looked at the device his father had given him, the "watch" strapped to his wrist. The diamond wasn't lit. The emerald wasn't lit. And the ruby's glow was dim.

No wonder he was exhausted. If he expended much more magical energy, he would pass out.

One of the dwarves was peering down into the crack through which the snake had disappeared. "Nothing down there. Anyone sense that creature nearby?"

A red-bearded dwarf scratched at his backside. "My rear end itches when it's nearby, and it's still itching. I'd be cautious."

One of the Ta'ah laughed. "Chromium, your butt has itched you for the last thirty years."

Ryan smiled despite his weariness.

"All right," said a voice behind them. "Enough merriment."

Ryan turned to see Elder Firewielder entering the cavern with several of the other elders. At that same moment, he felt a vibration in his ring.

Arabelle. I'm here too. Watching from the shadows. The elder doesn't know. I snuck out.

Ryan scanned the cavern, but if it weren't for Arabelle's magical energy signature, he would never have spotted her. She was too good at blending in, especially with so many shadows.

Elder Firewielder beckoned for Ryan to follow him toward the large stone door that the snake had been guarding. "It's time for you to become acquainted with Seder's vault," he said. He pointed at the glowing letters above the door. "That message is said to be written for the one who was meant to open the vault. I'm sure Grisham told you the tale. It was nearly a thousand years ago when twin orbs of power were discovered. We, the Ta'ah, were charged with the safekeeping of Seder's orb of power—and the prophecy spoke of you, the blue-eyed Archmage who arrived from above."

The elder placed his hand softly on the stone door. A shimmering sheet of energy hovered before it and extended over the inscription.

"As you can see, both the inscription and doorway are protected. Nothing was ever written about the protections, or exactly where the inscription came from, but..." he smiled at Ryan, "there are other ways to pass information down through the generations. When I sat on my great-grandfather's lap as a child, he told a tale that he'd learned from his own great-grandfather. That tale told of a human king who was a wizard. Under Seder's instruction, we allowed this great king and wizard of the humans to enter the vault. And according to the tale, this human, under Seder's guidance, was responsible for this inscription, and for the protection we now face."

Human wizard and king? Ryan wondered. *Could that be a reference to the First Protector?*

"So, Archmage," said Elder Firewielder, as the others gathered around. "Now you have come, as the prophecies have foretold. And now the inscription will tell you how to open the vault."

Ryan looked up at the inscription. It was definitely written with him in mind—but he had no idea what it had to do with opening the vault. He decided to start by reading it aloud:

"In the wake of demons and strife

"There exists a newfound life

"He comes from a place beyond the stars

"Yet knows the meaning of the planet Mars.

Ryan frowned. "The first two lines are nonsense. They could refer to anyone born during the time when the demons were in Trimoria. The third line, though… that one refers to me."

"Are you really from the stars?" one of the elders asked.

Ryan shrugged. "In a way. My family was brought here from… well, from very far away."

"It was Seder's will," Elder Firewielder said with a solemn nod.

Ryan contemplated the last line, it sounded ridiculous… even infantile. "I do know about the planet Mars. It's the fourth planet from the sun. But… I'm not sure what it means about 'meaning.' It's just a planet." He wracked his brain, trying to recall everything he knew about the planet, and thought out loud. "It's red. It's cold. It's named after a Roman god. I think he was the god of war."

A crack sounded from the door, and Ryan took a step back. The shimmering protection vanished, and the door cracked open a few inches.

"He did it!" said one of the dwarves.

"I did?" Ryan stared. "Did I unlock it by just saying the right words?"

"It must have been so," said Elder Firewielder.

It took several of the dwarves to open the door all the way. It was huge, and its unlubricated hinges protested loudly. Then they all stepped back, clearly intending for Ryan to enter first.

Ryan stepped cautiously through the door, sending forth an orb of light. The passage led to a much smaller cavern, empty and featureless save for another door on the opposite side. This door, too, had an inscription above it, and it was these shimmering runes that illuminated the space.

Elder Firewielder stepped up beside him. "Before we continue," he said softly, "perhaps you should ask your wife to join us instead of hiding in the shadows. If she insists on disobeying me, I'd rather she be near us."

"How did you know she was there?"

The elder put his hands on his hips. "She hides well, but her aura follows her even into the darkest places."

Before Ryan could send her a message, Arabelle materialized out of the shadows. "I'm sorry to disobey you, Elder Firewielder, but I vowed to Ryan's parents that I would keep my eyes on their son."

The elder shook his head and muttered something about strong-willed women.

Arabelle accompanied Ryan as he walked across the dusty cavern. Except it wasn't a cavern at all. Much like the living quarters of the Ta'ah, this place had clearly been carved deliberately out of the bedrock.

They stopped before the far door, and this time Ryan found he had trouble translating the runes, so Arabelle recited them aloud:

"I start my life on the vine
"For I am used when you dine.

"When eaten, my bearing is sweet

"Yet I'm only afforded, by the elite."

She turned to Ryan. "Do you think it's referring to wine?"

With a pop, the door opened, and this time it swung wide.

Elder Firewielder stared open-mouthed at Arabelle. "What is wine? Is this an Aboveworlder thing?"

As Arabelle explained what grapes and wine were to the dwarves, Ryan walked through the open door into a third chamber. This one was exactly like the one before it, except half as large. And once again, it led to another door—and another glowing riddle.

Ryan couldn't even recognize the runes on this one, so he waited for the others. Arabelle again translated and read aloud.

"Destruction is what I know

"In my wake, the metal flows

"I am welcome in your room

"Even though I'd seal your tomb."

Ryan puzzled over the message. "This reminds me of my father's smithy. Heat?" He paused, hoping the door would open, but nothing happened.

One of the dwarves chimed in. "Hammer?"

Ryan shook his head and smiled. "Fire?"

The door opened without a sound.

"I'd not welcome fire racing through my room," Arabelle said.

"You've forgotten about the fireplace you enjoy exercising in front of."

The next room was tiny—barely more than a closet. And the

door on the opposite wall was tiny as well, at only about three feet tall.

Ryan crouched before it, feeling a touch claustrophobic as a few of the others entered the confined space. Elder Firewielder read the inscription this time.

"In the darkest caverns I roam

"An evil spirit seeking a home

"Nothing lasts, for when we meet

"I disappear until you retreat."

Ryan wracked his mind, trying to solve the riddle. A few of the others muttered among themselves, apparently doing the same.

Then Elder Firewielder's wrinkled face brightened with a smile. "Loneliness!"

With a loud pop, the door vanished.

One of the Ta'ah smacked his palms together. "Of course. Our history books call these tunnels the Lonely Caverns."

But though the door was gone, the way forward was not yet clear. Crossing the doorway was a translucent barrier that hissed and sparkled with so much energy that Ryan felt the vibrations in his chest.

He knelt and looked through. On the other side was a cubical recess no larger than a crate. And at its center, resting atop a small black pedestal, lay a glowing orb of the purest white.

Seder's orb.

There were several smaller pedestals surrounded this central pedestal, each of them holding the same miniature statue—a statue that Ryan had seen many times before. It was the statue from the fountains, showing the First Protector with his arm raised, a gem clutched in his hand.

As Ryan looked on, a pulse of energy streamed from one of the statues' gems to the orb on the central pedestal.

Dad would love to study this.

The elder came up behind him. "This is the true test," he said. "Are you ready?"

Ryan thought of the people of Trimoria, the faces of his family, and of course, Arabelle.

My life, and everything I care about, depends on my fulfilling this responsibility.

He faced the elder. "I'm ready."

The elder nodded. "Before we begin, I would ask all of the Ta'ah to retreat to the first chamber. The energy in this barrier is intense, and if it explodes, none in a twenty-foot radius will survive. In fact, it might cause a collapse of the entire cavern."

Ryan agreed. The threads of magic shuddered with over-whelming amounts of energy, all of which could unravel explo-sively if triggered.

As the last of the Ta'ah departed, the elder turned back to Ryan. "This barrier is keyed to one specific individual. Let us hope that individual is you."

Arabelle placed her hand on Ryan's shoulder. "We're in this together."

Ryan's heartbeat thudded in his ears as he prayed aloud. "If there was ever a time for faith, this might be it. Seder, I hope your faith in me is deserved. Guide my hands."

He reached out and touched the barrier. Although it hissed and sizzled loudly, it provided no resistance. He pushed his hand forward, ignoring the barrier's angry protest, reached into the tiny space on the other side, and laid his fingers on the glowing white orb.

As he lifted it off its pedestal, he realized he was holding his breath. He tried to breathe evenly as he pulled it back through the barrier, which snarled and snapped.

And then the orb was through, and the stone door reappeared over the barrier.

"You did it!" Arabelle shrieked.

Ryan felt the orb's energy racing throughout his body. With just the slightest touch of his powers, he tapped at the energy— and gasped. Thousands of individual streams of power rushed through him, and to his surprise, those streams weren't coming from Seder. They belonged to other wizards, most of them dead for centuries, all of whom had poured a small part of their own energy into this orb. A blur of faces flicked past his mind's eye, moving through time, starting with the oldest wizards and moving up toward the present. He saw people he knew—RAM students, Arabelle, his father, even himself.

"How—how can that be…" And suddenly it all made sense. Those miniature statues feeding the orb…

"The fountains," he whispered in awe. "The First Protector was a genius."

Arabelle shook her head. "I don't understand."

He turned to her. "The First Protector's fountains—they're linked to the miniature statues that surrounded this orb. Every time we dipped our hands in one of those fountains, we not only received Seder's blessing, we also infused just a bit of our own power into this orb. That's why it's so powerful. Nobody's been near this thing in centuries, yet we've been feeding it all along."

Ryan raised his other hand, letting the sleeve fall back so he could see his energy gauge. Not only were the ruby and emerald full once more, but the diamond, which had never previously shown any signs of life, shone like a beacon.

With Arabelle and Elder Firewielder, they walked back out to rejoin the rest of the Ta'ah. Each time they entered a new chamber, the door behind them automatically creaked shut and the protective barriers came back to life. But when they reached the first antechamber where the Ta'ah awaited, a glowing white orb appeared near the ceiling, and a voice nearly blasted Ryan's eardrums.

"And thus the cycle begins, my children. Those who have called themselves Ta'ah, it is now time for you to join your brothers who think you lost."

The elder nodded solemnly.

But the disembodied voice was not done.

In the center of Eluanethra, a brilliant white orb materialized with a loud crackle. Many of the elven rangers retrieved their bows; others covered their ears.

Xinthian came racing through the crowd of onlookers. "It is a vision of Seder! It is a vision of Seder!"

And then the voice spoke.

"People of Trimoria. It is now time for you to lay your trust in those whom the prophecy foretold. For those brothers you

have come to know are now unmistakably the Lords of Prophecy. Trust in them, for your truest hope in the dark days to come will lie with them."

"The Riverton brothers," Xinthian whispered under his breath

He turned and yelled to those gathered about. "Gather the guard! We converge on Castle Riverton. The time has finally come, and we will not fail Seder's cause!"

Barnaby pointed at the talking orb that had appeared above them. "Rockfists, did you hear dat? Dat be our calling. It's off to Castle Riverton where we be gatherin' our forces."

His clan-mates cheered.

Barnaby turned to a dwarf who was celebrating by kicking a log into kindling. "Oy, Stompinguts. Race over to da Redbeards, da Hammerthrowers, da Alebellys, and all da rest. Tell 'em what we just be seein'. It's a call to arms for da dwarf nation, I'm tellin' ya."

Just at that moment, a mountain pony raced toward them, a large-bellied dwarf sitting astride it, yelling, "To arms! Seder be callin' and da Alebellys be answerin'!"

Barnaby yelled back, "Aye, dat we be doin'! Our people be gatherin' at Castle Riverton!"

He then turned to Stompinguts. "Well, no need to visit the Alebellys, and maybe the others neither, but spread the word just in case. We leave at dawn!"

In the royal dining hall, the same message had been heard.

"Throll, my friend," said Jared. "Whatever Ryan did across the mist barrier, it was what the spirit expected. It's begun."

The king stood, drew his glowing damantite sword, and raised it in the air. "To the last man!"

Castien stepped forward and touched the tip of his raised sword to the king's. "To the last sword!"

Jared stood and summoned a spear of fire to touch the two joined swords. "To the last thread of wizards' power!"

THE BARRIER FALLS

The population surrounding Castle Riverton swelled in the days after the shocking appearance of Seder's message. Aaron stood on one of the castle's balconies and looked out over a giant army of dwarves that was gathering in the courtyard. The rowdy race of soldiers made for a superb addition to the armies. Behind them was an equally large contingent of elves, and the human element of the army was the largest of them all.

Oda's voice carried up to him. "Stand ye back! Yer Rockfists, not Rockferbrains. Can't ye hear what Lord Riverton said? Clear da courtyard!"

Castien shook his head at Aaron's side. "I'm glad you made him a general. An excellent choice. Look at how he holds command over, what is that, nearly five thousand soldiers? I didn't think there were that many dwarves living in those mountains."

"It was your idea," Aaron said.

"I can like my own idea."

Aaron smiled at the elven sword master. "Was that humor? From an elf? You must be in a good mood."

"Oh, if what I've heard is true, you'll have a very happy elf. I might even smile."

At the center of the courtyard, the air shimmered with invisible energy. The din of the crowd hushed, and the people pushed and scattered out of the way. Then, with a pop, a gateway appeared, and Ryan and Arabelle stepped through. Ryan was surrounded by a pulsing glow of white that had never been there before.

"Wow. He's… really glowing," Aaron said. "What's that all about?"

"Look at his pouch," said Castien. "You can see the glow even through the leather."

Next through the gate were several white-bearded dwarves wearing brilliant white robes. And then, right behind them, came an entire parade of dwarves, stepping two at a time through the portal. Far more than just one clan. And after the dwarves came wagons of supplies. Dozens of them. It took nearly thirty minutes for the entire procession of dwarves and wagons to make it through.

This is a migration, Aaron thought.

Aaron's father stepped forward and raised his hand, sending thousands of sparks high into the air, drawing everyone's attention.

"I would like to formally welcome the Ta'ah nation to Castle Riverton," he said. He motioned toward Throll. "Allow me to introduce all of you to Throll Lancaster, King of Trimoria."

Throll stepped forward, and the entire Ta'ah nation bowed.

Throll returned the gesture. "People of the Ta'ah nation, I wish we were meeting in better times, but I welcome you to my lands." He held up a piece of rolled parchment. "As your ambassador requested, and as I have agreed, I've added a line making the Ta'ah nation an equal member of my ruling council."

One of the white-haired dwarves stepped forward and accepted the parchment from the king. He unrolled the parchment and put his mark to it.

Throll then raised his sword. "I will abide by this treaty, and will enforce it as written law so that all who've pledged to me will abide."

Castien also drew his sword, and his voice boomed from the balcony. "As a representative of the elven nation, I too pledge to uphold this treaty. Welcome, Ta'ah nation. May we one day break bread in the peaceful meadows of Eluanethra."

Arabelle spoke from the front of the crowd, and she held her glowing dagger high. "Representing the Imazighen, I pledge that the Ta'ah will always be welcome in our tents, and we'll abide by the terms of this treaty."

A red-bearded dwarf broke from the crowd at the edge of the courtyard, approached the white-haired dwarf and they stared at each other for a few full seconds before they roughly embraced and exchanged kisses on both cheeks. The younger dwarf stood back and raised his voice so all nearby could hear. "I, Silas Redbeard, welcome our much-missed cousins back from their wandering." Silas panned his gaze across the sea of white-robed Ta'ah and said, "Cousins, it has been too long that we've been apart, and know that the clans of the Iron Hills welcome you in our hearts and homes. And of course, we'll all abide by the terms of this treaty."

The white-haired dwarf who'd signed the treaty raised his right hand. "We are humbled by your warm welcome. Thank you all."

The dwarf bowed to Throll again, keeping his hand up. "I know that dark days are looming, and my people pledge themselves to the cause. We will use our skills to the best of our abilities, and to the last of us, we will fight to wipe the demons from Trimoria." From his upraised hand, the dwarf sent a scintillating ball of energy up to explode high above the crowd.

"He's a wizard," Aaron exclaimed. "Imagine that!"

As one, the Ta'ah yelled, "Death to the demons!"

And then hundreds of crackling balls of energy launched up from hundreds of the Ta'ah, exploding in a chorus of deafening reports overhead.

Aaron felt his mouth drop open. *They're* all *wizards.*

"Well," said Castien. "We've been saying we don't have enough war wizards to support the army." He smiled broadly. "Problem solved."

Ryan found Wat in the castle library, surrounded by books and parchments. "Wat..." he said, putting a comforting hand on the dwarf's shoulder. "I heard about what happened in Eluanethra. I'm sorry."

"If you don't mind, I'd rather not talk about it."

"I understand. But will you follow me? There's someone you should meet."

Wat sighed. "I don't think I should. I need to finish my research before we don't have the time for it anymore."

Ryan pulled the book out of Wat's hand. "Pretend the king ordered you to do it. Because if necessary, I'll make sure he does."

Wat grumbled and sighed again, but grudgingly got to his feet.

Moments later, the two of them were entering the dining hall, where many of the Ta'ah had gathered for a meal.

"Ryan, you know I'm not one for socializing," Wat whispered. "The dwarves don't care for those without a clan."

"Just come with me."

Ryan walked right up to the leader of the Ta'ah. "Elder Firewielder," he said. "I would like to introduce you to a friend of mine. His name is Wat."

The elder set down his food and looked at Wat—and took a sharp breath. "What trick is this?" he said angrily.

Ryan turned to Wat. "Tell the elder your clan name."

Wat looked awkwardly at his feet, then took a deep breath and lifted his chin. "Crazybeard."

Ryan frowned. "Wat, tell the elder your *real* clan name."

Red-faced, Wat stared at his feet once more. "I have no clan. I'm an orphan."

The elder stood and glared at Ryan. "I would expect better than such nonsense from you. Whatever foolishness you've put this young one up to, I'll find out." He put his hands on Wat's shoulders, closed his eyes… and then stepped back quickly, his hands shaking.

He looked at Ryan. "Why is this dwarf's memory blocked?"

"Blocked?" said Wat. "My memory's not blocked. I remember everything."

Elder Firewielder frowned. "Then why can't you remember anything from before the age of ten?"

Wat shrugged. "It's not unusual to not remember anything from early childhood."

Ryan shook his head. "Maybe very early, like two or three. But I remember lots of stuff from when I was younger than ten."

The elder yelled across the dining hall. "Madam Shimmerstone!"

A matronly dwarf stood and hurried over.

"Madam Shimmerstone, someone has placed a block on this young dwarf's memory. We don't know why. Can you see what you can do?"

"Certainly, Elder Firewielder."

Madam Shimmerstone placed her hands on the side of Wat's head, sending ribbons of energy floating about. As Ryan watched, she carefully teased a thread loose from a knot Ryan had never even detected. It was painstaking work; the process continued for nearly half an hour before she'd unraveled the knot completely.

And when the last thread came free, Wat gasped.

He turned toward Elder Firewielder, tears pouring down his cheeks. "Saba?"

The elder opened his arms, and Wat raced into them. Madam Shimmerstone began dabbing tears from her eyes.

"Saba?" Ryan asked her.

She smiled. "It means grandfather."

Ryan lay in bed with Arabelle's head on his chest.

"I'm so happy for Wat," she said. "But why was his memory blocked?"

"It turns out that Wat and his father were the first emissaries from the Ta'ah," Ryan explained. "Azazel's minions had them on the run soon after their arrival on this side of the barrier. Evidently, Azazel knew only about Wat's father, yet Wat refused to let his father make a last stand alone against Azazel. So to protect his son, Wat's father put a block on his son's memory. Not only that, he blocked many of Wat's latent abilities. As a result, Wat's first memory is of being an orphan in Cammoria."

Arabelle frowned. "That story is very similar to Grisham's. Though Grisham always knew who he was."

Ryan nodded.

"Did you know Ohaobbok brought that woman to the castle?" Arabelle asked.

"You mean Nyra? Yeah, I know."

"I don't trust her."

Ryan sighed. "Ohaobbok is watching over her, and we're all guarded day and night."

"She's Kirag's sister, Ryan. Weren't we just talking about how unpleasant the minions of Azazel can be? Kirag nearly killed me, and his assassins were trying to kill your family when you first arrived. How can I ever trust someone he called sister?"

"What do you suggest I do? Forbid Ohaobbok from seeing her? She's done nothing wrong."

"Just promise me that you won't let her accompany you and Ohaobbok when you depart for the Abyss."

Ryan closed his eyes. "Belle…"

"I'm serious. I don't trust that woman."

"Fine. I had no intention of anyone accompanying us anyway. Now, can we please get some sleep?"

Arabelle kissed him lightly on his cheek. "Thank you."

The dwarf standing guard outside the First Protector's cave heard a crackling sound coming from inside. Immediately he grabbed his spear and raced in to investigate.

A gray-haired woman stood next to the First Protector's dais.

"How in da name of all dat be holy did ye git in here widout me seein' ya?"

The woman gave him a toothless smile and cackled. "It is time, my young dwarf. Now shush, let me concentrate."

With a wave of her hand, the dwarf staggered back and the spear fell from his nerveless hands. He was frozen, unable to move a muscle.

The ancient woman then waved her hand over the shimmering cocoon around the First Protector.

It flickered… and disappeared.

The body of the First Protector twitched—then gasped. He inhaled deeply, for the first time in centuries.

"Rise, my embattled minion," said the woman. "It is time."

The ancient legend sat up with a groan. He put his hand to his head and cringed. "Seder, I cannot bear it any longer."

The woman placed her gnarled hands on the First Protector's shoulders, sending a white glow spreading through his body.

A look of relief crossed his glowing face. "Thank you. But—I've already done all I can…"

The crone bent her head down until their foreheads touched. "You have done all that could be asked of you. The rest is for others to do…"

Then in an instant the woman was gone, the First Protector was gone, and even the dais was gone. Whatever force had held the dwarf in place released him, and he fell to his knees.

A tremendous rumbling shook the ground beneath him, as if thunder rolled right through the rock. The dwarf scrambled out of the cave to warn the others—then stopped short at the sight that met him to the south.

The mist barrier was gone, its last fragments fluttering away in the wind.

As Ryan sat in the dining hall with Wat, Wat's mother, and Wat's grandfather, he could think only one thing.

Wat has a family.

"I'd always wondered why Wat had such unusual magical skill for a dwarf," Ryan said. "He's not only the only dwarf war wizard we have, he's one of the most powerful of *all* our war wizards."

Wat blushed, and his mother patted his cheek. "Our clan is quite strong with the offensive magic," she said.

"Perhaps I should have suspected something like this," Ryan said. "Wat always talked so different from the other dwarves. But I just thought it was from having grown up in a human orphanage."

"Bah," said Wat's mother. "He didn't grow up in an orphanage. He grew up with us, learning to speak proper. Not like some of the mountain folk I've been hearing."

Wat looked uncomfortable. "Mother, they're nice enough, even when they didn't think I had a clan."

"You have a clan now," Ryan said. "And a truly impressive one. To think, my orphan dwarf friend is now a member of a respectable clan, a war wizard, and a dragon rider."

Wat looked up. "A dragon rider?"

Ryan pulled a wooden box from his pocket. "Oh, didn't I mention that? Maybe your mother or grandfather would like to do the honors." He opened the box to reveal a dragon rider's rank pin.

Wat's mother took the pin and attached it to her son's collar. She wiped a tear from her cheek. "Your father would be so proud."

Elder Firewielder nodded. "He always was. As am I."

At that moment a tremendous rumble shook the castle. Ryan and Wat both leapt to their feet and ran up to the observation balcony on the south side of the castle. Ryan's father and Arabelle arrived at almost the same moment.

As they all looked at the incredible sight to the south, Arabelle said, "It's finally happened."

Ryan nodded silently.

Dad tapped a message on the ring that all the Trimorian officers shared, and Ryan felt it come through on his own.

Lord Riverton. The barrier is no more. It is time.

Then Dad put his hand on Ryan's shoulder. "Before you go, I promised that you'd give your mother and sister a hug."

Ryan nodded. "I'll do that."

Dad suddenly enveloped Ryan in his arms and squeezed him to his chest. "I can only begin to imagine what you're about to face. Just remember your training, and don't take any unnecessary risks. I love you, my boy."

As his father let go and rubbed at his eyes, Ryan felt more messages coming through on his ring. Castien was sending orders to organize the troops.

Ryan wrapped Arabelle in a warm embrace, and she squeezed her slender arms around him. "I can feel it, Belle. It's time. Time to confront my destiny."

***

As Anarane walked down the stairs into the underground darkness of the storeroom, she summoned a ball of light, sending the darkness fleeing from all corners of the dusty chamber. She waved her hand over the damantite chest, and using a thread of energy, released the inner locking mechanism.

The chest sprang open, revealing her treasure trove of flowing blue-white diamonds. She added one more to the collection, then knelt in silent prayer.

As she cleared her mind, she felt a vibration run through the rock beneath her. She spun around, energy crackling at her fingertips, scanning for an intruder. But the moment passed, and the vibrations subsided.

Anarane relaxed. She had just placed her hand on the lid of the chest to close it when a voice she hadn't heard in over five hundred years spoke within her mind.

"It is time."

"My lady? Is it really you?"

"Yes, and I have truly missed your company. I hope that you have carried out the tasks I set forth for you."

Anarane laughed. "Oh yes, my lady. I look forward to the day when I can show you the result of my hard work."

"Today is that day. The barrier is no more. Come to me, first amongst my disciples. We have much to do."

The connection evaporated.

Anarane sent a silent message to her enforcers, then pulled a drape aside, revealing a damantite arch directly behind the chest. She kissed her fingers, touched the arch, and smiled.

"I'll be back soon. It is time."

She climbed up the stairs and walked to the front of the temple. Nearly a hundred ogres had already gathered in front of it, all under her control. She waited a few minutes as more of the brutes raced into the cavern, out of breath. Only when the stragglers diminished to a trickle did she raise her hand and speak.

"Boys, I've called you here to tell you that I have one more assignment for you, and then you are free to follow your own wishes. It's time to seek revenge for injustices wrought against us. I want you to go now, and seek our revenge. Do this for me."

She sent them mental images of their quarry, and then gave

one final command: "Go!"

The ogres scrambled toward the exit, shoving each other in a race to fulfill their mistress's wishes.

Anarane whistled a lively tune as she walked back to the storeroom, planning her next move.

"What do you mean they're gone?" Sammael bellowed. "Where did they go?"

Malphas kneeled before his lord. "My lord, our scouts have walked all through the Ta'ah domain and found not a single one of them. I myself joined the search."

The temperature rose to broiling as Sammael growled, his scales glowing red with his anger. Malphas suffered in silence even as lesser demons raced away. Those who were too slow exploded in greasy puffs of smoke and sizzling gobbets of roasting flesh.

"They were there only a few days ago when they wrested control of the rock titan from me," Sammael said. "They couldn't have simply vanished."

"My lord, there is one other thing. I found one chamber that had been purposefully collapsed. I could smell explosives within the rubble. It was done very recently."

Sammael's color shifted from red to black, and the temperature plummeted. Malphas felt the ground rumble beneath him, and the demon lord held up his hand for quiet.

After a long moment passed, Sammael laughed. "It is time, Malphas. Gather the armies. We move now."

IT IS TIME

"One must not pretend that evil doesn't exist, for that is exactly what evil wants. Seek it out. Confront it. Destroy it. For if ignored, the evil festers and grows strong."

—Old elven proverb

Dust rose in the south, and Aaron knew it was time. It had been only an hour since the world cracked and the barrier fell, but already he was dressed in full battle armor, riding through his thousands of troops to observe the organized chaos of the preparations. He was pleased to see that not only had the Ta'ah split up their war wizards throughout the army as requested, but some of them were imbuing the common armor with the strengthening glow of their energy.

A wagon rolled past him, loaded with hundreds of leather flasks, and Aaron sent his horse trotting after it. "Hey! The men don't need any ale! Save it for after the battle."

The young dwarf leading the wagon pulled on the reins. "S-sir. It isn't ale. It's healing elixir, sir My mam is Healer Shimmerstone, head of our healers' guild. She thought it would be good for the troops."

Aaron looked over the hundreds of flasks. "Tell your mam that I can't thank her enough for what her healers' guild has done." He pointed to Castien in the distance. "Do you see that elf with the leather armor yelling at the officers? Please deliver this wagon to him and tell him that Aaron Riverton sent you to him."

The young dwarf flicked at the reins. "Yes, sir."

As the wagon rolled off, Aaron tapped a message into his ring.

Aaron. I have a wagon heading toward the officers' tent. It's full of healing potions. I trust you'll immediately distribute them.

Castien. Bless you. That was something I worried about.

Aaron. Make sure you thank the young dwarf who is delivering it, for it was his mother's idea. I'm really starting to love the Ta'ah.

Oda. Aye. Dwarf kin are the best kin to have.

As Aaron continued across the field, inspecting his battalions, a shriek erupted overhead, and Aaron looked up to see Pyre swooping across the army. The men raised their weapons and cheered.

At the far end of the field, he found the boisterous dwarves chanted gustily as they prepared for battle.

"Polish the armor, hone the blade.
Dance to the music, while it's played.
What's that we see, across the dell?
The barrier shimmered, and it fell.
Ready for battle, we'll make our day.
With our allies, they'll join the fray."

The nearby human and elven troops cheered.

"Look out boys, what's that I hear?
The crack of doom, enemies draw near.
Within their midst, an evil's come.
Pray for us and raise your spear!"

The dwarves banged their shields together before launching into another battle hymn.

Aaron shook his head with amazement. *Only a few years ago, there was nothing, and now this.*

He felt a vibration on the ring only he and his brother shared.

I'm signaling the dragons. Ohaobbok and I are off. I wish you the best of luck. We'll all need it.

A spark of fire launched into the air from a nearby hill.

Beneath that spark stood Ryan and Ohaobbok. Pyre raced toward them, and Ruby shrieked as she came in from the opposite direction.

Aaron kicked at his horse and tapped a quick message.

Wait! I'll see you off.

"Are you sure this is where you want to go?" Ruby asked as she held the portal open. Its shimmering image was of a bridge of fire leading into the blackness of the Abyss.

Ryan smiled. "It's what must be done, so that nobody else will ever have to do it."

Pyre blew a plume of fire into the air. "I'll go there with you. I can help."

"No, Pyre," said Aaron. "You're needed here. We'll soon have the enemy's army at our doorstep. Besides, Ryan's destination is underground, confined. Here, you'll have plenty of room to fly and cause havoc."

As Aaron clasped hands with his brother, the dwarves' battle chant sounded from the mustering fields. The two brothers turned toward the gathered troops, all of whom were now facing the hill.

"They're saluting you," Ohaobbok said. "They know what's about to happen."

The next lines of the dwarves' song were new:

"In this fight, we'll have no fear.

Look...

The Lords of Prophecy, they're here."

Aaron smiled at his brother. "Come back, or I'll have to go to the Abyss and get you."

Ryan laughed. "I'll do what I can." He tilted his head toward the mustering grounds. "Don't take any unnecessary risks out there. Remember, you're strong, but not invincible."

The brothers embraced, and then Ryan turned and stepped into the portal. Ohaobbok followed immediately after.

Battle horns sounded across the fields. Ruby knew what the battle horns meant. The enemy was approaching.

Aaron jumped on his horse and raced back to the mustering fields, leaving the two dragons alone.

Just as Ruby and Pyre let the gate evaporate, a shadowy figure raced through it.

"What was that?" Ruby growled.

Pyre flapped his wings, blasting fire from his nostrils. "I don't know, and I don't care. It's time to have some fun!"

Anarane clapped her hands. After she'd plugged a dozen of the charged diamonds into the tiny arch she'd constructed, the whole thing came to life—and now within the arch's span, the inner chamber of Lilith's temple shimmered into view.

Anarane pushed the giant chest through the gate, then

stepped in after it. She felt a moment of disorientation, then found herself in a chamber lit with purple light.

Her lady was smiling at her.

"Welcome back, first among my disciples. I am very pleased to see you."

With a wave of her hand, Lilith ripped the lid off the chest, spilling hundreds of diamonds across the floor. She laughed at the sight. "You have done well. Now it is time to finish what was started over five hundred years ago." She pointed to the giant arch built into the wall of the temple. "Place the diamonds in their sockets."

It took the help of many of Lilith's minions, but in time every socket in the giant arch was filled with a charged diamond. Lilith beamed with excitement as she looked upon the glowing arch.

"*Come,*" she said in Anarane's mind. "*It is time, my people. Our destiny awaits.*"

She must have sent her voice to all her minions, for within moments, Lilith's followers filled the temple.

Lilith waved her arms, and the gate hummed to life.

"Trust in me, for we go to a better place."

A shimmering image of a forest appeared beneath the giant arch, containing animals Anarane had never seen before. Her sisters marveled at its beauty and murmured about the joy of starting over. Then a man raced through the forest with a bow, chasing after an injured animal.

Lilith held up her arms. "Follow me."

And she stepped through the gateway.

Anarane thought of the possibilities.

A simple life, without prejudice or hatred.

She felt her belly and smiled.

Having a child the natural way.

She laughed as she followed the crowd into the gate, forever leaving Trimoria behind.

As Aaron approached the officers' tent, Castien came to meet him.

"We've seen the first sure signs of an army on the move," the sword master said. He handed Aaron a long tube made of shiny metal, with several dials and knobs on its side. "Look through this. It's a far-seeing device. Miriam, your sister-in-law's hand-maiden, helped our glaziers make it."

Aaron put one end to his eye and laughed. "It's a telescope. Brilliant!" he swung the telescope toward the south and saw the plumes of dust rising in the distance. "They're on the way."

Labri's voice broke in. "Would you like me to slow them down?"

"What did you have in mind?" Aaron asked.

Labri rubbed her chin, then smiled. "How about some torrential rains?"

"Mud?" Castien nodded in approval. "That would buy us several hours."

"Then I'll see what I can do." Labri closed her eyes, and after a moment dark clouds gathered to the south. Then lightning flashed across the skies. Aaron scanned the area with the telescope, and spied two funnel clouds.

"I'm glad we have you on our side," he said.

Several more moments passed before Labri opened her eyes. "I can do no more for now."

Aaron laughed as he continued to study the scene through the telescope. "You've done more than enough. In fact, I think those demons are going to be swimming into battle."

"Are you sure you know the way?" Ryan asked Ohaobbok.

"I do. One of the gifts I received on the mountaintop from the other paladins was their knowledge of the depths of the world. At some point, many years ago, some of them must have traveled throughout the abyss, seeking to destroy all that was evil in the world."

Ryan looked over the terrain with disgust. Hundreds if not thousands of demon bodies lay ripped open, with blood everywhere. "What killed all these things?"

Ohaobbok kicked a demon out of the way as he trudged through the cavern. "This is a nursery, where they breed new demons. So I'd guess these are the ones who were deemed too weak to be useful. The larger demons probably gorged on their still-beating hearts to strengthen themselves for the upcoming battle."

Ryan struggled through a swarm of gnats and nearly slipped in a pool of gore. "This is awful."

They moved past the nursery and into a massive cavern. The smell of brimstone hit Ryan's nostrils and a blast of hot wind blew into his face. The ground sloped upward, and as they ascended, Ohaobbok drew his glowing white sword.

And then they stopped. Directly ahead of them was a long stone bridge crossing a giant fissure in the bedrock. As they approached the bridge, the heat rose dramatically. From somewhere below there came a faint reddish glow. A roar sounded from the far end of the bridge.

"Brace yourself," Ohaobbok said. "It's time."

***

"Dad," Aaron said, "be careful up there."

His father smiled as he mounted Pyre's saddle. "This is just like flying a sortie in my pilot days. But you be careful too. Watch your men's six, and they'll watch yours."

"My men's six?"

Dad laughed. "Your six means your back. You know… a reference to a clock."

"Oh! Gotcha. Who's watching *your* six?"

Dad patted Pyre's neck. "Pyre, you've got your eyes open at all times, right? I'll watch your back if you keep mine safe."

The dragon laughed. "Just hang on, and we'll be all right."

"Let's go then. Giddy up!"

With a few flaps of his powerful wings, Pyre launched himself in the air.

As they rose into the sky, Dad yelled, "Hi ho, Pyre, away!"

Sloane touched Aaron's elbow. "Don't worry, he's taking this very seriously. He's just being amusing for your sake."

"I know, but I still worry. He's my father." He turned to her. "How are your preparations coming?"

"Well, I have nearly a hundred swamp cats and three hundred

wolves ready to go. With animals, there's not a lot to prepare. I also have two very nervous war wizards assigned to me, as well as two of the Ta'ah healers."

"Did you get some of the healing potions?"

"Oh, yes. Castien brought me a small cartload of them."

"Good." Aaron raised the telescope to his eye and looked into the distance. The rains had slowed the enemy, but it hadn't stopped them. They would be here in an hour, no more.

He tapped a message into his ring.

The enemy approaches.

THE FINAL BATTLE

Aaron aimed the telescope at the cloud of dust rising from the plain no more than a mile away.

"Do you see them yet?" Castien asked.

Aaron knew the keen-eyed elf could see that far without the aid of a telescope. "Yes," he said. "Kind of hard to miss them."

The demons leading the assault were enormous. Fifteen-foot-tall monstrosities obliterated any trees that stood in their path without even slowing.

Aaron used his ring to send a warning to the army's officers.

Aaron. Brace yourselves. Fifteen-foot-tall demons are at the vanguard of the first wave. Remember your training. The giants fall when you take their legs out from under them.

The armies were in position, and Aaron's heart raced as he waited for the action to begin.

"Patience, young general," Castien advised. "As a leader, you must allow yourself time to observe. While in the midst of the fight, you cannot have the perspective needed to guide others."

"I know, Castien. But isn't that why you'll be here? I can't just stand back and let others fight and die for me."

Castien sighed. "Very well. Go. Just don't kill them all before I get to bleed some—"

But Aaron was already racing down the hill toward the advancing horde.

Screams erupted as the front lines of the two armies smashed into each other. Aaron raced into the fray, aiming for the largest of the demons, which had just used a ten-foot-long mace to send a half dozen of his men flying.

"Watch the mace!" someone yelled. "The head of that thing must weigh a couple hundred pounds!"

When the demon swung again, Aaron dove at the brute's legs, his sword humming as it sliced the air. When his blade made contact he felt the impact all the way up his arm and heard the shattering of the scales on the demon's ankle. Then he rolled out of the way. The beast yelled, his right leg twisting sideways, and fell. Then the twang of bowstrings preceded the thudding of arrows into the demon's flesh.

A dwarf with spiked boots leaped atop the demon and jumped up and down, driving his spikes deep into the beast's neck and chest. Some of the other dwarves yelled in delight at their blood-spattered companion. "Stompinguts! Dere's more to stomp, leave dat one be!"

A shadow crossed over the battlefield as Ruby pierced the smoke hovering over the armies. Aaron ducked as a dual blast of fire decimated a group of demons trying to flank the main battle.

"Dere goes Wat Firewielder! He spews fire just like the dragon, he does!"

The smoke of wizard fire obscured much of the field of battle. Aaron tapped out a message to his generals. *Aaron. Can Labri summon a wind to blow some of this smoke away? I can't see anything.*

Within seconds, Aaron felt a breeze blow across his neck.

Castien. She is summoning it now.

Aaron raised his shield as a four-foot demon attacked. He swung his sword, beheaded the foolish demon, then searched for other demon captains to slay.

Ryan looked down into the chasm. Molten rock glowed red far below, and the waves of heat rising up nearly suffocated him. He tightened his shields, his power surging as he held Seder's orb.

Ahead of him, Ohaobbok raced across the bridge, his great stride carrying him quickly toward the beast who ran at him from the far side. Ryan's eyes widened as he realized that the opposing demon was significantly larger than the ogre, and the demon's sword was completely engulfed in flames.

Ryan gathered his power, preparing to attack the beast from afar, when he felt a chill run through his body, and the cavern's light dimmed. He shivered despite the heat, and even as he heard the clash of Ohaobbok meeting his demonic opponent, his attention was drawn to the other side of the chasm, where a large shadow was coalescing into the shape of a man.

The shadow man was massive—maybe three times Ohaobbok's height. Fire licked around him, and as he advanced toward the bridge, he left behind flaming footprints. But it wasn't his size, or his fire, or his darkness that made him so terrifying. It was the pure evil that emanated from him.

Ryan took a deep breath, stood tall, and raised Seder's orb.

Aaron grimaced as one of the Ta'ah healers sent a magic weave into him. "You're lucky, young general. I found no poison in the—"

Aaron dove out of the way, pulling the healer with him, as a giant winged creature crashed to the ground, crushing demon and Trimorian alike. Pyre's victory shriek cut through the din of the battle. He clenched in his claws the struggling wings of yet another of the huge flying demons.

Battle horns blew, and Aaron jumped to his feet. A phalanx of giant demons approached, larger than any he'd yet fought. He gripped his sword and advanced.

The sizzling bolts of a dozen war wizards streaked toward this latest assault. A maelstrom of exploding flame incinerated the first two rows of the demons, and their burning scales were peppered with hundreds of arrows from the archers.

Then a swarm of flapping creatures swooped in, releasing hundreds of spears into Aaron's troops. Aaron raised his shield just in time, and his ears filled with the screams of others who weren't as lucky.

He sent a message to his officers. *Aaron. Shields. Our troops are being skewered by flying spears.*

His dad replied. *Jared. I'm going to scan the battlefield for the supply of spears. They must be getting them from somewhere.*

Ohaobbok's arm vibrated painfully as his glowing white blade met the demon's flaming one. "In the name of Seder," he growled, "I compel you to submit."

The horned demon swung viciously at Ohaobbok, who leapt nimbly out of the way. "I'll never submit to a minion of my master's weaker brother."

Ohaobbok slashed at the demon, nearly knocking him off the bridge. "Your lack of knowledge is your weakness."

"Your faith in lesser gods is yours."

Despite Ohaobbok's tremendous size and strength, he strained with effort every time his sword connected with the demon's, and he'd occasionally have to take a step back. The demon was trying to smash through his defenses, and Ohaobbok was barely parrying the assault.

Then the demon bellowed and seemed to grow in power. His fiery blade darted toward Ohaobbok, striking with more speed and force than before. Ohaobbok parried and took a step back. And then another.

Yet even as he struggled with his opponent, it was impossible not to notice the massive power being exchanged across the expanse of the chasm. Tremendous spears of energy flew back and forth between Ryan and the giant shadowy figure.

Ohaobbok forced himself to focus.

One thing at a time.

He had begun this encounter with the swordplay he'd learned from Castien and Throll. But as he faced this paragon of evil, he felt the memories and training from another age bubbling to the surface.

The demon bellowed again and attacked with renewed strength and speed. The flames on his sword seemed to lengthen with every stroke. Yet, Ohaobbok found that his own slashes were crisper, his reactions happened without the slightest delay, and despite the furious assault from the demon, he now held his ground. He growled with determination, "Not another step back."

And suddenly he understood what was happening. In the graveyard, he'd received the blessings of ancient warriors. This was what their blessings entailed. He had their knowledge, their power, their skill. He'd become a creature of pure instinct and muscle memory.

He'd become Seder's paladin.

Ohaobbok smiled.

He stepped forward, slashing, parrying. Then with a perfectly timed move and a screech of scraping metal, he scooped the flaming sword with his blade, ripping it from the demon's outstretched claws. As the sword flew from the demon's grip, it evaporated.

Ohaobbok placed the tip of his own gleaming sword against the demon's neck.

"Alive or dead, you will submit."

The demon laughed, and its flaming sword reappeared in its hand. Ohaobbok barely danced backward, and the tip of the fiery sword scraped across his chest plate.

"You'll pay for that, soldier of Seder. Only I, Malphas, hold the seed of Sammael's power within me. You are no match."

"I am Seder's paladin," the ogre said quietly. "My name is Ohaobbok."

Then he lunged at the demon with impossible quickness—and all Malphas could do was grunt as he looked down to see the ogre's glowing white sword protruding from his chest.

Ohaobbok then withdrew the sword, and with all his might he swung it again, this time slicing through the demon's midsection and spilling his entrails.

Malphas's mouth opened soundlessly. He blinked, and fell to his knees. A blackened orb dropped from the wound and landed in the guts and gore. Then the demon general's lifeless body collapsed sideways, fell off the bridge, and plunged toward the hot molten rock below.

Ohaobbok stepped back from the orb. Palpable waves of malice pulsed from it. With righteous anger, he swung the sword of his ancestors at this symbol of all that was evil.

The world seemed to slow as his sword made contact. Cracks spread through the orb, and the air filled with the sound of shattering glass.

And then a tremendous release of energy sent the paladin flying backward in a storm of crystal shards, and the world dimmed to black.

Castien panned the telescope across the battlefield to find a swarm of dozens of giant demons cutting a path through the Trimorian troops. He sent a message to his officers there, but received no response.

His next message was for Aaron.

Castien. Aaron, we've lost contact with the officers on our southeast flank. They need reinforcements.

The reply came immediately. *Aaron. I'm on the southern front. Moving my troops to intercept.*

The shadowy figure across the chasm shrugged off Ryan's attack and sent a flaming lance of power streaking back at him. Ryan pushed energy into his shields and braced himself. As the lance connected and exploded, his ears rang, and when the smoke cleared, the rock around him was glowing red with heat.

How can he be so strong?

As he prepared another attack, another sight caught his attention. Ohaobbok's demon opponent went tumbling off the side of the bridge into the chasm below.

Ryan could have cried out with joy. His friend had done it! But he barely had a moment to celebrate before Ohaobbok let out a mighty bellow and swung his sword at something else on the bridge. A brilliant explosion sent a concussive blast against his shields, and Ohaobbok spun through the air and plummeted into the depths below.

"Ohaobbok!"

Across the chasm, the shadowy man laughed and stepped onto the stone bridge.

His throat tight with emotion, Ryan pulled more energy from Seder's orb than he'd ever attempted to hold before. The crackling of his power nearly deafened him, but in his mind's eye all he could see was the image of his friend falling to his death.

With a growl from the depths of his soul, he sent all of his energy at the figure who dared laugh at his loss.

This time, the shadowy man staggered back and howled with anger. It was the first time Ryan had actually seemed to cause him any serious reaction. The shadow shimmered, then boiled away, leaving behind a creature that was just as tall, just as powerful, but now in physical form.

He was over sixty feet tall. His skin was covered in black scales the size of shields. His eyes were pure fire. He had a forked tail that flicked powerfully back and forth.

He was the very picture of a demon.

And Ryan knew his name.

"Sammael."

As the demon heaved a wagon-sized boulder at him, Ryan pulled again at the orb and sent a spear of energy in return. Both attacks were easily dodged, but before Ryan could pull energy for another spear, two more boulders were already hurtling toward him.

And then the real attack came. Ryan felt claws in his head, trying to wrest control of his mind.

With a snarl, he strengthened his shields not only on his body but on his mind. The boulders bounced off his weave, and the pressure of the claws inside his head eased and then vanished.

But Ryan was weakening. He didn't need a device on his wrist to tell him that. He could feel it. If he was going to defeat this demon, he would have to do it now.

He dropped his shields. Now was not the time for self-protection. He would need all the energy he could muster.

He pulled deeply from the orb, without pause and without restraint. And as the power of thousands of wizards surged through him, he launched a continuous stream of white-hot power at Sammael. The explosive sound of the impact was nothing compared to Sammael's howl.

The demon lord sent multiple flaming lances of power at Ryan. Though he had no shields, his stream of energy was so strong that it evaporated the magical projectiles before they could reach him.

Sweat poured from Ryan's every pore. He could barely breathe from the heat, and he felt blisters raise on his exposed skin. Still he pushed harder, sending everything he had into the torrent of energy, pulling the orb's energy through him and striking straight at the heart of the demon.

Sammael staggered under the righteous fury of Trimoria's wizards, past and present. His scales cracked under the pressure of Ryan's attack. He threw another burning lance of flame, but it didn't even cross the chasm.

And then Ryan felt a change. It was small, but noticeable. The power of Seder's orb was waning. It wasn't unlimited.

Ryan pushed the last of his own reserves into the stream and silently prayed.

I hope it's enough.

Aaron slashed at a demon's ankle while Oda crushed the brute's knee with his mace. As the demon fell to its side, it was swarmed by the dwarves in Oda's command.

"Good job, troops, there's a lot more where that came from!" Aaron yelled.

Oda laughed. "You weaken der ankles, and I'll take der knees out. We be da perfect team."

"Stand back!" Aaron yelled just as a wedge of Ta'ah war wizards sent a searing blast of energy across the field, incinerating hundreds of lesser demons. The resulting hot blast of wind carried the smell of burnt flesh.

"Dem little demons aren't much of a challenge. It be the big ones you've gots to worry 'bout."

"Except if you let one of those little ones get away, they quickly turn into big ones," Aaron replied.

"Aye, I hear ya. Search and destroy."

"Besides, I think the *really* big ones are being fought where my brother has gone."

A swarm of cats raced across the battlefield, slashing at the demons as they passed. From their flanks came the howl of wolves. Explosions and battle cries sounded all around. His father had found the demons' supplies and turned them to kindling. It seemed, at last, that the battle had shifted in their favor.

And then, suddenly, a woman's voice boomed in his head.

"Those who have used the First Protector's fountains in the past, rush to them now, if you can. Simply stick a finger in the

water and keep it there. The need is desperate. We are almost out of time."

Aaron turned to Oda. "Did you hear that?"

Oda nodded.

"Go!"

Aaron was about to send a message to all the officers when a series of messages arrived.

Cranion. Sending four of my war wizards to the Castle Riverton fountain.

Justinian. I've sent six of mine.

As more messages came in from his officers, Aaron cut them off and sent a message back. A simple one.

Aaron. Send all of them.

Then he sighed. "I hope this isn't a mistake."

As if in reply, two more messages came through.

Wat. Two hundred of the giant demons are coming through the forest south and east of the battlefield. I couldn't engage because we have scouts in that forest.

Castien. Hundreds of ogres heading across the plains for our exposed northern flank.

Aaron immediately replied.

Aaron. Send your war wizards to the fountains. Everyone else, brace yourselves. This is going to be ugly.

Nyra had followed Ohaobbok through the glowing portal, but had lost him and his human friend in the tunnels. It had taken time for her to find them again, but now, at last, she had.

Sort of.

The tunnel she'd followed had ended on open air. She stuck her head through the opening, and found herself halfway up the side of a chasm that dropped down to hot molten rock below. Waves of heat seared her skin as she leaned out, but when she looked up, she saw Ohaobbok high above her, standing on a stone bridge and battling a huge demon. She witnessed the moment when the demon fell, plunging into the redness below.

And then something on the bridge exploded.

Nyra screamed as Ohaobbok's limp body came tumbling down from the bridge. She didn't think; she just reacted. She dug her fingers into a crack near the edge of her tunnel, reached out with her other hand, and grabbed his armor as he fell past. The shock of his weight pulled her shoulder out of joint, but still she didn't let go.

She would never let go.

Her hair curled and crackled from the heat, and as she heaved the paladin up into her tunnel, she felt the sinew in her shoulder tear.

She laid Ohaobbok on the floor. Blood trickled from his mouth, and one of his pupils was dilated. She unbuckled his breastplate and used her healing senses to examine him internally. She gasped at what she found. Blood was flooding his lungs, and he was bleeding internally in countless places.

She pushed her healing energy right into his chest, tackling his lungs first. He had to be able to breathe. Then she went to work sealing other injuries, but as she took care of two, another blood vessel burst. And her head was tingling, telling her she was running out of energy.

Please, just wake up so I can give you a healing potion.

She only had one potion, but she realized he would never live to drink it if she couldn't first continue her healing work. So she drank it herself, and felt her dizziness and fatigue fade away.

She infused him with new energy, but all too quickly she felt herself running low again. She cried out—her efforts weren't enough, and she had almost nothing left.

Then a calm feeling spread warmth to all of her limbs. Nyra felt herself separating from her body and rising up through the earth until she hovered over the chasm and witnessed the epic battle being waged there.

Seder's cause is in jeopardy.

Ohaobbok coughed and mumbled, and Nyra rocketed back into her body. "What, my love? What did you say?"

She pressed her ear to his lips, but he said nothing more.

At that moment, a voice spoke all around her.

"Those who have used the First Protector's fountains in the past, rush to them now, if you can. Simply stick a finger in the water and keep it there. The need is desperate. We are almost out of time."

The voice faded, and Nyra swooned. Just as she was about to tumble backward into the chasm, a gloved hand grasped her tunic.

The dizziness threatened to send Ryan to his knees. His stream of energy was fading with him, and the injured demon stirred.

Without Ryan's constant attack, Sammael was going to get back on his feet.

The orb dimmed and went out. With one last burst of his own paltry reserved, Ryan squeezed out one last, weak blast.

It's all I have.

He felt the world spinning, his body falling as he passed out. And then…

… a spark of strength.

The orb. It had… revived, somehow. Several streams of energy were beaming directly into it from within the earth. And as it throbbed back to life, so did Ryan.

The demon staggered to its feet. Ryan did the same. And as the energy in the orb grew, Ryan used all of it. He sent a tsunami of energy at the demon's chest.

Sammael's scales glowed white as the energy of Trimoria's wizards flowed through him. He opened his mouth in a silent scream.

And then, with a deafening explosion, he was gone.

The only sign of his ever having been there was the white ash outline of him burned into the rock wall where he'd stood.

———

Aaron arrayed his troops to fight a battle on two fronts. From the southeast, through the forest, came the demons. And from the northeast, over the plains, came the bellowing ogres.

The ogres would be the first to reach them. The ground vibrated with their charge. Aaron gripped his sword tightly and prepared to give the order to charge.

And then the ogres veered south, yelling and whooping, and to Aaron's shock and delight, they smashed directly into the approaching demons.

One of the ogres looked over at the troops, who were just standing there, dumbfounded. "Lady says smoosh baddies," he said. "You wants some too?"

Stompinguts yelled, "What we be waitin' fer? Let's smoosh the baddies!"

Aaron gave the order. "Charge!"

And as his army advanced, he heard the chants of the dwarves.

"Blood we've spilled, on this long day.

   "Loved ones lost, in the fray.

   "Look out boys, the ogres are here.

   "Slaughtering and killing, it's what they hold dear.

   "Ogres fighting demons, they're showing their might.

   "Can't let them do that, while we avoid the fight.

   "Come on boys, it's more battle I crave.

   "Let's put those demons in a proper grave!

Ryan knelt at the foot of the bridge and shed tears for his missing friend. "You'll forever be missed, Ohaobbok. I pray you're in a happier place."

"If we get out of this pit," said a voice behind him, "I think that would be a *much* happier place."

Ryan spun around to find Ohaobbok limping toward him, supported by Nyra and Arabelle.

"Ohaobbok!" Ryan rushed to embrace the ogre. "But—but I saw you fall."

Arabelle put her arm around her husband. "Let's walk and talk. There's a lot to tell."

THE AFTERMATH

As the dignitaries from all the lands filed into the council chamber, Throll personally greeted each and every one. Ryan stood in line with the others, breathing in the scent of newly applied wood stain and freshly painted walls.

"Can you believe they cleaned up Castle Thariginian so quickly after five centuries of abandonment?"

His dad winked at him. "It's all an illusion. Throll told me that only a small portion of the castle is in presentable shape. I think we've been carefully escorted through those parts."

The line advanced, and Throll clasped hands with each of the Rivertons. "I'm so glad to see you during these *less* trying times. I truly feared we wouldn't live to see it."

As Throll continued to greet the attendees, Ryan's father went over to visit with Silas, the clan leader of the Redbeards, while Ryan spotted Labri waving him over.

He sat next to the elf queen, and she leaned in.

"I haven't yet gotten a chance to thank you, Ryan—or to ask you about what happened! The tales you must be able to tell about dealing with the Avud… and battling Sammael himself! You *must* allow us to host you and Arabelle so that our historians can talk with you. And so I can talk to you too, of course," she added with a smile.

"I would love to visit with you, and I'm certain Arabelle would too."

A shushing spread through the room, and Ryan looked up to see Throll standing before everyone, his hand raised for attention.

"Welcome to Castle Thariginian," he began. "I'll make this a quick meeting, for I know we're all busy with the aftermath of the battle—and we've all lost many that we hold dear in this struggle against the demon horde."

He looked around, meeting the eyes of all the council members. "Our victory was a combined effort from all peoples throughout the lands. But I would like to recognize, in particular, the timely arrival of our new allies from across the former barrier. To those who have not yet had the pleasure, allow me to introduce you to the elder of the Ta'ah council, Flint Firewielder."

He motioned toward the elder, who looked uncomfortable as all eyes turned toward him.

"The Ta'ah contributed hundreds of war wizards and healers to our cause. In recognition of their vital assistance, and as a small repayment for the years they've spent underground in isolation, I've bestowed upon them a large tract of rich farmland to the south."

Flint stood and bowed formally.

Throll then nodded to Ryan. "I'm sure that all of you recognize our Archmage. Though none of us were there to witness his actions, I assure you that Ryan Riverton faced terrible odds in this battle. He was in the depths of the Abyss, fighting an evil none of us can even begin to imagine. I will not preach, for that isn't my calling, but I know that you're all aware of Seder. Our Archmage fought an agent of evil that was everything that our Seder was not. I won't profane these halls by even uttering the demon's name."

Throll frowned. "But though our victory is great, the struggle against evil is a never-ending battle—a battle that the common person is ill-equipped to deal with. This is why, long ago, buried in our histories, Trimoria had a society of paladins. Holy warriors, if you will. These paladins were charged with upholding all that is good in society and maintaining order. They were the bane of evil. In many ways, they were the original Protectors of our society."

Throll gestured toward the entrance, and beckoned for the ogre who stood there to come forward.

"I'm proud to introduce you to the first true paladin of Seder in over seven hundred years. Ohaobbok, paladin of the House of Seder."

The hulking ogre stepped into the chamber wearing the glowing white armor of the House of Seder. Three men followed behind him, carrying a size-appropriate chair, which they set in the area reserved for the ruling council. Ohaobbok bowed to the king, then took his seat.

"In this ruling council's charter," Throll continued, "I've

added the House of Seder as a peer member, with Ohaobbok as its standing representative."

Ryan stood and clapped for his friend, and the others in the council followed suit a second later. Ohaobbok bowed his head humbly, unused to the attention.

Throll raised his hand, and the room quieted.

"With the introduction of new members complete, I think we would all like to hear reports on the cleanup efforts that have taken place over the last two weeks." He turned to the elven sword master. "Castien Galonos, please tell us how your search for the remaining demons has progressed."

The sword master stood and bowed to the council. "King Lancaster, as you know, our troops were charged with scouring from the lands the fleeing remnants of the demon horde. Much like cockroaches that are exposed to light, they've fled in uncountable directions. We've killed several hundred, mostly pathetic creatures that cowered as the sword dispatched them, but I believe Master Redbeard has experience that differs slightly from mine."

Silas rose, and with a nod from Throll, spoke. "Master Galonos gots it right. Dems beasts are like cockroaches, and dey be spreadin' faster dan spilt ale. Our boys did encounter one nasty beast a bit over a week ago. He be da size of one of dem captains, and was terrorizing a village as we fell on 'im like Stompinguts stomps on a mouse. Me tinks we need to just keep at it till we finds no more."

Throll nodded his agreement, then turned to the Ta'ah elder. "Master Firewielder, what say you of the escaping demons? I know you've been looking low while the others have been looking high."

Flint Firewielder stood and spoke in a deep, gravelly voice. "Yes, Your Highness. My people returned to the Underworld, where we have existed for many centuries, and searched for those demons who might have retreated back into the dark. We exterminated only a few dozen, and they were all very small. It's our belief that they were hatchlings who were overlooked before the battle and left behind. Most demons aren't very smart, and I doubt they'd know how to get back into the tunnels unless one of the larger, more intelligent demons led them there."

The Ta'ah elder turned his gaze toward the elf queen and the elf sword master. "We also have other news to report—news that will be of particular interest to our elven friends. As we scoured the tunnels for demons, our scouts noted that the Avud tunnels, which are normally guarded, are now abandoned. So we searched their territory as well. Not only did we find no demons there, we found no Avud. The entire population has gone, and we believe we know how. In one large, central chamber is a spent gateway. A giant one. We can't know where it led, but we can tell it was used very recently."

Labri whispered in Castien's ear, then bowed to the Ta'ah elder. "Thank you for sharing this information, Flint. We must talk later on this topic."

"It would be my pleasure, Labriuteleanan."

The elder sat, and Throll nodded to Ohaobbok to speak next.

The ogre stood and addressed the assembly with a deep, confident voice. "You have no doubt all heard that ogres fought with us against the demons. This is true, as witnessed by our army on the battlefield. In the past two weeks, I've spoken to all the ogres that I could find, to understand their plans. Most have chosen to return to their clans deep in the mountains, but I'm pleased to announce that two dozen of them have pledged their service to Seder."

Ohaobbok pointed to the splayed hand emblazoned on his breastplate. "You will recognize these acolytes of the House of Seder by the vestments they wear, all of which will bear this, Seder's mark. I ask you to overlook any past, unpleasant experiences you may have had with ogres, for I have confidence that these acolytes will be the first in a proud new line."

As Ohaobbok sat, Throll nodded. "I could not agree more with Ohaobbok's request. If anyone has a concern about the ogres, bring it directly to me."

As the reports continued, Ryan met Ohaobbok's eye, and they exchanged a smile. They had been through so much together. They had faced down evil and survived. And now Ohaobbok, who had never been welcome as part of the ogre clan he'd been born into, was building an ogre clan of his own. One that he could be proud of.

The House of Seder.

A fitting house for a paladin, Ryan thought.

It was a few months later, and Ryan lay with Arabelle on the two-person recliner his father had constructed.

"Can you believe it?" he said. "Nobody is trying to kill us, and we don't have a prophecy staring us in the face with a mission around the corner. The adventure is finally over."

Arabelle smiled and cocked an eyebrow. "As soon as you're certain everything is settled, that is when things go awry."

Ryan poked her in the ribs. "You mean like when you were so certain about Nyra?"

"All right, you were right on that one. But it's lucky I was so suspicious of her. If I hadn't been following her, I couldn't have yanked her to safety before she tumbled into a pool of molten rock."

"I know, I know, I've heard it a thousand times. How you saved Nyra and brought Ohaobbok back from the brink of death. You were truly the savior of the day."

Arabelle elbowed him and laughed. "Stop it."

Sloane rubbed her swollen belly as she relaxed on her own recliner. Aaron had his head on her stomach, but suddenly jumped up. "It kicked me!"

"Welcome to the club," Sloane said. "He's been kicking me day and night."

Aaron looked over at Ryan. "The adventures might be over for *you*," he said, affectionately rubbing his wife's belly, "but I think *my* adventure is only beginning."

AUTHOR'S NOTE

Well, that's the end of *Lords of Prophecy*, and I sincerely hope you enjoyed it.

For those of you who aren't familiar with where this four-book tale originated, I'll note that when I wrote this story, years ago, I never intended for it to be published. After all, I'm a stuffy science researcher type and I don't go around talking about dwarves, elves, dragons, magic, and such. I just don't. The origins of this story really began because as a relatively younger father of two boys, I would come up with bedtime stories for them.

After a while, the details of the story began getting jumbled in my head, so I began writing things down. And the stories grew in complexity. It became a saga to entertain what at the time were seven and eight-year-old boys. And when I was done, those stories remained in my desk drawer for a long time.

And now that you've read these four stories, I should note that I expanded into genres that were more, not so much to my liking, but closer to what I read nowadays. Namely thrillers and some science fiction.

That doesn't mean I don't enjoy fantasy, far from it.

I especially love epic fantasy where the stories are large, complex, and often span multiple books to gain a complete insight into the bigger picture. After all, I grew up on Tolkien, Eddings, and various other authors who set me on the path of writing these fantasy novels in the first place.

But by the time you're reading this, I do have some things that I can announce:

Rothman is writing more fantasy as well as science-based thrillers.

In fact, it is my intent to have by the end of 2020 three more fantasy novels for you to read.

These are going to be a bit unusual, and they're definitely in the style of an epic fantasy, whereas the entire story may not seem to be what you think it is.

Let me give you a bit of insight into what you'll encounter if you read them, the first novel being *Running From Destiny*.

First, it'll be a new series whose books will have the subtitles of "A New Beginnings Novel" and I call the series that for a very specific reason.

The first three novels are a setup with seemingly different storylines, each of which has an ending which is satisfying, yet clearly indicates there's more. However, book two isn't the "more" for book one, and oddly enough book three isn't the "more" for book two or book one. I'm setting up what will end up being a bigger tale, one that evolves and may have outcomes that are unexpected at times. However, you'll find a couple of key elements that readers of the Prophecies series should appreciate.

— You're going to see Ramai (that elusive dwarf you read about in *Lords of Prophecy*) come back in a more prominent role.

— You're going to see what happened to Lilith's people.

— There will be a brief visit back to Trimoria.

As I said, the first three books are a setup for book four, which I'm working on. It is in book four where I'll be tying things together to move the threads forward.

I hope that's something you look forward to.

That being said, I do hope you enjoyed the Prophecies series, and I hope you'll continue to join me in the future stories yet to come.

Mike Rothman
September 2, 2020

I should note that if you're interested in getting updates about my latest work, join my mailing list at:

https://mailinglist.michaelarothman.com/new-reader

If you'll indulge me, below is a brief description of the first book in the New Beginnings series, it's called *Running From Destiny*:

Eighteen-year-old Jason Rogers' life is turned upside-down when he wakes up with burns from a car accident that claimed the lives of both of his parents. He finds himself in the custody of an unnamed government agency asserting that, despite his being a passenger in the rear seat, he was somehow at fault for his parents' death.

Anya is a seventeen-year-old who wishes she could be normal for once. But she's not... and a secret government agency, headed by none other than her father, knows how to leverage the dangerous capability she was born with. All goes well for her until one of the agents turns on her.

Jason and Anya find themselves an unlikely duo as one escapes from an unjust incarceration, and the other runs from the people who betrayed her.

Ultimately, Jason's escape makes him confront the impossible. Was his destiny really written in a musty tome more than a thousand years old?

Anya's trust for those she holds most dear wavers as she realizes her escape may have fatal consequences.

Trying to run from the burden of his destiny, Jason learns it could cost him not only his life, but the life of everyone he's ever known.

The fate of the world lies in the balance.

Jason Rogers

1

An Unexpected Summer

Gazing across the food court of the Arundel Mills Mall, Jason watched a girl with pink hair who was leaning over a plate of chili fries. She was cute despite the neon-bright hair, with a slightly upturned nose and full lips.

Then he cursed as a stream of people walked between them, blocking his view. The mall was packed today with people trying to escape from Maryland's hottest and most humid June on record.

"Dad, I'm trying to lip-read," he said, "but none of it makes any sense."

His dad was seated next to him, sipping at a vanilla milkshake. "Watching someone's lips is only a small part of interpreting what they're saying, son. Try extracting some meaning from other context clues, like her facial expressions and mannerisms." He leaned in a little closer. "I'll give you a hint. She isn't speaking English."

Jason raked his fingers through his mop of brown hair. "You're kidding me. I can barely figure out what's being said when people are speaking English. You expect me to read lips in a foreign language?"

"It's not like we only speak English at home, Jason. Think outside the box, use what you know, and try to match things up with what you're seeing. Your mom can read lips in over a half dozen languages. If she can do it, there's no reason you can't."

"But she's been practicing for most of her life. I've only been at this for a couple of months. And anyway, why is it so important that I learn to read lips?"

But as Jason looked up at his father, he saw that he wasn't going to get an answer to that question—or any other questions. The crease between his dad's eyebrows and the set of his jaw spoke volumes. Some people were easy to read.

Jason turned back toward the girl. She was becoming agitated now. Her face was getting redder as she talked to the guy sitting with her.

And then something clicked. As he matched the movement of

her lips with her facial expression, the words *"Ich bin fertig"* materialized in his mind.

She tossed her soda in her companion's face, stood from her chair, and stormed toward the exit.

"Well, so much for the parakeet," Dad quipped.

"I think she was speaking German," Jason said. He turned to his father. "Am I right?"

"What do you think she said?"

"The only thing I think I caught was, 'I'm done.'"

His father looped his muscular arm over Jason's thin shoulders and laughed. "Pretty good. Though considering the scene she just made, it wasn't too hard to figure out that she must have said *something* like that. I think she gave you some fairly major context clues."

"Hey, give me credit, I did figure it out. I just need more practice. Now, answer my question: why is this so important to you?"

His dad smiled. "Jason, you're like me in more ways than you can imagine. We both love challenges. That's what drove you to get accepted to Yale. And this… well, I thought you'd find it to be an interesting challenge."

"Somehow I doubt Yale cares whether I'm any good at lip-reading."

"It's not for Yale." Dad stood, signaling the end of today's lesson. "Just trust me. You'll find a use for this."

Jason shrugged. "If you say so."

"I do."

Sitting at the desk in his bedroom, Jason took a deep whiff of the bundle of herbs his mother had prepared to help with his headaches. The strong scents of cedar, lavender, and sage were soothing, but nothing ever truly rid him of the blinding headaches he'd been getting so often lately. He tried to ignore the pain as he pored over his World History textbook. He'd kept a 4.0 grade point average through his first three years of high school, and he refused to succumb to the "senioritis" that lots of his friends were suffering from. Besides, his family had instilled within him a sense of responsibility for his own education. *Education is your key to the future* was an oft-repeated mantra in the Rogers household.

Even at an early age, Jason had always pushed himself to excel. He knew that hard work was going to help prepare him for real life, get to the schools he wanted to attend, and ultimately land him his choice of jobs. His acceptance into Yale had been just one more step on his life plan—an important step, to be sure, but one of many.

He tried to read his textbook, but the words on the page wavered and his vision was streaked with flashes of white. A wave of nausea washed over him, making him salivate uncontrollably, and he feared he would throw up again. And then the dizziness hit. As the room tilted, Jason closed his eyes and pressed his clammy forehead against the book. He breathed deeply, hoping to make the episode pass more quickly.

He felt a strong hand on the back of his neck. "Jason? Are you all right?"

Jason shot up into a sitting position, and he barely kept his stomach contents down as the room spun. He felt cold sweat dripping down the side of his face.

"Sorry, Dad. I'm just feeling queasy."

It would be impossible to hide the fact that he was sick. It was probably obvious, but even if it weren't, his father was extremely perceptive. He'd even taught Jason a few tricks to use in paying attention to what others did. Were they fidgeting? Did their eyes dart about? Dad never spoke about what he did at work, but Jason suspected it had something to do with interrogating people for the government.

Now Dad put his hands on Jason's shoulders and turned him so they faced each other. "What are your symptoms?"

"It's another headache. But they're getting worse. More often than not they now also make me feel dizzy, which really turns my stomach."

"When did these new symptoms start? The dizziness and the nausea?"

"Umm… I'm not really sure. It's been quite a while."

Dad frowned with concern. "Did you take a spill on your bike or something? Have you had a fever I don't know about?"

"Well…" Jason paused. "About two weeks ago I fell off the ladder when I was fixing the satellite reception, but—"

"You did what?" Dad grabbed Jason firmly by the arm and escorted him from his bedroom. "What the hell, Jason! You get yourself hurt and you don't bother telling us about it? What were you thinking?"

"Dad, it's no big deal. I don't think my headaches have anything to do with the fall."

As they walked into the kitchen, Mom looked up. She was

deaf, but could easily see from body language that something was amiss. "Zahseen? What's going on?"

"Zahseen" was the name on Jason's birth certificate, but only his Mom called him that. He'd given up trying to make her stop.

It was Dad who answered. "I'll tell you what's wrong, Mirela. He's been walking around with a concussion and never told either of us. I'm taking him to the emergency room."

Jason thought this was a massive overreaction, and his feeling on the matter didn't change when they arrived at the ER and a nurse asked him a ridiculously long list of questions about his symptoms. But his dad didn't say a word until the nurse prepared to take Jason's blood.

"Is that really necessary?" he asked.

The nurse swabbed Jason's arm and fanned it with her hand. "Doctor Smalski asked for a CBC—a blood count, as well as a few other tests. The headaches might be coming from an infection. Is there any reason I shouldn't be taking blood, Mr. Rogers? He doesn't have hemophilia, does he?"

Dad waved away the question and shook his head. "No, nothing like that. Go ahead and do what you must."

After the blood test, an MRI, and even a lumbar puncture, Jason felt like an abused lab rat. But as a doctor carefully studied the computer images of his skull, neck, and brain, Jason started to feel as worried as his father looked.

Maybe Dad was right to bring me here.

Finally the doctor turned to Jason and winked. "I think you'll live."

Dad put his hand on Jason's shoulder and gave it a squeeze. "Did he have a concussion?"

"If he did, I don't see any evidence of the trauma. I'll prescribe something for the headaches, along with a muscle relaxant and something for nausea." He smiled at Jason. "You'll be fine, son. But if you continue to have issues even with the medicine, contact my office."

As the doctor wrote out the prescriptions and talked to Jason's dad, Jason felt his vision blurring with those white streaks again. He prayed the medicines were going to take care of everything.

Jason was cutting across a park on the way home when one of his headaches stopped him in his tracks. He clutched the bark of a nearby sycamore to steady himself, but still the world tilted and his nausea was overwhelming.

He wondered if this was what a migraine was like. He'd read about them in the school library, but migraines were supposed to give some kind of warning before they hit, whereas Jason's headaches came on so suddenly it was like being smashed with a sledgehammer out of the blue.

He grimaced against the pain, and the park blinked out of existence. For a moment, all Jason could see was white.

And then, just like that, the world snapped back to normal. The pain was gone just as quickly as it had arrived.

How can it come and go so quickly?

Starting off again, he tried to dismiss the incident. He'd just completed his final day of high school, and he was looking forward to a summer of watching TV while relaxing on his dad's massage chair. Maybe that was all he needed. Maybe he'd put too much pressure on himself in maintaining that perfect 4.0 average.

Yet as he continued to walk home, things felt… out of place.

He'd been walking the same route for years, and he knew exactly what to expect. Mrs. Patterson's garbage cans at the end of her driveway, even though garbage pickup had been two days ago. The usual kids' bikes on their front lawns. Mrs. Dougal yelling at one of her dogs for digging holes.

Jason was good at noticing such ordinary things—thanks to his dad's training. The two of them used to play a game where Jason would walk into a room after Dad had changed a couple of things—the angle of the TV, the placement of a magazine, the absence of a book on a shelf—and Jason would have to figure out what it was. So when something was off, he noticed it.

Such as the silver-gray sedans with tinted windows currently idling on the street. One of them had a Department of Defense sticker—just like the one on Dad's car. That was different.

And when he turned onto his own street, he saw something else different His dad was home, and both Dad and Mom were leaning against his father's car.

Why is Dad home so early?

And Jason walked up the driveway, Mom waved excitedly and Dad smiled.

"Congratulations, son. You're now a college man. Now get in the car—I made an early reservation at the Old San Francisco Steakhouse to celebrate. It's not every day that my only child finishes high school."

Jason grinned as Dad ruffled his hair and Mom pulled him down and kissed him on the forehead.

As they drove to the restaurant, Jason's parents chatted about how this would be his last summer of freedom before college. Mom wanted to go on vacation somewhere as a family. But Jason was having a hard time listening. Something was still wrong.

He twisted in his seat and saw a car driving about fifty feet behind them. He swore it was one of the same sedans that he'd seen on the way home from school. He was just about to say something to his father about it… when the world flashed white.

There was no sound. The car, the trees, the road… everything disappeared. And for the briefest of moments, a sandstone cliff towered over Jason like an ominous sentinel. At his feet, a stream snaked across desert scrub and into a dark cave at the cliff's base. Jason felt himself being pulled toward that mouth of darkness.

Then everything went white once more.

Flooded with panic, Jason screamed—but he made no sound in the endless white abyss.

Slowly, his senses returned.

First he heard the crackling of fire. Then came the acrid smell of gasoline and burnt hair. Jason blinked, and the whiteness transformed into flame-streaked clouds of smoke.

He felt the heat then, heard the sound of breaking glass and the creak of metal scraping against metal.

"Grab the kid and let's get the hell out of here!" yelled a deep voice.

Jason felt hands pulling him from what he now realized was

the wreckage of his dad's car. Searing pain hit him, and the world blinked out of existence.

Anya Fitzsimmons

The Freak

Staring at herself in the bathroom mirror, Anya frowned and rubbed her cheeks in a futile attempt to get some color into them. "It's pointless," she huffed.

She was always going to look like some kind of freak.

She pushed her lip up and gritted her teeth. Only yesterday she'd visited Dr. Livingstone, her dentist at Fort Meade. He'd filed her canines down so that they were flush with her other teeth, just like he'd done every week for as long as she could remember. But already, her fangs were showing signs of growth.

She tried to calm herself. Her teeth only grew more quickly when she was stressed.

But who *wouldn't* be stressed at this time of the school year? The junior prom was coming up. Everyone was either stressed about getting ready, or stressed about not going.

Anya, of course, was in the latter category.

Mom came up behind her, plopped her chin on Anya's shoulder, and smiled at her adopted daughter in the mirror. "Baby, why so gloomy-looking?"

Anya wished she looked more like her mother. Wavy brown hair. A smattering of pale freckles on the bridge of her nose. And that warm smile…

Anya would never have a warm smile. Even with her teeth filed even, she was at best a pale-faced girl who looked as if she were about to snarl.

"Do you think I should try bleaching my hair again?" she said.

Mom frowned. "I doubt it'll work any better than last time, honey." Last time, Anya got an itchy rash that lasted for three days. "Besides, your hair is gorgeous. Straight, raven black, halfway down your back and yet never gets knots. Most people would kill for your hair."

"Mom, I look like a freak. Like something Buffy should be slaying. I'm sick of it."

Anya's mom wrapped her arms around her and gave her a kiss on the cheek. "Baby, you're beautiful."

"You only think that because you're my mom. It's your job to ignore the weirdness in your kid. But I know what I see in the mirror: paper-white skin, black hair, and purple eyes. I mean, really—purple? I know you guys found me in some orphanage on the other side of the world, but I can't even imagine how they put this combination together. Honestly, I wish I'd get pimples just to add color to my face. But I can't even do that right!"

"Oh honey, I know it's tough at your age, but believe me, you really are beautiful in all the ways that count." Mom rubbed her thumb along Anya's cheek. "How about I talk with your father about some makeup?"

Anya shook her head. "You can talk to him all you want. He'll still say no."

Her father was a former colonel in the Army's Special Forces, and he'd always told her that being pretty was a curse, and that her abilities—which only he knew about—were what she needed to focus on.

"In that case, I won't tell him. You're seventeen—that's old enough to be wearing a bit of blush. I'll get you the lightest shade possible; it'll help with your paleness, but maybe not so much that he notices you're wearing it. What do you think?"

Anya wrapped her mother in a tight embrace. "Mom, that'd be great! Thank you so much."

As Anya's algebra teacher, Ms. Claypotch, droned on about quadratic equations and parabolas, Anya's attention was on Greg Miller. He was the goalie of the varsity lacrosse team, and every time she looked at him, she felt that odd warmth inside of her grow.

Anya, get yourself together. Stop thinking about boys.

Her dad had told her to be careful around boys. Most fathers warned their daughters about boys because they were afraid of what might happen to their daughters. But Anya's dad had warned her because he was afraid of what might happen to the *boys*. Even with a boy like Greg, who was enormous, Anya knew she could knock him out easily. She'd done it before—though not to Greg—and the knowledge scared her.

That was why she'd turned down the three boys who'd actually asked her to the junior prom. She couldn't risk having another incident like the one that happened last year with Tony.

It had happened after a football game, when they met under the bleachers. Tony's version of events was that Anya had "worn him out"—and that was why he was found unconscious there an hour later. Anya's version of the story… well, Anya didn't have a version of the story. She couldn't exactly tell people the truth: that she'd knocked a football player unconscious with her bare hands.

And so Anya, who'd previously been known as a loner and a weirdo, became a slut overnight.

It took Anya over a week to figure out what was going on. The attention she got from some of the guys skyrocketed, while most of the girls she'd gotten along with before stopped speaking to her. Eventually she put two and two together.

Even now, the incident brought up feelings of anger and betrayal. She couldn't believe she'd actually kissed the jerk.

Over time, her reputation as a slut had slowly faded. But recently, she'd heard new whispers. Evidently, since she'd been declining offers of any kind from the guys at school, she was now being labeled a lesbian.

If those idiots only knew how wrong they are.

As soon as the bell rang, she hoisted her backpack on her shoulder, strode directly to the student parking lot, and hopped into her yellow Volkswagen Beetle—a gift from her parents for her seventeenth birthday. As she slowly weaved her car through the other students, anticipation built within her.

She wondered what today's mission would be.

As the guards waved Anya through Fort Meade's entrance, she glanced at the scrap of paper where she'd jotted down the details of her assignment.

Northeast training field, 4 p.m.
Report to command Kinney at the bunker.

Despite her age, her father had made special arrangements for her to participate in a secret project that was unknown both to the Army and the National Security Agency, which was headquartered on the base. After the Tony incident, she'd told her father about her strange powers—and in turn he'd told her about a secret government agency that worked with unique people. People like her.

Her father, it turned out, was the director of something called "Project Gandalf." He was charged with finding people with hidden powers and helping them cope with their abilities. In most situations these people were young, and once they gained control over their powers, they were released back to their families—hopefully to live out relatively normal lives. Many of them saw it as nothing more than an extended stay at "Camp Gandalf."

As Anya parked near the firing range, she saw a small crowd huddled near the concrete bunker and a lone girl standing in the middle of the field. She immediately understood what her mission today would be.

It would be her responsibility to keep the girl from killing herself—or anyone else.

Anya tapped the girl's shoulder. "Are you ready to start?"

Sabrina, who was only nine, sent her blond ponytail bobbing as she nodded. "I won't lose control this time. I swear."

Anya still felt a sense of awe at the power Sabrina possessed. Anya wore the proper safety gear, including rubber-soled shoes, and she stood on a rubber mat with a wire trailing from her to the ground. Still, nothing was certain when it came to Sabrina.

She squatted so she was eye to eye with the girl, then pointed to three targets about two hundred yards away. "Just remember, you're supposed to keep the lightning strikes right on those targets. If the lightning strays at all, the test is over."

Sabrina hopped excitedly from one foot to the other. "I know. Can I start? I feel the pricklies calling me."

As Anya nodded for the girl to begin, Commander Kinney's warning played again in her head. *The girl has altogether too much love for her power. You need to keep her under tight control, or who knows what'll happen?*

Sabrina raised her arms in the air. Anya felt like ants were crawling all over her as Sabrina called upon her power—this was the feeling the girl called "the pricklies." She felt Sabrina's powers build almost in slow motion.

And then, up in the sky, thousands of threads of light streaked across the cloudless blue and merged into a brilliant ball of shimmering energy directly above them. The crackling ball of actinic white sent a sudden burst toward the first target.

It was a direct hit.

Sabrina jumped up and down and clapped, turning to Anya with a grin.

Anya returned the smile and motioned for her to continue. Commander Kinney had asked Anya to run the girl through a dozen strikes—provided she made no mistakes.

But that was the problem. Sabrina was likely to get lost in her power the more she used it. That was typical of kids in the project.

Again and again, Sabrina pulled lightning from the sky. It has a distinct odor that reminded Anya of the chlorine bleach her mom sometimes used. By the seventh strike, Sabrina's eyes were glowing with a silvery light, and as she raised her arms for the eighth strike, she laughed and yelled, "Watch this!"

Thousands of silver threads twisted from every direction and gathered into a shimmering ball of power. But this time, instead of sending the coalesced energy toward one of the targets, Sabrina pulled a lightning strike directly onto *herself*.

"Sabrina!" Anya shouted.

But Sabrina was unharmed, apart from now glowing brightly from head to toe. She had absorbed the energy.

A voice spoke over the loudspeaker: *"Cut off the testing. Terminate."*

Sabrina's smiling face took on a manic expression, and the nimbus of energy that she'd captured crackled and popped. She turned to Anya and said, in a voice charged with portent: "The pricklies say you aren't my friend anymore."

Luckily, Anya knew the protocols for handling out-of-control lightning-callers. She yanked a wire-mesh blanket from under another rubber mat and flung it onto the glowing girl. The electricity she'd been holding exploded in a violent storm of light and sound. The mesh sizzled and partially fell apart.

Sabrina screamed. "I knew you wanted the pricklies all to yourself. You can't have them!"

Anya leaped toward her and sent her own hidden demon roaring into action. As she touched Sabrina, it was as if a gate inside her blew open, and the caged beast leaped forth. A crackling fountain of energy cascaded through Anya's hand and into Sabrina's body.

Sabrina's eyes rolled into the back of her head, and she collapsed in Anya's arms.

The voice spoke again over the loudspeaker. *"Move in. Test subject is neutralized."*

ABOUT THE AUTHOR

I am an Army brat, a polyglot, and the first person in my family born in the United States. This heavily influenced my youth by instilling in me a love of reading and a burning curiosity about the world and all of the things within it. As an adult, my love of travel and adventure has driven me to explore many exotic locations, and these places sometimes creep into the stories I write.

I hope you've found this story entertaining.

- Mike Rothman

For occasional news on my latest work, join my mailing list at: https://mailinglist.michaelarothman.com/new-reader

You can find my blog at: www.michaelarothman.com
Facebook at: www.facebook.com/MichaelARothman
And on Twitter: @MichaelARothman